Smokey Pete and the Festival Fiasco

Peter W Whitehead

Published by Peter Whitehead 2022

Copyright © 2022

First edition.

ISBN:

For Anne-Marie

Preface

Green lanes are ancient byways. They crisscross the country for no apparent reason. They usually don't go from town to town.

They link random places.

They have never been paved. Always grass topped and never rutted. Never paved because no carts have ever journeyed along these tracks.

Carts made their deliveries by roads. Roads went to destinations.

It was not always apparent where you would end up if you went down a Green Lane. The journey was as important as the destination.

Beginnings and endings have no meaning on a Green Lane.

It was the heady summer of 1971 when the young couple tentatively drove the powder blue Ford Consul Estate car, lent to them by his mother for its soft suspension, onto one of these Green Lanes. They went in search of a Free Festival that was supposedly happening a few miles away from his parents' house in Somerset. The sun was still shining brightly after three weeks of continuous beautiful weather!

"Can't we just take the road?" she asked.

"No, this track should bring us out near Pilton right behind the Festival," he answered with the brimming overconfidence of youth. The car bounced lightly over the track without destroying the ancient grass surface. The lane twisted and meandered between the fields. They knew where to head by keeping Glastonbury Tor on their left. Just at the point when they were about to give up they heard music coming from behind the hedge. Seeing a gap he launched the car through it and immediately had to brake hard to avoid running over a group of people who were sitting on the grass, smoking dope and looking at the band playing on a tiny pyramid shaped stage. The noise of the music drowned out the sound of the car's engine and when they turned round, in their stoned state, it was as if the car had silently dropped down from the sky!

"Far out!" one of them said incredulously.

"Awesome!!" was all another guy could say.

"How did you just get here?" a girl asked looking up at the sky to see if any more cars were dropping in.

The young couple were delighted to have arrived straight into the festival with such ease and be parked right beside the stage.

"Oh my folks live about five miles over there and we just drove through the fields on an ancient track," he explained.

"What you just drove from your house across the fields and came through that hole in the hedge?"

"Pretty much, yes."

This explanation impressed them far more than if they really had dropped out of the sky.

"Far fucking out."

After sharing some joints with their new friends, the two new arrivals wandered off to see what was going on. What was going on blew their minds. They had never seen anything like it in their short lives. Bright sunlight bathed the field. Right in front of the stage there were tents, people dancing or lying around listening to the music, smoking dope, sleeping, cooking food on open fires, laughing, blowing bubbles, riding their Triumph motorcycles for fun. Some felt the need to take their clothes off before they rode their motorcycles.

It was like being in a mediaeval fair. It was as if all the bad things happening outside the festival had been taken away and replaced with good. All the uptight people who made the rules had no influence here. For one weekend you could do whatever you wanted and no one would stop you. There was a little alcohol around and some free milk supplied by, the ever so humble owner of the fields, Michael Eavis. There were plenty of Hippies dressed in velvet and silk. Plenty of Loon Pants and a sea of denim. Plenty of dope being shared. Terry Reid was playing 'Dean' on the stage.[1]

"This guy is a genius," the young man exclaimed. "Believe me. He'll soon be the biggest name in the music business." Making the first of his many unbelievably wrong predictions.

When the sun started to set behind the Tor the two got into the car and set off back through the gap in the hedge and down the lane. This was a monumental day for them. It was never going to be repeated. It could never be repeated. Times change. Laws change. Society changes. There would never be a festival like that again! It would never be 1971 again.

As they drove past the high hedges in the middle of nowhere, Glastonbury Tor appeared rising like a mirage in the distance.

"Look at the sun going down on the Tor," he said.

"Oh yeah, that reminds me. Stop the car now," she said.

1 Terry Reid 'Dean' live, YouTube, to see amazing film glimpses of the festival.

He stopped the car and turned off the engine as she curled up on the powder blue bench seat with her head in his lap. Without saying a word she undid his jeans and slowly took him in her mouth, in her unique, shy, gentle way, as he watched the sun setting behind the Tor. Soon he was seeing stars as well.

"You've just made a wonderful day a perfect day. Thank you so much," he said.

"I'm so glad," she replied. "It was my pleasure." And she smiled a secret smile to herself. What she didn't tell him was that she was leaving him in a few days and this was his final goodbye present, but she was kind, and didn't have the heart to spoil the moment for him. She would tell him later.

You never know where you will end up when you set out on a Green Lane.

CHAPTER 1

Looking for adventure.

The leaving celebrations had started the previous evening in the flagstone bar of the Castlebrook Inn, with a few friends coming to see Peter before he left Somerset and went to seek his fortune in London. A few drinks turned into a few more. Then a few more and Bob, his brother-in-law, had loomed up to him and said, "I can see you're drunk, your face is blurred."

And it was, so they decided to drink Wilkins Farmhouse cider and gin as there wouldn't be any of that in London. You take a sip from your pint of farmhouse cider and pour a shot of gin into it. As you drink it anyone who wants to buy you a drink just tips a gin into your glass, so the cider gets clearer, and soon you end up with an almost clear glass of what is probably the most lethal mix of alcohol that you can buy legally. This was, after all, his leaving bash. Who knew when he was coming back, and after a few pints, who cared? The night was deemed to be over when most of the drinkers had lost the capacity to speak and it was left for Bob to do his party trick one last time. He removed his front false teeth for safety's sake and poured his pint of gin and cider straight down his throat in under three seconds flat.

"Bloody lovely," he said. There was rapturous applause from the drunken crowd who then stumbled off home as best they could. Some had to drive because they were incapable of walking.

"Sweet Jesus. I swear I will never drink cider and gin again," he said to himself, not for the first time and probably not for the last, as he drove off into the rain the following day.

Black storm clouds had conspired to meet over the gloomy Somerset countryside and were hurling down rain with the hellish fury of a woman scorned. It crashed down onto the black roof of the little yellow Mini Cooper that swooshed its way through the rapidly rising water. The numbed brain of the driver slowly began to realise that he had only just made his escape in time. All this angry water running in rivers down both sides of the lane would soon join together and completely flood the roads, making them impassable in all directions. The water ran in streams down the windscreen making it hard to see down the lanes and this was only the very beginning of the four-hour journey to London.

The hammering of the rain on the roof echoed even louder inside the head of Peter Whitehead, the 21-year-old driver, as he wrestled the little car through the treacherous lanes. Why had he allowed himself to be persuaded to drink Farmhouse cider with shots of gin in it? Everyone knew that was a sure-fire way to get completely annihilated, but the occasion had warranted it.

The noise inside the car was intolerable. The roar of the big bore exhaust magnified the sound of the engine, the stiffened and lowered suspension jarred and crashed over every little pothole which just amplified the raging headache of the cursing driver. 'Why did he feel so ill?' he wondered.

The small villages and towns in that picturesque part of Somerset, that were an anathema to the fleeing youth, flashed by the window and were greeted with a malicious farewell.

Hornblotton, "Shithole."

Castle Cary, "Shithole."

Wincanton, "Bastard Shithole."

This journey was the only thing on Peter's mind. The mantra was 'Get to London'. That's where the excitement is. That's the only place to be if you are 21 years old and have been brought up in a tiny village of 600 people and you've got Big Ideas.

The only problem was that he had no idea what it was he wanted to do when he got there. Maybe he could sell a bit of dope.

The last three years had been spent at a Teacher Training College in Warrington. During that time he'd bought a two bedroom house for £175 and done it up, sold a lot of dope to fellow students, slept with as many of the girl students as he could and surprisingly scraped through the exams to become a qualified teacher of Drama and English. The qualification he had so eagerly sought three years before, now meant so little to him. The prospect of teaching Drama to a bunch of surly teenage kids in inner-city Birmingham, for £13 pounds a week, held no interest to him whatsoever. Shit, he had made more than four times that selling dope to those super straight student teachers, without even trying.

The upside to the years spent semi-attending college was that he had met Gill there as she arrived as a pretty, fresh-faced, newly arrived first year student. and he was an experienced, worldly-wise second year student. He was prepared to pass on some of his wonderfully useful knowledge to her, if she wanted it. He thought she was gorgeous. She had medium length curly brown hair, a cute face, skinny body and her pert breasts were a source of wonder for Peter. She wore tight needlecord jeans and snug tee shirts that only increased his curiosity.

To be fair to her she wasn't in the slightest bit interested in him or any of his bullshit. This came as a bit of a shock to Peter who hadn't met with much resistance before to his charms and his offers of spliffs in the house he owned in Newton-le-Willows. Who on earth could resist that? Gill could and she did.

He realised that she wasn't just a dumb chick who could be bullshitted into bed and then started another charm offensive.

First he ignored her.

She didn't even notice.

That worked well didn't it?

He'd pretty much run out of ideas and realised that he really fancied her. Not just fancied her but was really attracted to her in a different sort of way and really wanted to get to know her and he was infatuated by her lovely sexy body. Surely that would be enough to enamour her?

Finally, after a few weeks trying to put her out of his mind he sat himself next to her in the student common room and explained that he found her really interesting, very pretty, could not stop thinking about her and did she want to come out for a curry with him and a couple of friends that evening and smoke a little dope afterwards. Unbelievably she just said "Ok, what time will you pick me up?" and that was the start of an ambivalent off/on relationship that carried on for the next ten years. More off than on though.

These thoughts blurred through his addled mind as the car made its slow departure from Somerset. Gill. Sweet, lovely, sexy Gill who at the moment was studying at some polytechnic and was renting a house somewhere in London. At the moment their relationship was pretty much non-existent. Not that it had broken up, it never did, they had just drifted apart again.

He had been Trade Plate driving in Somerset. Delivering brand new lorries to garages in Cornwall and VW campervans around the country and earning about £100 a week which was a fortune for a newly qualified teacher in 1971. Gill had left the Teacher Training College at the end of her first year claiming it was a waste of time and "You are all a bunch of fucking idiots." He thoroughly endorsed that idea but did not have the guts to walk away from the possibility of obtaining a 'Qualification.' Also his mother didn't own most of Barry Island so he didn't have the luxury of expressing himself quite so freely.

He'd enjoyed seeing Gill again, after a gap of six months when she came down to stay for a couple of weeks, spending lazy afternoons in bed together while his parents were out and he was not driving all over the south of England delivering lorries. Enjoying the freedom of the job. There was no one telling him what to do all the time and the money was good.

Buoyed by the success of buying and selling a house while at college, and ever wanting to impress Gill, he stopped by an estate agents in Glastonbury and asked if they had any cheap houses for sale. It so happened they did have one house for sale at the very reasonable price of £350. "A bargain" was the consensus of opinion. The house was in a little village called Batcombe, a place completely unknown to Peter as it was the other side of Evercreech.

In 1971 Somerset was a much different place. It had not yet been 'discovered' by the Notting Hillbillies and unlike now, places like Batcombe and Godney and Frome were pretty much no-go areas. If you went to visit and had more than three teeth you were called a sissy.

Certainly not places a sane local would buy a house to live in. Nevertheless they jumped into the car and started trying to find Batcombe. For some reason they hadn't been given an address.

"It's the third house in the only row of four. You can't

miss it." After driving around desperately searching they came across the house. It was indeed the third house in a terrace of four pretty stone cottages. They entered through the cottage-style front garden into a flagstone floored kitchen complete with Rayburn. Three bedrooms upstairs and a back garden all in amazingly good condition. You could have toshed it out and moved in within a week.

"What do you think?" Peter asked her. "I've got the money to buy it outright if you like."

"It's amazing! So pretty and we could almost move in straight away with very little work... Where are we?" she replied.

"I think Batcombe is acknowledged as the geographical Arsehole of Somerset," he announced.

"Who says that then?"

"It's common knowledge to anyone who was brought up in and around Glastonbury."

"Oh that's lucky then," she said "Cos I'm starting my course at the City of London Polytechnic next week and if you move in here you'll have to do it on your own, Buster!"

"Oh thanks for that. What am I gonna do in this house on my own?"

"I have no idea but the very best of luck," she said laughing as they got back into the car and drove away from the property. If they had bought it, it would be worth maybe £900,000 at present day prices! Batcombe became Millionaire's Paradise.

Starting a course in London next week eh? He kept his mouth shut and the small beginnings of a major plan were ticking over in his mind.

The narrow lanes joined up with the A303, the main road to London, just after Wincanton and Peter began to believe he was getting away at last.

This was in 1971 and the A303 was not a smooth dual

carriageway to London but a winding bumpy lane that twisted its way through the small villages like Mere, and then was clogged with slow moving, smoke belching lorries that could hold you up for miles as they laboured up the hills at 15 miles an hour in crawler gear. As the car's speed slightly increased so the noise of the exhaust rose to a roar inside his head. The overriding emotion was to turn around and start again tomorrow but he knew if he did that, the escape would be put off day by day until it was forgotten completely.

If he could keep going until Andover there was a transport cafe by the side of the road where he could stop and get a mug of coffee and some breakfast which might do something to quell the sickness and pain he was feeling. The thought of eating a greasy fried breakfast was even worse than the thought of four more hours in this bastard car but experience had taught him that it was a very good way of getting rid of a hangover. Also he needed to be in good form when he arrived unannounced at Gill's door.

It would hardly convey the right message if he puked all over the step as she opened the door. That is how he felt now. Like puking.

Eventually the truck stop in Andover hove into view and Peter slid the car in between two brand new Volvo lorries and then set off for the cafe trying to hold down the contents of his stomach in order to eat something to settle it.

The cafe was a cosy Greasy Spoon with steamed up windows and a comforting blue fog of cigarette smoke hanging just below the yellowing ceiling. The Formica tables each had one grimy plastic tomato filled with ketchup on them. It was full of truckers who were smoking and eating breakfast before setting off again to clog up the road and delay everyone's journey by at least two hours.

Ordering a Full English with a mug of coffee, he was

surprised when he was asked for 30p for this meal. Jesus, how prices shot up the closer you got to London. He sat brooding at the table until a pretty, if not slightly greasy young girl arrived with his breakfast. It was indeed a Full English. That would either kill or cure him and the way he felt right now, he didn't care which.

After attempting to eat a good half of the breakfast and drinking two mugs of strong instant coffee he started to feel slightly better as he got back into the car.

Pulling alongside the petrol pumps he put five gallons into the tank and had to dig into his pockets for some money. Fishing around he found a £1 note, a 50p piece and then searched for another 15p to pay for the five gallons. It was still not easy to come to terms with decimal money and everything seemed to have doubled in price overnight. How much was 33p a gallon in real money? One good thing about the Mini was it did about 40 mpg. Even so it would still cost £1 to get to London. It did look the dog's bollocks though, with its de-seamed yellow body, black roof, lowered suspension, Cooper badges and a really loud big bore exhaust. No one could tell just by looking that it wasn't a real Cooper and just had a standard 850cc engine. Anyway when he got to London there wasn't much chance to do much more than 40 miles an hour was there?

He was now more than halfway to London and starting to feel a little apprehensive about what he was doing.

What was he doing? Why was he launching himself into a city he had only visited a few times? How would he survive and more importantly what would he say to Gill?

Later he arrived at the outskirts of London with the confidence of a cocky kid who thought he knew it all but actually knew nothing. Peter swung the car left when he arrived at the North Circular and suddenly felt scared. It wasn't the amount of traffic or the aggressive way everyone drove or even the fact he didn't exactly know where he was going, it was the sheer looming enormousness of this huge sprawling place to which he had decided to come and try to make a living. Where did you start? The place to start was apparently Hendon or that is what it said on the piece of paper on which he had written Gill's address. He had managed to obtain the address by saying he might need it if he was ever in the neighbourhood and felt like dropping in.

"Yeah, right!" she had said. "You can drop by for a cup of tea!" And that was enough of an invitation. Wasn't it?

Anyway, the problem now was to find Hendon using a tatty A to Z map of London. This was the only way to get around in the seventies. You had to try to drive with one hand at the same time as looking at the different pages of a book of maps, held in the other, that depicted the millions of London's streets, while trying to arrive safely at your destination. Finally, after many wrong turns and frustrating one way systems, and signs saying No Right Turn, he turned into the right street.

What a major fucking disappointment.

"I thought she was supposed to be living in London." And this didn't look anything like the London he imagined. 'Hendon looks like boring houses full of old people' were the thoughts going through Peter's head. "Oh my God why would anyone want to live in a place like this?"

CHAPTER 2

Let me take you by the hand and lead you through the streets of Hendon

Pulling up outside the house he realised that discretion was the better part of valour and put these opinions to one side as he quickly assembled his thoughts to start the charm offensive that was up to now the most important thing he had done in his life.

Trying to clear his head from the remains of the residual noise of the engine's roar, he rang the bell and stepped back. The door was opened by an amiable student looking bloke with a full bushy beard and long brown hair. He wore faded denim jeans and an equally faded jean jacket. He smiled. Peter already liked this guy.

"Yes mate. Can I help you?"

"Hi…I'm an old friend of Gill. Is she in by any chance?"

"Yeah, sure I'll go and get her."

Now he was really nervous. What would she say? What should he say? What was the best way to plan this? It was really important he got inside as this was the only place where he knew someone living in London. Although it wasn't exactly the London that he had been dreaming of coming to for so long. Hendon seemed to be a boring suburb full of boring looking houses nowhere near the London he was expecting. One thing he did know however was that sometimes it was better to keep your opinions to yourself. He heard a door open and glimpsed Gill rushing towards the front door. She was smiling with anticipation and expectation. For a second he felt so good. The fear of rejection left him and he almost felt a thrill of anticipation. Then she saw him and for a brief second Gill's face lost its smile and there was almost a flicker of disappointment.

Quickly the smile returned. If he didn't know better it was as if she had been expecting someone else and hadn't been too happy to see him standing on the doorstep.

'Oh shit, this isn't going to be easy,' Peter thought to himself.

She was flustered but had managed to regain her composure and with a cheeky smile said, "Oh my God it's you!"

"That's right, it's me. How did you guess?" Peter said weakly, desperately trying to inject some levity into the conversation.

"Oh no I just meant it's a shock to see you. You're the last person I expected to see here. I thought you were driving buses in Glastonbury or something."

"No, it was chassis cabs in Shepton actually, but I've chucked that job in. It's not really what I wanted to do."

"That is really fascinating." Gill muttered a little sarcastically. "So what are you doing now?"

"Well, I'm standing on your doorstep after having driven all the way from Somerset with a raging hangover hoping you will invite me in."

"Well what I really meant was, what are you doing here in London?"

"Let's go inside and I'll tell you all about me and my plans."

The lightbulb visibly went on in Gill's head and she exclaimed, "Oh my God you want to stay here with me, don't you?"

Not wishing to play all his cards at once he was floundering for the right answer.

"Well maybe for a day or two would be nice," he offered.

"Why didn't you phone me before you came?" she asked, already knowing the answer.

"Cos you'd have told me to fuck off, obviously."

"Well suppose I do tell you to, now."

"I don't think you would be so cruel. Remember all the times you stayed with me in my house in Newton-le-Willows. All the dope you smoked. The times you came to my parents' place in Somerset. Don't make me beg." He was beginning to sound desperate. It was time to play the trump card. "It'll only be for a couple of days till I get sorted and I've got a half of righteous dope in my bag which you can help me smoke if you like."

"A half ounce?" she asked.

'Gotcha.' he thought. "No a half weight. Eight ounces of primo Afghani dope from a couple of those rich Hippies passing through Glastonbury in a designer gypsy caravan on their way back from the Pilton Festival. It'll get you so stoned you'll try to take your jeans off over your head."

That did the trick.

She was fond of smoking dope and she was particularly fond of smoking good dope.

"Let me see what you've got."

"That's what you said to me in that house in Batcombe that ended up with us having a quick shag with you bending over the Rayburn."

"Shut up," she whispered loudly. "Where do you get these stories from? You're such a lying bastard and I don't want the whole street to know about it."

"You didn't seem to care about the whole of Batcombe knowing about it," he said with a leer.

"My God you are such a liar," she continued.

"Oh am I? Well how come the estate agent refused to sell me the house after all the complaints of your screams from the neighbours?"

"STOP IT NOW! Come on. Get inside before the whole world knows my business. And don't you get any ideas about helping me off with my jeans, either. Over my head or otherwise."

"The thought had never crossed my mind," he lied through his teeth.

Off he went to get his bag and took it into the house. Once inside he was shown into the living room where Eric, who was the bearded one, looked quizzically at Gill who introduced Peter to him and said he was staying tonight. There was a couple who were also students, from some god-forsaken place in the North, whose names would later be indelibly etched in his brain. Meantime the pair went off to the kitchen muttering something about "Making us teas."

Eric seemed like a nice guy and had obviously been ear-wigging the conversation outside because he had already got out a pack of Rizla Reds which he had nonchalantly placed on the coffee table. Feigning surprise Peter picked them up and said innocently, "Anyone fancy a spliff?" To her credit Gill agreed it would be rude not to and Eric asked if it was anything nice.

"Well I met a couple of hippies who had just arrived in Glastonbury from a trip to Afghanistan. You know, the Hippy Trail. They told me they had renounced money and wanted to live the simple life. You know the saying …

'Dope gets you through times of no money, better than money gets you through times of no dope!' You should have heard the stories they told about Afghanistan. It sounded so beautiful. Places like Basra, the Helmand Valley, Kabul and Mazar i Sharif. It sounds like such a peaceful paradise. I would love to go and see those places and stay there smoking their amazing dope amongst all the peace and tranquillity. They brought back a couple of kilos from Mazar i Sharif and were prepared to suspend their principles and exchange a few ounces for some filthy lucre as they hadn't got any food! Needless to say, I bought eight ounces as I thought maybe there were some people who would be interested in trying some dynamite dope for a change."

Eric's head was nodding in agreement and Gill's smile returned.

"You bastard. How do you always manage to come up with lumps of such brilliant blow?" Gill asked rather grudgingly. Eric was already sticking a number of skins together ready to roll up. Peter fished in his pocket and pulled out a tola of dark pungent dope and tossed it to Eric.

The first joint was being rolled by Eric who was meticulously assembling five papers and crumbling the oily hash into the tobacco. Meanwhile Peter nicked a few papers and quickly skinned up a skinny joint loaded with the dope and a bit of tobacco. It was alight and being eagerly toked by the pair of them as Eric's magnificent construction was only half completed.

"I don't know exactly," Peter answered. "It's just a knack. I can't help bumping into people who have excellent dope and they want to sell it to me. I think it's a gift."

"Bollocks it's a gift, it's just that everyone feels sorry for you. You pathetic wanker!"

"If that's the way you feel I'll jump back into my car and take my dope to someone who properly appreciates it," Peter said with a mock pained expression on his face.

Eric, who wasn't aware of the relationship between them, for one awful moment could see the lump of Afghani going out of the door before he could get to try it.

"Hang on Gill you're being a bit hard on him there." Which caused both Peter and Gill to collapse with laughter at the absurdity of him actually leaving the place he'd worked so hard to get into.

"You'll need a bloody big crowbar to get rid of this one," Gill said with not a little serious concern.

"Here Eric have a toke on this," Gill said. "It'll help you make that one."

"What?… How?… Oh never mind let me try it." And taking a deep lungful he immediately coughed and choked and coughed again. His eyes were running and his face turned bright red.

"Cough, cough and you're stoned," Peter remarked. And he was.

They were all immediately totally wiped out by the wonderful example of Afghanistan's finest.

Eric regained some of his composure and managed to come out with, "Er Peter. Is there any chance you might be able to sell me some of that?"

Gill answered for him.

"I'm sure he will be able to spare some for both of us, won't you Peter?"

"Yes of course I can and you both get special Mates' Rates!"

Peter knew then that his accommodation problems had been temporarily solved, but only for a few days.

There were not many options left for that evening now that the three of them had started smoking hash of that quality. It is just not necessary or possible to smoke huge amounts of primo Afghani hash and when the other two came back from making their tea they saw that Eric, Peter and Gill were completely wasted. They weren't interested in smoking anything and weren't able to get any sense from anyone and announced they were tired and were going to bed.

After they had left, Eric and Gill started giggling and then laughing uncontrollably.

"What?… What?" Peter asked but they couldn't speak and just made signals to be quiet and wait. They waited and soon muted sounds started coming through the floor from the bedroom above them. First the rhythmic squeaking of bedsprings, slowly getting faster, building speed and then in a rich Yorkshire accent they heard two voices.

"Ooh Geoffrey!"

"Ooh 'Elen!"

"Ooooh Geoffrey!!"

"Ooooh 'Elen!!!"

"OOOh Geoffrey!"

"OOOh 'Elen!"

"Ooooooh shut the fuck up," Gill said between paroxysms of stifled laughter wiping tears from her eyes.

"Every night this happens! I couldn't care less about the shagging but it's the 'Oooooing' that does my head in."

The evening passed in a dreamy, wonderful haze, listening to The Stones and *Astral Weeks*.

"Man, I've never heard Van sound like this before. It's amazing!" Eric managed before he stumbled off to his bed. Only just remembering to reserve a half ounce of the blow to buy tomorrow.

"Sure thing, mate. See you tomorrow." Peter said snuggling down next to Gill on the sofa.

"Listen Pete, you really can't stay here long. I've just started my course and I promised Dad that I would see it through and not get distracted, particularly by you, again."

"Oh that's not fair, it was your decision to leave college, I had nothing to do with it," he said.

"Maybe you didn't but you know I can't be around you for long. You drive me completely nuts and he is paying for everything. I don't get a grant you know."

"Yes I do know. And I didn't get a grant either. I worked my fingers to the bone to pay my way through college," he said with a pained expression.

"Oh sure you did. Weighing out all those quarters and half ounces must have exhausted you." She laughed at the memories they had but not allowing herself to slip back into what was essentially a bad relationship. She was attracted in a strange way to his freewheeling lifestyle but guilty about not living up to her father's expectations. "She is still too young to throw her life away for a complete waste of space like him" was her father's opinion and at the moment he was holding the purse strings.

"Seriously though, Peter, what do you want to do? How are you going to make enough to live on? You can only have saved a few hundred from your job and that won't last long."

"You know what. I don't have a clue. I thought maybe I could sell some dope. You know, build up to a couple of weight a week and make £300 clear. That should be enough to get by even at London prices."

"Ok. Even if you could do that you need somewhere to stay. You need to find people to sell to, even if you could find some dope to buy. You need somewhere to live and you can't stay here. It's just not possible. There are three other people in this house and I'm going to finish my course this time. I am not going to be a loser. And that is a fact!"

"Alright we can talk about it tomorrow. Let's go to bed."

Gill had the downstairs bedroom that was once the dining room and had scattered her familiar belongings around in that cute untidy way she had. Disappointingly, in one way, she only had a single bed and that would not be easy to sleep in.

"Listen I'm serious. This is only for a few days and then you get out. Promise?"

"Promise," he said lying through his teeth for the second time that day.

They squeezed together in that little bed and soon felt that electric sexual tension flicker between them.

Soon the gentle squeak of bedsprings could be heard, followed by the broad mock Yorkshire accents.

"OOOh Gill!"

"OOOOh Peter!"

"OOOOOh Fooock!"

When he opened his bleary eyes the next morning he had no idea where he was.

Whose room was this? Where was he? Slowly it came back to him. He was in London.

At last. The world was his lobster and the streets were paved with gold. First things first though and he skinned up a little joint to smoke with the cup of coffee he made in the kitchen. Gill had obviously gone off to college at sparrow's fart without waking him and there was no sign of anyone in the house. What a shame Eric had gone as well. He liked Eric and it was always nicer not to smoke on your own. However this little one would help him sort out what he was going to do. What it sorted out was that he wasn't really able to do anything after smoking it. This lump of dope was the real deal. He was an idiot not to have bought a whole kilo from those hippies. He could have made a fortune selling it in half ounces and then bought some more. Maybe he could buy a van and drive it overland to Afghanistan and get a few keys for £50 and smuggle them back and sell them for loads of money. Maybe he could persuade Gill to come with him so he didn't look suspicious while travelling. Maybe she could get some money from her dad to finance the deal. They wouldn't need much and it was a great investment. They could tell him they were buying carpets or something. His mind was flying off in so many directions he forgot about the basics like what was he going to do and where he was going to stay.

Much later Peter had not moved from the spot on the sofa and Gill came crashing through the front door.

"Jesus look at the state of you. You haven't moved all day and you're stoned out of your tiny mind."

"Yeah it's great isn't it?" he said lamely.

"No it is not great. You're a fucking menace. You've just been sitting here all day smoking that stuff. After all those things you said last night you haven't done one of them." She was raving.

To be perfectly honest, he couldn't remember much about what had been said last night. There was something about not staying for long and something about getting a job.

Luckily at this point Eric got back. Grinning at both of them he said, "Hi man. Can I buy a half ounce of that amazing dope?"

"Yeah sure you can. I'm afraid I'm gonna have to charge you thirty quid though. It cost me a lot. Those hippies may have renounced money but they certainly haven't forgotten the value of it!"

"That's cool. I haven't ever smoked anything like that before. Here you are," passing over six fivers.

"And here's something I made earlier," Peter said, passing over a cling film wrapped lump to the eagerly waiting Eric. "It's a pleasure," he added.

"No, the pleasure is all mine," said Eric

"No, no the pleasure is all mine," countered Peter.

"Will you two stop it now? We were talking about something serious," Gill said.

"This is serious to me," Eric replied, scooting out of the room before he became involved in the upcoming discussion.

"Ok, here's the deal," Gill started saying. She had a folded copy of the *Evening Standard* in her hand.

"You find a job in this paper today or you are out of the door now. If you get a job you have one week to find somewhere to stay. That is how it is and there is no room for discussion. Also if you don't get a job you don't get to touch me either. *Comprendo* Buster?"

Peter felt as if all the air had been sucked out of the room.

To be made to get a job was bad enough but sleeping with Gill and having no sex was unthinkable. One thing he did know was that Gill was as good as her word and if she wanted something she got it.

"Ok then give me the paper, though I'm sure there won't be anything in it," he muttered.

He sat down on the sofa to make it look more like he was seriously looking and opened the paper at the Situations Vacant section. My God there were hundreds of jobs there. How was he going to get out of this? Starting at the top he skimmed through the ads dismissing them each with a reason he could not do the job. Not qualified. Not a waitress. Can't type. No HGV licence. And so on. After a few minutes of furiously pretending to look he said, "There's absolutely nothing suitable here."

"Give me the paper," Gill said and snatched it out of his hand. She scanned the ads for about half a minute and triumphantly announced,

"Here's one that's perfect and you can start immediately."

"Show me then. What is this marvellous job?" He realised this was not going to be easy.

"Here," and she pointed to an ad that simply said,

" Person wanted to deliver leaflets. Start immediately." With a London number.

"It sounds dodgy to me," Peter tried. He was desperate.

"There's nothing dodgy about delivering leaflets. Everyone does it."

"I don't and I don't think you ever have either," he countered.

"I'm not jobless or homeless so I don't have to. So get on the phone and talk to them or…"

"Alright I'll call them but they still sound dodgy to me."

CHAPTER 3

What's it like to be completely unknown?

He gingerly picked up the phone and dialled the number from the ad and waited for six rings before it was answered.

The voice on the other end of the phone barked in a heavy Scottish accent.

"Concorde Showers," and then waited for an answer.

Peter was not 100% sold on the idea of getting a job, but could not really get out of it right now.

"Er… I'm phoning about the advert in the paper."

"And which advert might that be?"

Now things were getting confusing for the stoned Peter and he was considering hanging up the phone.

"Don't you dare hang up," Gill hissed. It was like she could read his mind.

"No, no I won't."

"No you won't what?" the Scot demanded.

"Sorry I wasn't talking to you."

"If you don't want to talk to me would you be so kind as to get off my fucking phone and stop wasting my time," the voice shouted with brutal directness.

"No I'm sorry. I'm phoning about the advert for leaflet deliverers."

"Ah you want to deliver leaflets, do ye?"

"Well I suppose so."

"Just make your mind up son and stop wasting my time."

"I do. I do want to deliver your leaflets."

"Ok, when can you start?"

This question threw Peter right off balance. It appeared that he had just been offered the job within ten seconds of talking to the man.

Firstly, he didn't want to get a job.

Secondly, he didn't want to deliver leaflets.

Thirdly, the man on the phone sounded like a lunatic and he didn't fancy his chances with him.

"Er… How about tomorrow. When do you deliver leaflets?"

"Any fucking time you can get here son." All vestiges of politeness had immediately disappeared now he was as good as on the payroll.

"Right. What time should I get there?"

"Can you get here for 5-ish?"

"I guess so. Is there somewhere for me to park nearby?"

There was a brief pause while the penny dropped on the other end of the phone.

"You have a carrrr?" The voice asked incredulously. The Scottish accent had just gotten a little more Scottish.

"Yeah I've got a car."

"How many people does it seat?

"Four, other than me."

"In that case son you have just been promoted to driver of the leaflet deliverers. Get your sorry arse down here tomorrow to 118 Tottenham Court Road. I can't wait to make acquaintances with you and your lovely car." With that the voice abruptly hung up leaving Peter looking at the receiver in disbelief.

What had just happened?

That man was a certifiable nutter and should be avoided at all costs!

Gill was absolutely delighted. She was jumping around laughing and shouting, "Peter's got a job! Peter's got a job! Chief driver of the leaflet deliverers!"

"Shut up will you. Give me a break. I'm only doing it because you forced me."

"You're so right I did and by the way your week's notice starts tomorrow."

"You didn't talk to him. He is absolutely crazy. He was shouting and effing and blinding like a trooper and calling me son and he sounds like a Glaswegian hoodlum. I'll probably get my throat sliced with a cut throat razor and it will all be your fault."

"Well if that does happen you will get a full apology from me."

There was obviously no chance of getting out of this 'job' so Peter gave up and rolled another skinny joint and they all got stoned again for the rest of the night.

The following morning all the student members of the household got up fairly early and went about their studies leaving Peter home alone. That was just as he liked it. No one telling him what to do. He stayed in bed till midday and then got up to make a sandwich. In truth he was really nervous about starting the job. Not so much being scared of the Scottish man, though he was a little wary, but this was not the reason he had driven such a long way to be here. There had to be a better job. Why hadn't he looked harder in the paper and not taken the first job that came up? What would he be doing next? Cleaning toilets probably if Gill had any say in the matter.

He hung around all day until he decided there was time for a little one skin joint to calm his nerves before he walked into the Madhouse at five o'clock and the time flew by and before he knew it he was negotiating the pre-rush-hour traffic between Hendon and the Tottenham Court Road.

It wasn't long before he realised just how far away Hendon was from where he needed to be.

'Why would anyone choose to live all the way out there?' he asked himself as he wrestled the Mini through the clogged streets. It didn't seem to matter the traffic was mainly going in the other direction as no one seemed to be moving. He really didn't want to be late on his first day.

Finally he got himself going the right way up the Tottenham Court Road, spotted 118, and managed to squeeze into a parking space just round the corner in Goodge Street.

Walking back towards the shop he passed several Used Car Dealers standing around their cars. Maybe he could be a car dealer. He loved cars and it would be so much better than delivering leaflets but the salesmen didn't appear to be doing any business and probably didn't need his help. It was two minutes to five when he found himself standing outside number 118 Tottenham Court Road. It turned out to be a shop. On a dusty shelf in the window was a lone shower propped up on a cardboard box surrounded by leaflets. It was not particularly impressive but it did tell the story. Showers for sale.

Peter took a deep breath and pushed open the door and entered a scene of complete chaos.

The man with a strong Glasgow accent was shouting at the top of his voice to another man about not completing enough leads and:

"How the fuck am I going to pay the rent if no fucker Is selling any showers?" The floor area was piled with showers in their boxes reluctantly being stacked by an effete young blond man in a blue needlecord suit. Brown paper packages of leaflets were stacked alongside four nondescript people who were obviously the other deliverers. Curiously in the corner away from all the action was another young man.

He sat cross legged on the floor and oblivious to everything around him was playing beautiful classical Indian ragas on a sitar.

The shouty man noticed the new arrival and smiled a huge welcoming smile.

"Come in, son. We won't bite you. What's your name, son?"

"My name is Peter… er Peter Whitehead," he replied

"Welcome Peter Whitehead. My name is Bruce Dunnet. Everyone calls me Bruce."

He managed the whole sentence without swearing once, Peter noticed.

Bruce was wearing a brown suit, a nylon shirt and tie and had a slightly stooped appearance, a lantern jaw and a foul mouth. He had a frail frame but also the hard appearance that came from a tough upbringing in Glasgow.

"So you have a car then, son?"

"Yes it's parked in Goodge Street."

"Well go and get the fucking thing and let's get to work."

The car was brought round and the boot was loaded with leaflets and four people squeezed in and they were sent off, by Bruce, to the suburbs to deliver as many leaflets as they could. Peter, it turned out, had to deliver as well as drive and as yet no mention of money had been made.

After a couple of hours of traipsing up and down people's paths and sticking leaflets in the door it was agreed they had done enough and returned to the shop. It was in darkness but the others were not new to the job and said that Bruce would be in the pub next door if he wanted to see him, which he did, and so Peter headed through the pub door.

He heard Bruce's loud voice over the hum of conversation in the crowded bar and squeezed through the throng until he was standing in front of the small group. Bruce spotted him and instantly asked what he wanted to drink.

"Sit down. Sit down. How did you get on today? Are we going to be getting loads of enquiries from the good folk of Croydon?"

Peter sat down with his pint and surveyed the people sitting at the table. The person who had been playing the sitar was sitting there. He was called Clem Alford. He was also Scottish and was apparently either the fifth or sixth best sitar player in the world.

"So where does Ravi Shankar rate in the listings?" Peter asked.

"If you mean Shankar the Wanker we don't talk about him thank you very much," Clem muttered into his pint but he shook Peter's hand and said "Hi" in a friendly way, obviously not taking offence to Peter's apparent gaffe. That was something that just had to be brought up at a later date.

There was another man, about the same age as Bruce, sitting at the table who seemed a little reluctant to get too involved. He was introduced as Malcolm Nixon. He was a short stoutish man who had an air about him of a Dickensian Pickwick character. At first glance he seemed immaculately turned out but under scrutiny his expensive looking clothes looked ever so slightly worn. He seemed to be less well off than he tried to appear to be but still looked like he was doing ok.

He didn't shake hands but also with a strong Glaswegian accent made a welcoming remark along the lines of: "So you're Bruce's new protegee are ye? The one with the wee car?"

"Well I don't know about protegee but I have got a car."

"We'll see then won't we?" he said mysteriously.

The Sulky Young Man with the corduroy suit was introduced as Jurgen and Bruce said he was German and Malcolm's PA. This was delivered over the top of Malcolm's head punctuated with a huge stage wink and mimed laughter.

Peter was completely lost. He felt so out of his depth. Jurgen didn't talk much which was lucky because Peter was about to ask what it entailed being a PA for Malcolm. It wouldn't be until a little later that he worked it out for himself.

"Who's ready for another one then?" Bruce bellowed at the same time thrust a fiver into Peter's hand saying, "Get them in Son. I'll have a light ale and get one for yourself."

Peter never saw Bruce drink anything other than light ale except for the time he introduced him to the wonders of drinking a bottle of Laphroaig. But that was at a party weeks later.

Bruce and Malcolm entertained the little group with anecdotes, stories about Scotland, union members, Communists, tales of the folk clubs they had run in London and 'tearing the back out' of lots of people, most of whom Peter had never heard of, who were well known faces and enemies of either Bruce or Malcolm.

The pub closed at ten-thirty and all the others lived in reasonably close proximity to the pub and set off to walk home. As Peter got into his car he heard Bruce shouting, "Make it four tomorrow. We've got a shedload of leaflets to deliver.

Driving back to Hendon he had plenty of opportunity to mull over the events of the day. The leaflet delivering had not been very interesting, but although he was as mad as a hatter, Bruce seemed like a genuine bloke who was trying hard to make a crust. Malcolm was an odd one. He seemed to be extraordinarily clever and quick-witted. At one point in the evening one of the customers upset him with a derogatory remark and Malcolm flayed him alive with outrageous sarcasm and invective, coloured with inventive obscene abuse. Peter decided never to get on the wrong side of him as he had never seen anyone be so verbally humiliated before. He was obviously homosexual at a time when, although it had been made legal, it was still frowned upon by some people. He didn't give much away and he and Bruce seemed to be incredibly good friends and united on some kind of crusade.

"What have I got myself into?" He pondered following the signs back to Hendon.

Arriving back at the house he was greeted with a note in the living room saying,

"Gone to bed. Don't you dare wake me up!!!!" with four exclamation marks.

He crept into the bed trying not to disturb the sleeping body and Gill either did not hear him or pretended to be asleep. That was fine as he was exhausted and needed to sleep.

At ten the next morning the whole house had disappeared off to their studies and after getting up and making a sandwich from whatever he could find in the kitchen Peter began to wish he was at the shower showroom.

"Don't be so stupid," he told himself. "It's much better doing nothing. Just lounging around" But he watched the clock ticking over the minutes and hours until three, when he left for work. He couldn't decide what the fascination was with those people. None of them were very successful or famous or rich but they all had magnetic personalities and were driven by some hidden agenda.

All except the German lad who was just a sulky poof!

Three o'clock came and he got into the car and set off to work wondering what the day would bring. Walking through the door there was the usual rag tag group of people. Some faces were familiar, some were new. Peter was greeted with the usual friendly jibes and was sent downstairs to remove some clutter from the storeroom. Downstairs was a large room and leading off it at the back was a little room. In it was a small grey-haired man, who was hunched over a typewriter, pecking away at the keyboard. He took absolutely no notice of anything going on outside his room and Peter made no move to talk to him. After shoving a few boxes into the corner he went back upstairs.

"Who's the bloke downstairs?" Peter asked Bruce. "He looks like a little mole peering out through the gloom."

"Och that's just Michael," Bruce offered. Peter wanted to know more.

"So what's he doing down there?"

"Oh I don't know exactly. I think he's writing scripts for the television. He's a really nice bloke. His name is Michael Bakewell and he was once quite big in The BBC." And this is where Bruce had put two and two together and made 400.

"He married Joan Bakewell when she came down to London from Oop North. Once she was famous and had learned how to talk with a plum in her mouth, she walked out on him and now he's down there trying to write something to get his career back on track again."

This was typical Bruce. A perfectly plausible story but probably without an ounce of truth in it. However it didn't stop them saying, "You fucking bitch" every time Joan Bakewell appeared on the television. It was part of the code. Even though Michael Bakewell never entered into conversation with any of them except to softly say goodnight to Bruce as he left the office, he was 'one of the chaps' and didn't deserve to be treated like that. Whether it was true or not.

That was the trouble spending time with Bruce and Malcolm. Their true stories were as fantastic as the ones they made up for the shock value of entertaining the group.

The days rolled past. Leafleteers were driven to the suburbs. Leaflets were delivered. Then they all met back up in the pub. People dropped by the table. Some left a light ale.

Some asked where their money was. Some just said hello. Always received with a joke or a profanity from either Bruce or Malcolm, who was not there every night and seemed to be involved in a secret mission.

Bruce and Malcolm's story was told to Peter over a series of sessions in the pub by Clem the sitar player when Bruce wasn't around.

Bruce and Malcolm were brought up in Glasgow. They were both card carrying members of the Communist Party and very active in it. At various periods in their lives they had run a music booking agency in Scotland, run folk clubs around Shaftesbury Avenue, managed Pentangle, fallen out with Bert Jansch and even fallen out badly with Ewan MacColl.

Malcolm had been First Secretary of the World Federation of Democratic Youth, travelling all over the world organising huge Communist youth rallies, but he didn't talk about that. Now they just wanted to make a little money for themselves. Bruce was, at the moment, the one making a bit and was helping out Malcolm financially.

The way it worked was simple. In the seventies lots of houses in London had not yet got a bathroom. If they hadn't it was usually because the residents didn't have the money or the room to install one. It didn't mean they didn't want one, so this is where Bruce came in to help. He had leaflets delivered to the sort of areas that didn't look too upmarket, offering to supply and fit a self-contained shower anywhere in the house. Under the stairs. In the box room. On the landing. Anywhere. The cost could be paid in very reasonable monthly instalments. If you answered the advert someone would call round to discuss the best place to site the shower. It would be fitted by qualified plumbers with very little inconvenience and little fuss. Just fill out the coupon with your address or phone the showroom for more information.

What actually happened was if someone returned the coupon for more information, filling in the box with their address, a salesman would arrive on the doorstep and try not to leave without signing up a hire purchase contract for a new shower. There was always space somewhere for the shower and once the credit agreement was confirmed the whole amount was paid in full to Bruce. A shower was bought and a plumber was sent round to crowbar in the brand spanking new shower. The salesman got his cut, the plumber got paid, the customers got their shower and Bruce made some money. It was not a scam and everyone was happy.

It was a great idea but not one unique to Bruce. There was a bigger company called Dolphin Showers who ran bigger brighter colour adverts and always seemed to have already leafletted the streets Bruce wanted to do. Most people preferred the colour advertisements and glossy leaflets from Dolphin and woe betide anyone who mentioned their name. It drove Bruce mental and he would rant and rave about them "Taking the food out of my mouth and stealing my business with their Shitey Showers."

It became evident that Bruce's heart was not completely in the business and he had another idea that he was trying to get off the ground.

One Saturday it was arranged for Peter to collect Bruce from his flat in Gordon Mansions. He pulled up outside and was impressed with the building. It looked really posh and had a lift as well. The flat was huge and comfortably furnished. His wife and young son were very briefly introduced to Peter and the two men left immediately.

"Right son. You are about to be amazed. I can personally fucking guarantee that you will never have heard anything like this before in your whole pathetic life." Bruce said as they entered a small rehearsal room in Camden.

Inside there were amplifiers and microphones, mixing desks and speakers. Sitting cross legged on an Indian cushion was Clem who was gently playing a beautifully ornate Sitar. Leaning against a small stack of Marshall amps was a skinny, black-haired Indian bloke who was strapping on a Fender Stratocaster. It turned out his name was Amancio D'Silva and he was a guitar playing genius.

"Get it? Do you Get it? East meets West. One of the best sitar players in the world, a Scottish lad, and one of the best electric guitarists in the world, an Indian lad. Put them together and you've got it, 'East meets West', however you see it," He was in his element and called out for them to get a move on as he was paying for this room: "By the fucking hour."

Firstly Clem started to weave a Raga on his sitar. The notes swam through the room and immediately it was obvious that he really was an impressive player. Soon the guitar joined in and the two wove a beautiful melody soaring, both solo and together, in complete harmony.

Bruce however was not happy.

"For the love of fuck!" he howled "Stop sitting there playing with your dicks and put some feeling into it. This is costing me money and you're not even trying. I thought youse twos were supposed to be the best. Well fucking show me some emotion."

They started again and played with such fire and passion Peter had never heard anything like it before. It was mind-blowing music played by two superb musicians in complete harmony with their instruments and each other.

Bruce's gentle words of encouragement seemed to have done the trick.

They rehearsed a few numbers until Bruce announced he had to get back to take his son out. Peter stayed there as instructed and as soon as Bruce had gone a joint was skinned up which helped take the music to another level again.

When the rehearsal was over Amancio had to go home so Clem and Peter adjourned to the pub and over a couple of pints Clem told him how he came to play the sitar.

Growing up in Scotland he had started playing the bagpipes and had become pretty good at it. One day a friend played him a recording of someone playing the Sitar. He was smitten. There was such a similarity, he realised, with both instruments using a drone to great effect. He was immediately obsessed to the point of selling everything he had and going to India. He did some research and found there was an ashram where he knew a famous sitar teacher worked. He just turned up there and explained that he wanted to learn to play. The teacher was not over impressed with a white Scottish guy wanting to learn the sitar but Clem would not be put off and eventually was accepted as a pupil for a trial period. It soon turned out that Clem had a natural flair for the Instrument and after a year or so he was the star pupil. They lived, breathed and slept sitar. The first week was spent playing only the opening note of a raga. This was meant to show how important the note was and how it must be played exactly right. Clem got it. He absolutely loved it and stayed for five years and became a virtuoso. There was nothing more he could be taught there so he left to share his gift with the world and continue trying to get even better.

Returning to England at a time when the sitar was in ascendancy, with George Harrison being so keen, he thought it would be easy to get a few gigs as he was acclaimed in India as one of the best players. A tour was arranged by a promoter and Clem was ready to start a brilliant career in music. Then something came out of the blue. The tour was cancelled.

Ravi Shankar had heard about this Scottish person who

was an acclaimed player and announced that someone one who was not of Indian birth could ever play the sitar properly. This Scottish man was a clown and could not be listened to. Also if any Concert Hall booked Clem to play they would never hear the great Ravi Shankar play there. This effectively put an end to any hope Clem had of playing anywhere in the world. That's how he gave him the nickname Shankar the Wanker.

They drank their pints and Clem left to get back to Bloomsbury to his Japanese wife.

"You must come round and meet her," Clem said as he jumped on the bus. "I take it you like Japanese food."

"You bet I do." Peter said not having a clue what kind of food it was but always game to try something new.

Days turned to weeks. Peter's job turned more into a gofer/chauffeur and less leaflet delivering. Bruce and Malcolm liked him for his willingness to help. He would go anywhere and do anything cheerfully without question. He also never hassled Bruce for his wages. People believed that Peter had far more knowledge and expertise than he actually did. It often happened when they first met him, when he knew absolutely nothing, he appeared to be knowledgeable about any subject. Part of the trick was not to let on that he knew nothing and only need to be shown something once.

It didn't take long to work out that Bruce's finances fluctuated wildly but if you were owed something he never forgot and paid up when he'd got it. Peter wasn't expecting to get rich working here but it was never dull.

He had moved out of Gill's house in Hendon as promised and hadn't seen very much of her with the hours he was keeping and it was a pain in the arse driving up and down to work. He had remembered that someone he was at school with in Somerset at least five years ago had moved to London and was apparently living in a flat in Shepherd's Bush.

When he dropped by, he discovered that luckily, John, his friend, had got a box room going spare and Peter could rent it for £3 a week. The flat comprised of four rooms on the third floor above the busiest 24-hour Kentucky Fried Chicken takeaway in London. It had until recently been over an old-fashioned gents outfitter which had been lovely and quiet until the Colonel's people took over and put huge extractor fans on the flat roof which pumped out the stink of greasy fried chicken. The upside was that the KFC administrators had no interest in the three flats above their hugely profitable shop. As long as the £7 a week rent was paid by each of them they never bothered anyone.

John had a bedroom as did Claire, who was in the final throes of becoming a barrister, which left Peter with the smallest room. John was studying engineering at Brunel University and was being sponsored by Vauxhall Motors. He was getting a wage every week to go to university and seemed to have plenty of money and he was also very careful about spending it.

Peter could not have been more delighted. Shepherd's Bush! That was more like it. It was 'Proper London'. Overlooking the Green. A space to park the car in the side street. Two minutes to walk to the tube and a 20-minute ride into town.

His flatmates went out early and came back late so it was a really great place to stay.

One day at the showroom Bruce said he wanted a word with Peter. He told him that they were stopping leafleting and doing more ads in the papers. This meant there was not so much work available for him. However he thought it was time Peter stepped up a grade and started selling the showers instead. This idea was not great news for Peter who had carved a cosy niche in the firm and was not doing much real work. The upside was that there was a lot of money to be made on commission for selling the showers.

"If you only sell three showers a week, you'll make £210, son."

He had to agree that it was possible to sell many more than three showers a week. The other salesman could sell six or seven so how hard could it be? But he was worried that he had never sold a shower in his life. He had sold quite a lot of hash but this was different. Selling showers entailed going into a stranger's house and selling them something they didn't necessarily want, which was the exact opposite of what Peter did when selling dope. But the money was good and he didn't really have a choice.

First he accompanied the salesman as he went to follow up the leads.

"Don't ever leave without signing them up," was his advice. "They have expressed an interest so they want to buy. Don't let them change their mind. Get their signature on the agreement even if it's the only way they can make you leave the house," he emphasised. That didn't really fit with Peter's way of selling and he visited four leads on four days without signing anyone up. Bruce however was very encouraging.

"Have a bit of faith in yourself, son. Anyone can sell these things. Just push yourself. Just have a little belief."

He did have a little belief and managed to close a deal for a shower. It was Friday night and when he told them in the pub they were delighted for him. Drinks were bought and much celebrating was done but on Monday morning the buyers had cancelled the deal and bought a Dolphin Shower!

He was devastated. How could they buy a shower from Dolphin Shitey Showers?

It was immediately agreed that Peter was not really cut

out for the shower business and it was time for him to go his own way.

"You're a good kid and I know you'll do well. Keep in touch with us. I really mean keep in touch because Malcolm is working on something big and if it comes off he'll have something for you."

Yeah, I'm sure he will. Peter thought and promised to stay in touch as he scribbled his new number on a scrap of paper and passed it over.

"All the best, son. I owe you one," Bruce said and he walked away from shower selling forever.

CHAPTER 4

You can go your own way

Living in Shepherd's Bush was brilliant for Peter. He had his own room. He had time to himself. There were people around who were doing exciting things and starting to make their way in the world. Living below in the first-floor flat was Nick who had a Saturday morning show on Radio London. The BBC not the pirate station. He managed to persuade lots of famous people onto his Saturday morning kids' show and got invites to all kinds of events, new films, shows and parties. Peter often went along to these dos and was really impressed meeting celebrities, musicians, footballers and the like. It really felt like that in the early seventies London was an exciting place to be.

People were always coming and going from the flat and soon a large group of people began to meet up in the local pubs and immersed themselves in the pleasures of living in London. Most Friday nights they all met up at a restaurant. Their favourite was The Stockpot in Earls Court. It was like a real Italian cafe that was also really cheap so they could eat lasagne and drink cheap chianti, that was served in raffia wrapped bottles, and not break the bank. No one had much spare money as they were all just starting out on their careers. They really enjoyed the restaurant and it made them feel very cosmopolitan to order from all the Italian dishes on the menu.

The number of people Peter came into contact with was growing at a furious pace that was considerably helped by the fact that he always had a piece of good dope to smoke and it was always possible for anyone to buy some from him as well. It wasn't long before he was selling several ounces of hash a day, while John was working or at college, and had done all his business before five in the afternoon, so no one was fully aware of what was going on. He had been round to visit a guy who had sold him a weight of dope when he was at college. He lived nearby in West London and so Peter went to revisit. As it turned out the guy had stopped selling dope, due to a scare with the police, but they sat around smoking a little Thai Grass some travelling Australians had supplied Peter. It was amazing weed and did the trick because after a little prompting Peter left with the phone numbers of some people called Dave and Ernst who were still selling lots of dope. That was just the lead he was looking for and he turned the numbers to good use by starting to buy dope from them.

Claire, their flatmate, was struggling to qualify as a barrister and get a job, as it cost her quite a lot of money which she did not have, and Peter had been helping her out with her rent and food for a couple of months. She was appreciative of this and also she was aware that Peter was starting to move quite a bit of weight from the flat. He had moved up to arranging the sale of pound weight deals by getting the sellers to wait in Claire's room, with the buyers in his room and the deal done in the kitchen so the two never met. Claire wasn't there and was happy with the arrangement and racked up a debt of about £200. One day Peter and John came back from the pub and found she had done a flit.

Her room was empty and she had just moved out with no word to anyone. It was no big deal as the rent was so low but they felt a bit miffed that she hadn't told them she was going.

Peter thought it was because she owed him so much money but it later transpired that she had got herself a job. The only job she had been able to get was as Prosecuting Barrister for Her Majesty's Customs and Excise Drugs Department! That would explain why she didn't want to carry on sharing a flat with a dope dealer and although he wished her well he had no desire to meet her again in her new official capacity and promptly moved into her bigger room.

Gill had been dropping by occasionally, sometimes to buy or sell some dope, and often stayed the night but they didn't have a serious relationship. It was a good business partnership and also fun to be with her although he hadn't heard anything from her for a few weeks.

One day Clem phoned and asked if Peter was doing anything and would he come over to the flat as there was something he needed some help with. Peter drove over to Bloomsbury and was met at the door by Keiko, Clem's Japanese wife, who seemed very happy to see him.

"Come in. Come in. Clem not here right now. He teaching sitar to his student but I have a favour to ask you."

Peter was curious to know what the favour was.

"Sure thing. If I can help I will. What do you need doing?"

"Come in and I show you." And she led the way into their living room. Sitting on the sofa was a very petite Japanese looking girl. She was absolutely stunning and tiny like a pretty little doll. She had black hair that was cut short and her skin was the colour of clear honey. He soon realised where this was going.

Peter was introduced to Yasuko who was not actually Japanese but came from South Korea. She was 19 years old but looked younger. He thought she looked amazing and was really beautiful.

"Yasuko has just been thrown out of her flat by her

boyfriend. He's very unkind to her and she has nowhere to stay. Clem thought maybe you would help her out?"

"What do you mean? Does she want to come home with me?"

"Yes, I would very much like to come home with you," Yasuko said "Keiko says you a nice man. Not like the Peter who threw me out. He was crazy man. He was a musician with big ploblems." All of this was spoken with a singsong Japanese style accent that was driving Peter crazy.

A while later Clem got back and was delighted that his problem guest had been found a new place to stay.

"The moment Keiko told me about her I knew you were the one to help us out."

"Are you sure she wants to come with me?" Peter asked.

He had never been in this kind of situation before but was delighted with it.

"Yes she wants to go with you but I must warn you she is as crazy as a box of frogs," Clem told him ominously.

Her bag was already packed and off they went in the car. Keiko waved and smiled and Clem laughed as the pair drove off back to Peter's flat.

What had he let himself into he wondered as they drove out of Bloomsbury. They talked about her ex-boyfriend who was a really famous guitarist who took some bad drugs many years ago and that had pretty much ended a brilliant career.

"He was a good man but he sometimes beat me up," she said.

"I can assure you I would never do that."

"Oh but sometimes I like it. You know, being hurt a little."

No he didn't know but was interested in giving it a go, if that's what she liked!

They drove in silence wondering how this would turn out.

"What are you thinking about?" she asked as they passed Notting Hill Gate tube station.

"Oh, I was just wondering what you looked like with your clothes off."

"You like I show you now?" she said laughing. Then she whipped her tee shirt off over her head displaying the loveliest pair of honey coloured breasts. He had never been so turned on by a girl before. Her tiny size made her even sexier. Peter couldn't believe his luck. He was taking home the loveliest Oriental girl he'd ever seen and she was absolutely wild.

"I don't think the good people of Holland Park are ready to enjoy the delights of your titties. Let's wait till we get back to the flat so I can enjoy them properly."

"Alright then. But from the bulge in your trousers we had better hurry home," she said, pulling her tee shirt down tightly so he could clearly see her nipples straining through the material. He couldn't believe she was prepared to undress in the car and show him her body right in the middle of Notting Hill. The last thing he needed was a pull from the police. Otherwise he may have let her take all her clothes off in the car. Why not? Maybe she was mad but he didn't care. This could turn out to be a lot of fun.

When they got back to the flat he showed her his room and said she could put her bag away and she sat on his lap and kissed him.

"Thank you for taking me into your house Peter. I think you are a kind man. You want to look at my body now. I show you."

Slowly and gently he undressed her and looked with wonder at this beautiful tiny body. She looked like a porcelain doll, that would shatter if you were too rough, but really she was not at all delicate and she displayed herself with the self-confidence of a young beautiful girl.

"You know I will do whatever you want me to. I don't mind. You just tell me what you like and I do it. You know. Anything." She said to him with a big grin.

Peter was stunned. His mind was spinning. He couldn't believe he was hearing this angelic looking girl saying something like that. There had never been anyone like her before. Although he had slept with quite a few girls at college they all needed to be persuaded into bed and then they were mostly fairly shy and a little inhibited. He wasn't sure he would be able to come up with enough interesting ways of pleasing this little oriental firecracker but he was prepared to give it a go.

What did happen was the slow beginning of an introduction to sensual and sexual pleasure. The difference of attitude between the West and the Far East was unimaginable to the naive young Peter but he was a patient and enthusiastic pupil willing to learn and practice the art of lovemaking. Oriental Style.

"I think it take me some time to help you," she said in her cute way.

"You can take all the time you need. We've got all the time in the world."

And then she blew his mind.

They were still in bed when John got back from work and stuck his head round the door.

"Wowee," he exclaimed, "Where did you get her from?"

"Well I'm looking after her for a friend. She is Korean. Meet Yasuko. She is going to be staying with me for a bit."

"You are one Jammy Bastard," John said as he shut the door.

"Doesn't he like me?" she asked.

"Oh yes he likes you. And now I'll show you just how much I like you," he whispered. She just giggled and they started over again.

At first for them the sex was like being caught just off the beach by a giant wave, being picked up flung around and washed-up exhausted back on the shore. Then after the initial excitement she introduced him to the long slow secrets of pleasuring each other and they spent hours practising the art. Then came the spells of boredom.

At that particular time arranging the sale of pounds of dope was a slow waiting game. Days are spent waiting beside the phone until the stuff arrives, then there is a short spell of adrenaline rushed activity. The dangers of being ripped off or busted are ever present and until it's all over and the money has been counted there is no safety. The buyers have to be contacted so they can put the money together and then get round to the flat. Then the sellers have to be persuaded to bring the gear round, at the same time, to be sold. It would have been so much easier if he had enough money to just buy it and sell it in his own time. For now it had to be like this. He stayed by the phone for days waiting to hear if the gear had arrived. He couldn't leave the flat while a deal was being planned for fear of missing the opportunity of making some money. The only phone was a landline and he had to sit close to it because if he went out and was not there to take the call he could miss the whole deal.

The upside of this was that he had Yasuko with him all of the time, although she always went away when the deals were being done. She wanted to see no part of what she said was "that bad thing." Otherwise she was always around and always ready to play the rest of the time. Nothing surprised her. Nothing but nothing shocked her. It was true she would do anything for him and during the long times spent waiting she pretty much did as she continued his education. There was a downside though. She was actually as mad as a box of frogs as Clem had said. She would disappear for hours at a time and not say where she had been. She got very possessive. She got very moody sometimes to the point of being depressed. Nothing would bring her out of these black moods. There was no way to connect with her and after a while, like all good things, the novelty began to wear off.

One afternoon while she was out Peter went downstairs to see Nick. He was sorting out his radio show but made a cup of tea and they sat on cushions on the floor drinking it.

"What's up, mate? You look a bit pissed off. Is that girlfriend of yours wearing you out?" Nick asked.

"Well, to be truthful, she is beginning to get on my nerves a bit."

"What! I thought she was the real deal."

"Yeah she is the real deal but she is also mental. I get so angry with her and all she says is 'Don't hit me or I'll never leave you.'"

This really got Nick intrigued.

"Are you saying you can't hit her because she likes it too much?"

"Yes I am."

"But you don't hit her, do you?"

"No of course I don't but she seems to want me to."

"Oh really. Can I have a go?"

"Course you can. What are friends for?" Peter said ironically. "I'll try to get her to drop in on her way out."

"But what does she like? I've no idea about that sort of thing."

"You don't need any idea. She has enough ideas for everyone," Peter said with a dead straight face as Nick was looking wistfully into the distance.

It wasn't long before Yasuko tired of life in Shepherd's Bush. She did stop off into Nick's flat on the way out, but what happened there was never talked about. It was assumed that she went back to the rock star who was making a bit of a comeback. Peter was happy for them as he thought that her Peter was one of the best guitarists he had ever heard play and he deserved a crazy chick like Yasuko to inspire him.

Peter did have one huge regret and that was he was unable to get in touch with Gill while Yasuko was staying with him. She had moved to a flat just opposite Olympia and hadn't given him her new number yet. He wanted to persuade her to come round and get it on with the two of them. Although Gill had only ever expressed a passing interest in making out with other girls Peter could tell she was interested and it would have been so much fun with the three of them in bed together.

"Oh well!" – to quote a well-known song of that time.

The supply of dope seemed to dry up around that time and a few weeks had gone by with nothing to sell but the lousy Moroccan, so-called Penny Stamp, our Irish political friends had stockpiled by the hundredweight in North London and nobody would buy unless there was absolutely nothing else for sale. The name came from the impression of a Moroccan coin that was on every kilo block making it instantly recognisable. It was rumoured that the money made selling it was used to buy arms and explosives so nobody was very keen to buy it. Also it was absolute dross.

The phone rang and John called out to Peter: "It's for you. It's one of the Sweaty Socks."

Peter assumed it was Bruce ringing about some party or gig he wanted a lift to and he was surprised when a familiar voice said, "It's Malcolm … Nixon, you know?" The familiar Glasgow accent was unmistakably Malcolm's voice. "What are you doing now?" he asked, not really wanting to know.

"Oh you know a bit of this and a bit of that. You know how it is."

"Aye so you're still pushing drugs are ye?" Peter realised

Jurgen hadn't been able to keep quiet about the joints they all smoked together.

"Yes. Just a few bits and pieces. You know. Just to keep the wolf from the door."

"It's not the wolf you need to keep from the door it's the polis you have to watch for ye stupid wee barmpot." Malcolm's accent always got broader the more excited he got. "Anyway I want you to come to my office tomorrow. I've got something happening that is the Real Thing."

"Oh have you really?" He'd heard so many schemes and plans being cooked up with Bruce and none of them had come to anything. Peter was mildly interested as things were a bit quiet at the moment. But that wouldn't last. The next shipment would arrive soon and it would all kick off again.

"Listen to me," Malcolm barked into the other end of the phone "What I've got going is fucking huge. This is not pissing around like Bruce and his stupid showers. I've been working on this for a year and now it is happening. I've got an office on the eleventh floor of a building overlooking the Thames. I've got a secretary. I have a budget to pay wages and expenses for a wee eejit like you to come along and help work on the biggest pop festival this country has ever seen. Yes or no. Are you in?"

"I'm in." What a no brainer. Malcolm's work and planning had finally come up trumps. This was the big one they had all been waiting for.

"Get yourself to the eleventh floor of Alembic House on the Albert Embankment tomorrow at nine and don't come looking like a tramp. I'll tell you all about it and we can discuss your wages and expenses then. All the money is sorted for us to start work on this Festival. So get some sleep and I'll see you tomorrow." Peter was visibly shaken. What had just happened? John could see something monumental had just occurred.

"What's happening man? You look like you've had a shock"

"I think something huge is happening. It doesn't sound like the usual Mickey Mouse scams those two get up to," Peter said. "I've got a feeling this is the big one. But who knows, it might just be some of Malcolm's bullshit. I'll have a better idea when I get to see him tomorrow."

"Good luck then. Maybe this will work out for you."

"I hope so. I really hope so."

CHAPTER 5

Our choices were few

If Peter was afraid of walking into the shower saleroom to meet Bruce, he was terrified by what he saw on the Albert Embankment. Arriving by Tube he walked alongside the Thames looking for Alembic House. There was no number and he had to look at all the office buildings on the river side of the road. He read the name Tintagel House. Wasn't that a place in Cornwall? What did they do in there? He thought to himself and there it was, right next door, Alembic House. Set back from the road and towering above him was the building. In front was access to the underground car park and a driveway for a car to access the front door. Parked outside was a big silver Rolls Royce and chauffeur waiting for someone to come out. The main doors opened and a man who looked dark and menacing, had a prominent brow and moody eyebrows, swept through being trailed by a dark-haired girl who Peter for a foolish moment thought was his daughter. Peter recognised the man as the actor Stanley Baker who had made lots of British films in which he had played Gangsters and 'Hard Men'. He was obviously in a hurry and didn't want to be spotted leaving the building. Peter waited for the Rolls to leave and walked to the front door and pressed the 11th floor buzzer. A disembodied voice asked who he was. He told the voice he was coming to work for Malcolm Nixon and was informed he could come up to the 11th floor. He was buzzed in and got in the lift and pressed the button and alighted when the lift stopped. There was a vestibule with two front doors in it. He picked the right hand one and rang the bell. The door was opened by a secretary who showed him through what was essentially half of the 11th floor turned into offices, to the room where Malcolm sat at a desk looking up to The Houses of Parliament from the south side of the river. What a view. Malcolm was grinning from ear to ear. This cat had certainly got the cream. Peter had never dreamed a place like this existed let alone imagined himself working in it. There was a vacant desk under the window overlooking South London, which turned out to be his, and another desk where a pretty young woman sat in front of her typewriter. She was introduced as Linda. She was Malcolm's secretary who would also assist him when it was needed.

"A secretary when I need it. What is this job?" Peter thought.

Malcolm as usual was two steps ahead of him and said to Linda, "We're going out for a while," and they went back to the lift together. As they passed the other door he said, "That is where the Booking Agent John Martin is. He's an utter wanker. You won't have much to do with him as he keeps himself to himself."

They took the lift and went up a floor and Malcolm started to explain a little of what was going on.

All Peter needed to know right now was that Malcolm had sold his idea about putting on a pop festival. He had arranged the backing from a group of businessmen who were allowing it to be run from these offices. The building was completely owned by Stanley Baker's company and Stanley kept a grand bedroom there as a pied-à-terre for when he couldn't get home to his wife and family and needed to stay in London! There was an underground parking garage, which Peter could use on the occasions his car would be needed, that housed the Rolls and a magnificent Citroen Maserati which Stanley used as his runaround. It was impressed on Peter the need for discretion which meant no mention of Bruce and his gang, and if he wanted to work here, he would have to commit 100% for which he would be paid £100 a week by Stanley's secretary and to keep all receipts for expenses which would all be reimbursed weekly. Peter asked what he was expected to do.

"Well, you'll help set up the biggest and best pop festival ever seen of course. Why else would I get you here?

While Malcolm was explaining the deal he opened the door to the upstairs flat and they went inside. It was the Penthouse Suite and Peter could not believe his eyes. It was so much more impressive than the floor below. He stopped listening to what Malcolm was saying and tried to take in the place. For a start the living room was two stories high and occupied the top two floors on the corner of the building. It was completely empty with absolutely no furniture or sign of habitation. Both of the outside walls were made entirely of double height glass and had an even more spectacular view over the Thames, overlooking the MI5 building and up to the Houses of Parliament. The building was built right over the Thames and from this height appeared to be surrounded on three sides by water. There were open stairs up to a mezzanine area with bedrooms that were behind single-storey walls made completely from mirrors which also reflected the spectacular views of London. This experience was completely mind blowing for the boy from the country. He'd never seen anything like this but kept quiet so as not to seem too much like a hick. Malcolm just laughed and said, "Pretty impressive huh?"

"You could say that. So does Stanley own the whole building then?"

"Yes I believe he does. Him and his company."

"Jesus I didn't think anyone could make that much money. And he doesn't even live in the place." And so it started.

They went back down and Peter sat at his empty desk waiting for a clue about where he was to start and Malcolm as ever started giving him a mountain of tasks that involved looking up the names and addresses of people, companies and businesses that would be contacted in the future. This process entailed laboriously looking through telephone directories and the *Yellow Pages* for individual numbers and addresses and writing them down on paper until they needed to be contacted. It took ages to find a measly 50 addresses but Malcolm didn't care. He didn't want it to look like he ever had nothing to do. Look busy was the watchword and Peter always complied and in no time at all he was snowed under with things to do.

The office they were in was on the south side of the building and had magnificent views up the river up to Westminster Bridge. The East End and the Docks lay in the distance to the east. There was a smaller room which housed three of Stanley's secretaries next to a huge L shaped room with an 18-seater table and beautiful views across the river to the South Bank and up to the rear of the Houses of Parrliament. This was the room that had featured as the office in the film *The Italian Job* and could easily be recognised from the fabulous views and the very seventies floor lamp. Also there was Stanley's bedroom but that was completely off limits for them.

According to Malcolm a company had been set up, to organise the festival, consisting of Stanley Baker, Lord Harlech, Michael Deeley and Barry Spikings.

Michael Deeley had produced *The Italian Job* which had been, until then, moderately successful for him and he appeared to have made plenty of money. Lord Harlech was a friend of Stanley and his name on the headed note-paper added dignity to the company. Stanley Baker was putting up all of the seed money and allowing some of his building to be used as office space and Barry Spikings was a completely unknown quantity. He had apparently been a reporter on a local paper in Lincolnshire and had made a short film for which he had won the "The Golden Ear" award from the *Farmer's Weekly*!

Building on this prestigious start he was looking to make his mark in London and had a way about him that made you feel like he would do anything to get it.

As this was the start of the project everyone was very friendly and they all worked well together with the united wish to get the festival off the ground. At the moment the festival was in its infancy. There was no site, no bands and no proper finance in place.

The idea was to do a festival absolutely 100% properly and that meant everything was to be paid for up front. The Bands, the site owner, the onsite facilities like loos, caravans, lighting, sound, contractors and services. Everything! This was totally unheard of at this time, when everything was usually on credit until all the money had come in and if enough didn't come in, nobody got paid. The idea was to run the best festival possible and if you paid up front you could get the best. At the moment it was Stanley who was covering all the costs.

Malcolm had been asked to go to Michael's house that evening and told Peter that he wanted him to come with him. He was enjoying hobnobbing around town with his new wealthy friends and liked the idea of someone else seeing it as well. They took a cab to Belgravia and found a very discreet Mews running behind the street. Apparently this was a really expensive part of town and the Mews was a very fashionable place to live. All this meant nothing to Peter who was just sucking up all these experiences like a sponge. He was learning so many new things and was determined to use all this knowledge at a later date. They entered Michael's little cottage and climbed a small staircase to the living room. It all seemed so small to Peter who wondered why he didn't buy something bigger. The whole house could be no bigger than a double garage. He had no idea this little place in Belgravia had cost an absolute fortune. He waited at the top of the stairs and was introduced to Michael and his lovely wife Ruth who were very welcoming. Malcolm and Michael immediately signed some papers and had an animated discussion about something while Peter looked at the artwork on the wall. One picture took his fancy and he saw it was done by Picasso. When they had finished the discussion, Michael asked if he was alright. Peter said he was fine and was just admiring the Picasso print.

"Picasso print?" Michael laughed "That is a real fucking Picasso. Not a print." They all thought it was hilarious and Peter learnt then and there not to assume anything with these people.

When he got back in the cab with Malcolm he apologised for being so stupid but Malcolm just laughed and said, "How could you know it was real? Anyway he got a big kick being able to tell someone it's a real Picasso. He's loaded and wants to make more and I'm going to help him."

The cab dropped Malcolm off at his flat in Regent's Park and then drove Peter home to the Bush. He felt posh getting out of the cab saying, "Thanks… it's on Stanley's account" and everyone in the flats was impressed when he said he had come home from work on his first day in a taxi.

Next day he had been told to bring his car and he parked it in the underground car park next to the Rolls and went upstairs to his office. Apparently the number one task was to find a suitable site for a festival 'as soon as'. They spent the next few weeks travelling around the country looking for a suitable venue. They looked at County showgrounds and any other interesting sites in Essex, Sussex, Kent, Berkshire and all points around London. Peter was elated because he was getting paid by the mile at a very good rate and made more money travelling around the country than his car had cost him.

Everywhere was wrong for some reason or other and it was getting to the point when it was embarrassing that there was no site yet. The press had got wind of this odd consortium trying to put on a pop festival and was trying very hard to discredit them with their usual subtlety and charm.

In the early 1970s it was normal for the Establishment to try to stop anything that allowed young people to enjoy themselves. They were trying to stem the tide of long-haired, unwashed kids doing anything that upset the Established Order. The Government legislated wherever they could. Jobs were not given to people with long hair, and having a good time was looked down upon. Enjoying rock music and smoking drugs was particularly discouraged and the police were encouraged to plant dope on famous musicians. Most of the newspapers toed the party line and gave their full backing and publicity to the right-wing archaic views of the day.

On one of their trips Peter told Malcolm about his trip that summer to the free festival in Somerset. He said the site was really beautiful but it was very small and all access was through the tiny village of Pilton. It would not be possible to get access for more than 10,000 people and they were looking at getting nearer to 300,000!

Malcolm told Michael Deeley about this magical little festival site and Peter was sent for and asked to describe the site. He retold the story saying it would be too small and with no access would create bad publicity as well as major congestion problems but it was decided that Barry and Peter would go down there on Sunday to have a look. Things were getting desperate and maybe, with Barry's 'superior festival know how' they could find a way to make it work.

The owner of the site was the farmer who had allowed some young 'poshy' people to organise a free festival on his land last summer. His name, Peter told them, was Michael Eavis. Eavis was duly phoned and it was arranged to visit him on Sunday. It didn't start well as Peter was an hour late arriving at Barry's flat in Queensway because he forgot to put his clock forward for the end of British Summer Time. Eventually Peter, Barry, his wife and baby daughter piled into a little Lancia and they set off for Somerset. It was not long before they picked up a puncture and Barry had started to get angry. The day was hot and Barry didn't want any help with the wheel and the baby was crying and they were only halfway there. The inside of the car heated up as did tempers but finally they arrived at the picturesque village of Pilton. Both Barry and his wife thought the village was gorgeous with its lovely cottages and gardens basking in sunlight. They weaved through the narrow lanes until they arrived at the entrance to Worthy Farm. Driving down the track the farm looked a bit tumble down and had a shabby look about it. Obviously the farm was not making any money and if it was suitable the owner would bite their hand off to get paid to put on a festival there.

Michael Eavis met them at the door and leaving his wife and baby in the farmhouse Barry walked down the hill, with Michael and Peter, to the field where the free festival had been held. The site was beautiful and was a natural amphitheatre and the perfect site for a small festival but the juggernaut that was being planned in London could in no way be crowbarred into the few acres of Worthy Farm. They thanked Eavis for his time showing them around his lovely farm. It was just too small for the affair that was being planned and with no real access to the site the complications would be too great to overcome and Barry said he was really sorry but they couldn't fit the festival here. They wished him well if he planned any more festivals and they shook his hand and left. Barry did not want to hang around looking at a site he couldn't use so they all jumped back into the car and headed back to London.

"Why didn't you say the site was so small?" Barry asked Peter as they drove out of Pilton.

"But I did say it was small. And that the access was too limited for anything larger than a 10,000-person festival. I also said it was perfect for a little free festival."

"Well we've wasted a day and got no further finding a site," Barry snapped back. The heat and strain of the crying child and the pressure to find a site all seemed too much for him.

The atmosphere was colder than the temperature in the car and they eventually got back to London without further disaster.

The next day when the papers arrived, the headlines on one of the tabloids read:

'The Festival Company With Nowhere To Go! Someone had phoned round the papers to sell the story of the big festival company still looking for a site. It wasn't such a big deal, it was just that the papers were all over the company with bad publicity. Every time they could find a story to make them look bad they published it. They took great delight mocking Lord Harlech and Stanley Baker and it seemed there was always something for them to mock.

Everyone grumbled about the whistle blower and wondered who could have sold the story for 50 quid to the newspapers.

Malcolm reminded everyone that Peter had said the site was too small and so it was Barry who copped the blame.

From then on Barry seemed more determined to prove himself as someone special and look out anyone standing in the way!

Still there was no finance in place, no site and not one band had been booked.

CHAPTER 6

We fought the Law...
and we won

Then along came a problem that threatened to not only put an end to their festival but to stop all festivals forever. The Conservative Government of the time, run by Edward Heath, was very concerned that young people were having too much fun. They were listening to pop music, dancing, taking drugs, making love indiscriminately and generally enjoying themselves far too much. Moral standards had declined and it was time to put a stop to it. Pop festivals were the breeding ground of all this decline and someone very high up in Government decided to introduce a law to stop them. Of course it wasn't presented like that.

A Private Member's Bill was passed through committee stage after some revision. According to the National Campaign for Civil Liberty this was the outline:

"The original formulation of the Night Assemblies Bill made it a criminal offence to hold a gathering of 1000 people or more in the open air for any period of three hours between midnight and 6 am without applying to a local authority four months beforehand and without giving certain financial guarantees."

The Bill was introduced by Sir Alfred William Wiggins who was known as Jerry Wiggins after his grandfather, the man he aspired to be. Representing the safe seat of

Weston-super-Mare for the Conservatives he had been to Eton and Trinity College and sat on the far right of the party. He was a member of The Monday Club, a supporter of Ian Smith in Rhodesia opposing sanctions in Rhodesia and South Africa, and regularly called for the restoration of the death penalty. A True-Blue Conservative.

This upright pillar of the community later turned out not to be so squeaky clean. He was later called 'Junket Jerry' by *Private Eye* because of so many fully paid trips abroad for all the useless committees he sat on.

He at one time put Sebastian Coe's name on an amendment to a Bill, without either notifying or consulting him on behalf of a lobbying group for which he was a paid consultant and stood to make a lot of money from. Had he tabled it in his own name he would have had to declare an interest and the amendment would probably not have carried. He did however come up with a sound defence.

"That is always the way I operate," he said.

The then Tory whip Giles Brandreth called him a 'greedy tosser' and in the spirit of policing MP's behaviour towards money grabbing, an independent oversight to MP's expenses was created. That turned out to be useless as well.

This was the stalwart the government had going in to bat for them. This was the respectable upstanding politician that everyone was supposed to respect and his dishonesty had yet to rear its ugly head. Jerry Wiggins said that the Bill was aimed at controlling pop festivals although there was no mention of that in the Bill. Mark Woodnutt, one of the Bill's sponsors, explained his difficulty in drafting a Bill relating to health and safety at pop festivals and said that organisations such as the NCCL should propose amendments to limit its scope.

The other obvious dangers of passing a Bill like this was that all sorts of other assemblies would be included.

Political demonstrations, trade union rallies and charity meetings even Boy Scout jamborees would be affected. The general public needed to be informed of the draconian laws that were being slipped through the back door to curb their freedom.

Keith Waterhouse said in the *Daily Mirror*: "The Bill does not have the guts to say it's intention is to stamp out pop festivals. It can only magnify the appalling relationships already existing between the young and old."

It didn't take long for everyone at Alembic House to realise that if this Bill went through there would be no festival and therefore no big profits for them. The wheels of the festival company suddenly started turning.

A campaign was mounted to let the public know about what was happening. In the days before Twitter and Facebook, it was not easy to contact a lot of people at once so it meant Peter was given the job of contacting as many people as possible, individually by a Royal Mail letter, to create a media storm so that public opinion forced the stopping of this outrageous new law. A list of sympathetic names were drawn up. Everyone in the office, including Michael and Stanley, suggested names of people who would be helpful and could get this Fascist move by the Government stopped before it was sneaked through. The many names of pop stars, comedians, film stars, left-wing politicians, barristers, judges, peers of the realm (thank you Lord Harlech) and every relevant name and address in everyone's Filofax was duly dumped on Peter's desk. They were sorted in order of importance and influence, the really important ones were contacted personally by their friends, and a letter was composed by Malcolm. The letter was a masterpiece of left-wing outrage about the freedoms of the public being stolen by the smug Tories. How if this Bill got through it would be illegal to have a barbeque at your village fete at night. So make some noise. Write to your MP. Write to your newspaper. Tell your friends. Stop this Stupid Bill!

The letter was typed up and Xeroxed by their long-suffering secretary Linda, and Peter personally signed all 1500 of them, rendering his signature to a straight scrawl, and all the secretaries in the offices were drafted in to type the addresses and everyone filled the envelopes and stuck the stamps on. This took them days to physically achieve. The first reply came by letter from Spike Milligan who offered his support and signed off the letter saying: "Fuck 'em all! Spike." They loved him for that.

Lord Harlech was called in to use his influence in the House of Lords and the general public began to get outraged by this obnoxious piece of subterfuge. The publicity grew bigger and bigger and the more people who heard about the Bill registered their protest and after weeks of campaigning the Government and even Heath were embarrassed to be associated with such an unpopular piece of legislation and it was left to wither and die without being submitted again. Ted Heath and his cronies were run over by the steamroller of public opinion. The festival company was ecstatic. Now we can make some real money was the byword.

There was much celebrating in Alembic House. As well as the success of stopping the Night Assemblies Bill a new site for the festival had been found by Malcolm. A farmer had offered his land in a place called Tollesbury near the coast in Essex. It was a start but everyone knew that there would be lots of wrangling to do before the site could be used. The usual public outcry and complaints would start soon and everyone would have to be placated and assured of their safety with offers of financial compensation. Malcolm and Peter went off to the site to assess its suitability and while Malcolm looked over the fields with the farmer Peter was sent to do a recce around the village. He stopped in the shop where they were excited about the prospect of thousands of kids coming to the village to listen to music. The pub felt the same way. Both places obviously felt there was an opportunity to make some money. And why not? Other villagers were not so happy about a horde of long-haired, unwashed drug addicts rampaging through their village wreaking havoc. When Malcolm got back he said, "It's not perfect but it's big enough and in a pretty area close enough to London. We can secure the site with no problem so it's all good. How were the natives?"

"Well the pub and the shop obviously were all for it and some customers in the pub were hostile but mostly they didn't think it was such a bad thing as long as they could make a few quid out of it."

They drove back to the office discussing ways of making the idea of a festival less of a threat to the villagers and thinking of ways they could be included or compensated for the inevitable inconvenience.

All too soon the Village Action Committee was formed and a meeting was arranged to discuss whether the festival was to be allowed to happen there. It was very important that the village heard how this festival was going to be so well financed and organised and to get the point across Stanley Baker and Michael Deeley drove to Tollesbury in the Rolls to attend the meeting and put their side across. The meeting went well and although several villagers were vehemently against the event taking place most people thought it wasn't such a bad thing and maybe it was an opportunity to bring some money into the village.

As well as Stanley coming from London the BBC had sent a television news crew in the hope of filming some violent protest or at least angry shouting and fist waving. Unfortunately for them, this didn't happen but this did not deter them. They rounded up some vocal anti-festival villagers and pulled out the makings of a bonfire and two effigies from the back of a BBC van. They built the fire and set it alight and filmed the villagers shouting, "No to the festival," and shouting, "We don't want a festival here," and such slogans. They told the villagers to angrily throw the effigies on the fire, while they filmed it, to publicise their cause. This was done and the two effigies went up in flames. One of them looked mildly like the Welsh actor as it had a monobrow but no one had a clue who the other one was. The only people apart from his family, who knew what Lord Harlech looked like were the people in the props department of the BBC. They had obviously been commissioned to make these effigies, to give to the good people of Tollesbury, who would throw them on the bonfire to make a good visual news story. Whoever would have guessed The Beeb was so biased towards the right-wing establishment?

Even without the help of the BBC it was decided at the meeting the festival could go on with certain provisos and compensation which could be worked out later. The Good People of Essex had prevailed and now could earn a bob or two! The publicity machine went into full swing and announcements were made about the new site.

Stanley had a son who was about 18 or so. He had the same brooding good looks of his father, but none of his brains, and he too thought he was a ladies' man. In the interests of finding him a job, or something he could actually do, he was dispatched to Tollesbury as a sort of trouble-shooting ambassador. He was to smooth the way and stop any problems which may pop up.

Several days later the catastrophic news came through that the farmer in Tollesbury had changed his mind and the festival was off. There was nothing that could be done to make him change his mind and that was that. All hell broke loose and Peter was sent to find out what had happened and it was finally confirmed that nothing could change his mind. No reason could be found as to why he was so adamant about this change of mind. There was however a rumour going around, which nobody believed, that Master Baker in his job of spreading goodwill around the village had been overzealous in his attentions to the farmer's young daughter.

They had allegedly been caught in bed together by the farmer who was unsurprisingly not amused to the point of cancelling the festival and threatening to shoot any member of the Baker family who set foot in the village. Nobody believed that story as the lad seemed such a likeable, sensible boy.

Once again the press had a field day. They crowed about the Festival Company with no festival site and took great delight in ridiculing the hapless Baker and Harlech. What they didn't know was that not only was there still nowhere to hold the festival, not one single band had been booked nor was the finance in place yet.

CHAPTER 7

He ain't heavy, he's my father

Malcolm's reaction to this monumental cockup was surprisingly mild. He only spent about five minutes raging about the stupid, incompetent, cock happy, spoiled, idiot boy who had fouled up everyone's hard work and didn't deserve to be let out into the real world without his nanny. Soon enough he was concentrating on a new site.

The papers were full of news about the festival company looking for a new site and there were quite a few people who were prepared to bear the brunt of the anger of their neighbours in order to allow a festival to be held on their land. In exchange for an amount of money, to compensate for their inconvenience, you understand.

One such gentleman was Lieutenant Colonel Michael Underwood, formerly of the Queen's Own Cameron Highlanders. It was now January 1972 and Underwood owned 45 prime acres in a village in Kent called Bishopsbourne and had offered it to be used for the festival now planned for the May Bank Holiday three months away.

The villagers of Bishopsbourne were not as delighted with this news as the good Lieutenant Colonel and set about expressing their disaffection for him. His wife's car was surrounded by a baying mob who rocked it while shouting at her. He received threatening letters, bomb threats and was even sent a shit parcel in the post. Malcolm was delighted with this site. It was close enough to London for people to travel there easily and it was on a pretty estate. He was determined not to lose this one and made a statement to the press saying, "There is no way this festival can be stopped from taking place. We are on a private estate. We have done our homework, legally and in every way. The fact that people don't like it is unfortunate."

If the good people of Bishopsbourne had been angry before they were now incandescent with rage. They doubled their attack on the courageous Lieutenant Colonel, who had shown bravery in the face of war, making his life hell and threatened to demolish his house brick by brick. After considering all of the possibilities the wily ex-soldier decided to retreat and pulled out of the fray. It was again reported by the press that the festival company had nowhere to pitch their tents.

The mood in the back office was now pretty gloomy. Malcolm briefly had visions of his money-making idea turning into nothing with the company dropping out from all the bad publicity. He spent a lot of time chasing around the country, with Peter looking for other sites and seemed to grow even more determined. It was his idea and it would work!

Peter was just being swept along by the tidal wave and could not believe how complex business could get. He was also loving all the expenses he was making while driving hundreds of miles a week.

Linda was snowed under with a deluge of letters and memos from Malcolm and had become very protective of him and particularly Peter who she appeared to like very much. He didn't really understand how this attraction worked. Girls were attracted to him and people seemed to think he knew more than he actually did. He did nothing to stop either happening and felt it was a blessing.

One day when things were quiet and Malcolm was away from the office Linda came over to Peter's desk.

"Can I ask you something?" she said.

"Of course you can. Ask away," he replied wondering what was coming.

"Well I'm not sure how to say it. But here goes. Would you take me out for a drink one night?" Peter nearly passed out. It was slightly unusual for a girl to ask someone out in the seventies but he thought that was sweet. The idea of going out for a drink with Linda also seemed not a bad idea. The fact she had a five-year-old son was not a problem. All these things raced through his mind in a split second as she was waiting for him to say "Yes." The problems that Peter had were this. If they went out together and one thing led to another and they started to get it on they would have to work in the same office together. This may not be too much of a problem but if they then broke up it may be a little difficult. If they broke up acrimoniously this could be really serious. However all this paled into insignificance. Linda's father was a good friend of Stanley Baker. His name was Albert Dimes, otherwise known as 'Italian Albert'. Stanley liked to hang out with the criminal fraternity and many East End gangsters could be called his friend. Reputedly the Stanley Baker film *The Criminal* made by Joseph Losey, had been partly based on Albert. His reputation had been legendary in and around Soho in the 40s and 50s. He had been born in Scotland to an Italian father and a Scottish mother and then moved to Clerkenwell which was called 'Little Italy' at the time. He went to work for gang leader Billy Hill getting involved in loan sharking and bookmaking. He was convicted of attacking a man in a club in Wardour Street and was bound over for three years. In the attack a man was killed by another gangster.

The most famous legend surrounding him was that in

1955 during gang wars between a Jewish gang, run by Jack Spot, and the Italians. Albert and Jack had a very public and vicious knife fight on a Soho street. Albert had been defending Soho against the other gangs who wanted a piece of the very lucrative area. Both men were critically wounded and although they were both seriously injured and on the floor bleeding to death, they were still both attempting to kill each other. As could only happen in Soho an angry Jewish grandma ran out of a nearby shop and laid into them with a very large and very heavy metal ladle and stopped the fighting till the police arrived. No charges were made as both men denied anything untoward had happened. Apparently it was all an accident.

It was alleged that in 1966 Dimes arranged a meeting between New York mafiosi and the Corsican Francisci brothers in order to arrange investing in London casinos. It was said that it was only his association with Charlie Richardson that kept the Krays out of Soho for years.

All of this flashed through Peter's brain along with visions of an irate Albert avenging all the wrongs done to his poor daughter, by the dastardly young Peter, with the knife he had used on Jack Spot.

"Well?" she said, wondering why he wasn't answering.

"Er, no I can't," he muttered. Working for Malcolm who was although not overtly, but was undeniably, homosexual did have the downside that people might think Peter was too. He didn't care what people thought and wondered if this was a put-up job by the other secretaries to find out whether he was straight.

"Why not?" She was now in the swing of it and was not prepared to take no for an answer. She had gone this far and didn't want to give up now.

"What can I say? I can't, that's all," he said feebly but this wasn't good enough.

"Ok I understand you can't but I just need to know why."

It was as if someone else was speaking for him, and he forever deeply regretted the words that came out of his mouth, but he said it, "I'm scared of your dad."

"Why are you scared of my dad?"

"Well he has quite a reputation for being a heavy."

"I would just like you to know my father is not a heavy, he's a pussycat," and with that the conversation was forever over. She was such a sweetheart and it was never mentioned again. A couple of weeks later Albert walked into the office and gave Linda a big hug. Although he was about 60-something and six feet six inches tall he looked like the hardest man Peter had ever seen, and he obviously loved Linda deeply. He didn't even glance at Peter who was hoping nothing had been mentioned to him about his daughter's conversation and Albert went off to discuss some business with Stanley. She was right, he was a pussycat, but cats have really sharp claws if they need to protect their young!

CHAPTER 8

Just do what you think you should do

One of Peter's main interests was music. He loved going to concerts and seeing all the new bands playing in the pubs and clubs all over London. What interested him was the office occupied by John Martin, the guy who was booking the bands. Absolutely nothing had been heard from him. No bands had been booked and not even a rumour of negotiations with a big name had been mentioned. This really pissed off Peter. John Martin had an unlimited bundle of cash to get any artist in the world to come and headline the festival and he hadn't yet got hold of anyone.

"So what's the deal with John Martin then?" Peter asked Malcolm.

"What do you mean, what's the deal?" Malcolm replied obtusely.

"I mean why hasn't he booked a band yet?" Peter continued.

"Och there's plenty of time yet. Give him a chance. I've just got to go and see Michael just now," and with that disappeared to the front office.

The situation with the booking of bands had started to become a standing joke. The word was that John Martin was not only a lousy booker but was so disliked by everyone that, when he got through on the phone to the secretary of whoever he was calling he could never get put through to who he wanted to speak to. He was supposedly unable to talk to anyone in the business. That was the extent of the dislike for this man.

One of Malcolm's problems in the past had been the lack of money to maintain his lifestyle so he could float ideas to people without looking like he was desperate. In the journey through life many people rise up through the business only to fall back down again. Malcolm had both risen and fallen, and on his journey he had obtained favours from people who had helped him out in all sorts of ways. Some favours were small and others had been huge. Nothing was forgotten and all favours were religiously repaid in kind if the opportunity arose. Peter knew of Malcolm's integrity and could not begin to imagine what the debt was that he owed to John Martin but it must have been a whopper. To give such a huge opportunity to such an incompetent halfwit, putting his reputation on the line, must have been repayment for a huge debt or he would have not have given him the job. All of Peter's questions were met with a brick wall of silence and he never got to know the story behind these two men, who obviously hated each other with a passion, however much he probed.

Arriving back at the office after the weekend, feeling very much worse for wear, Peter was greeted by an extremely happy Malcolm.

"Ah there you are. Good. Good. You look like shit. Have you been on the wacky baccy again? You'll fry your brains, so you will, you stupid little shit." He was obviously the bearer of some good news as he was normally not so chatty.

"Alright then tell me the good news before you explode."

"Well it's not so much good news as fucking great news. The finance for the festival was arranged over the weekend. We have all the money we need in place and available to spend now. All of the money is Right Here, Right Now!"

He could hardly contain himself. His whole plan had worked. Having an idea and a plan was nothing until all of the money was in place and apparently this had happened.

"You've worked your butt off for us all and I'm going to take you out to dinner tonight as a way of saying thank you." He was like a cat that had got the cream. Both offices front and back were buzzing with the news. The money was in place. Stanley wasn't seeding any more. The whole package was sorted. Now they could get down to business. There was no limit to what could be paid for, just get the best. The money is in place.

The day flew by and Malcolm told Peter to meet him at The Capri restaurant behind Regent's Street at eight that night. Peter wasn't all that keen to go out for dinner with Malcolm but one thing was for sure it would not be boring. Malcolm's catalogue of stories ranged from the hilarious to the heartbreakingly sad. He had a huge fund of lurid tales that he would sometimes tell involving all sorts of famous, and not so famous, people and most were absolutely scandalous. He also had three screenplays he had written and was desperately trying to fund so he could make them into films. In his usual way he would not let anyone else make the film as they would lose the integrity of his stories. Peter believed he was only doing the festival as a means of funding his films. Anyway, Malcolm was always a generous host with great taste in restaurants and the night was bound to be interesting.

CHAPTER 9

Man, you must be putting me on.

A few minutes after eight Peter pitched up at the Capri. It was an old-style Italian restaurant sitting just behind Regent's Street in Swallow Street, an expensive looking side street. It looked like it had been there for years and that look continued inside. The tablecloths were crisp white linen and bottles of chianti bound with raffia were the main decoration of the place apart from colour prints of views of the Italian coast. Full bottles lined the back of the bar and empty ones were suspended from the beams and the ceiling in true seventies style. Peter was impressed as it looked both understated and expensive and he knew there was no chance he would be asked to pay for anything. The waiters were Italian men who were all over 60 and extremely good at their job. They were standing around Malcolm's table laughing and joking with him as if he were an old friend, which of course he was. He spotted Peter in the doorway and called him over.

"Come in. Come and sit down. We are over here at the best table in the house. These are my friends who work here and they will make your meal as memorable as they can." They all agreed, laughing, as they bustled off thinking to themselves, "Malcolm is in the money again." And they were right.

"I've ordered a bottle of very nice wine for us and do you want an aperitif? I'm having a scotch."

"I'll have a Pernod with ice and water if they've got it," Peter said, fondly remembering drinking Pastis, on summer evenings, in a little cafe in Paris with his French girlfriend in 1969 just after the student riots of 1968.

"If that's what you want, fine. I'm having a large Laphroaig to celebrate my good fortune."

"Cheers," Peter said, raising his glass of Pernod. "Here's to a successful festival and I hope we all make some money."

"I second that and even you might make a bob or two."

Malcolm ordered for both of them as this was a favourite place of his and he knew what was really good. Peter was happy to eat what was brought and it was absolutely superb. The waiters were also skilled at their job in a way only older Italian men can be.

It was again evident that Malcolm had something on his mind and Peter knew better than to ask what it was. All in good time he would learn what was going on.

They drank a bottle of dry white wine with their starters of fried whitebait and a good chianti was ordered to go with the breaded veal escalope when Malcolm got serious.

"I'm going to tell you something that I want you to know about that is not to be repeated to anyone. Do you understand?"

"Sure. You know I don't talk about things to anyone," Peter said.

"Yes I know and that's why I'm telling you."

It was then he began the story. "In the fifties London was being controlled by criminal gangs. It always has been in one way or another, only then the gangs were not so obvious. They controlled the gambling and moneylending and the violence did not really extend outside the gangs. If you didn't cross them you were pretty much left alone."

Peter sat there fascinated wondering where this was going.

"In the sixties it became a bit more of a problem. The Richardsons were controlling south of the river and the Krays started to move into the more lucrative parts of the West End. The Richardsons already controlled Soho and the Krays wanted it. The Krays were also entering into business with the American Mafia who were keen to get involved with the gambling in London as it was an easy place to launder money. At that time London was so corrupt that it was impossible to stop the gangs because of the protection they had from all levels of bent policemen. The Krays were hobnobbing with celebrities, the aristocracy and the Mafia and the Richardsons were nailing people to coffee tables if they crossed Charlie. The situation got out of hand but mainly the threat of the Mafia getting a foothold in London led to some extreme measures being taken.

"An entirely new gangbusting squad was formed. In order to find policemen who were not on the payroll of any of the gangs they had to be drafted in from far flung corners of the country where they had been out of reach of the lure of large 'Bungs'. This elite squad had been housed in an office block called Tintagel House which, coincidentally, was next door to the one Stanley had bought where they were now working."

"This new squad, headed by Inspector 'Nipper' Read worked hard and long to clean up the streets of London. By the end of the 1960s the gangs had pretty much been broken up. The Krays had been put in prison, their power had been diluted, and the open warfare had been ended. The government's overriding concern was that the Mafia should not be allowed to get a foothold in London with particular concern that they shouldn't be allowed to control the gambling and that effectively closed all avenues for money laundering."

"There was absolutely no way they could get major interests in the casinos so there would be no possibility that London could become a major centre for large scale money laundering."

"This is all very interesting Malcolm. Thanks for taking the time to tell me this story." Peter said a little sarcastically. He knew there would be a point to the story but just wanted to gee Malcolm up a little.

"I'm sorry if this piece of social history is too much for your pea brain, son, but let's have another bottle of wine and I'll continue. If I fucking well may?"

"Go ahead I'm all ears, really it's very interesting."

"OK then. London has been closed up as tight as a fish's bum and the Mafia are being squeezed out on both sides of the Atlantic and are always looking for new ways to launder their dirty money."

"Alright I see that. It must be a big problem for them."

Malcolm was now getting slightly pissed and enjoying the situation of having enough money to not care how much the bill would be. He wanted to enjoy himself and tell his story and that was what he was really good at.

"Now we come to the present day," Malcolm continued. "Rock and roll is the new cash cow. Everyone wants a piece of it. New bands are getting signed up and their contracts just give all their money away to their management. Their publishing deals are the same thing and they give away all their royalty earnings just because the groups are stupid enough to sign a bad publishing deal. They don't know what they are signing and they get given all the money they need to throw around while the managers take huge sums of money from royalties and the artists get nothing. The bands are making their managers millionaires. There's so much money at stake that contracts are being exchanged by threats of death, even by hanging people by the feet from seventh storey windows to make the manager sign over a good selling band."

"Yeah we've all heard that story and ones about the 'Arden' contracts signed with a gun to the head" Peter said.

"That's right" Malcolm continued taking a hefty sip of wine. "There are so many crooks and heavies in the business it is almost impossible for a young band to get an honest deal these days. At the moment even The Rolling Stones don't have a pot to piss in. In reality they have a few cars, a house each and as much pocket money as they want to spend but their royalties for publishing should have earned them millions. One day they will wake up and try to buy back their deals and make some serious wedge."

"What a shame they don't have you helping them with their money," Peter joked.

"Aye, right!" Malcolm laughed and briefly considered being in control of The Stones' finances.

"But I digress. So now we come to the 'Great British Music Festival'."

Malcolm punctuated the quotation marks in the air with his fingers.

"Hundreds of thousands of eager fans are prepared to spend a fiver to watch bands for a weekend in a muddy field. Many people have tried to arrange these festivals but have usually failed ending up with no one getting paid and the festival losing tons of money. Take the Isle Of Wight festival for instance. The story goes that Fiery Creations, who organised the last one, inflated all the prices they said that they paid for the bands, inflated all other costs apart from the profits made by the catering company, which was owned by Fiery Creations. When the sums were done they declared a huge loss. Estimates of the crowd are ridiculously hard to make but some people said there were six to seven hundred thousand people there. It was bigger than Woodstock.

During the festival the French Anarchists demolished the fence and a load of people got in free. Nobody except the organisers know how many did not pay and before the end of the festival someone was seen boarding the ferry with a large carpet bag. The festival allegedly made a huge loss but it was said that someone had made off with a bag stuffed with £150,000 in cash from the takings on the gate even before the money was counted. There is no evidence to confirm that rumour. Also there was none to prove their previous festival hadn't made a huge loss even though the three brothers managed to each buy a large mansion on the island after posting notice of losses, Fiery Creations moved to a brand new huge office and the staff increased to about 70 employees."

Malcolm stopped to take a brief rest and Peter was totally confused as to what the outcome of this story was going to be.

"Two large brandies Luigi if you please," Malcolm called over to the waiter.

"Do you get the link yet?" he then asked.

"To be perfectly honest I haven't got a clue what this is about!" Peter said sniffing the fumes of a very good VSOP brandy.

"That is because you are a thick wee boy straight up from the country."

"Yeah yeah. I know and you are Number One music promoter in England at the moment."

"Aye well I just might be." He paused while he considered that statement.

"So you can't join the dots on those two stories." Malcolm said quietly. "Well, I'm not surprised because it's taken me years to come up with such a brilliant idea for a film. It is a perfectly simple way to launder illegal money in an almost fool proof way without going through the casinos."

"Well, that is a good idea." Peter said sarcastically. "And whose money are you thinking of laundering?"

"Anyone who has a million or so of cash they want to legitimise! Bank robbers, bullion hijackers, drug smugglers or high-end diamond traffickers." Malcolm said.

"Jesus Christ, haven't you got enough on your plate organising this festival without planning a massive money scam film?" Peter asked incredulously.

"You know me. I've always got ideas flying around in my head. You know. Crazy ideas.

Film screenplays, a book or just pipe dreams."

"That is good as long as you keep them in your imagination and don't try to pull them off. Anyway, what's the story. How can you launder a million pounds?"

Malcolm stared at him and then said, "If I told you I would have to kill you."

A few seconds passed and they both started laughing. "Maybe I'll let you know more about it sometime in the future when I've decided what I'm going to do with it." He appeared to be very pensive as he called over Luigi to pay the bill. He whipped out a bundle of notes that would choke a donkey and paid with a flourish adding a good tip for the waiters who all seemed very happy to see Malcolm again. "I'll expect you bright and early tomorrow Young Man so get some shut eye and be ready for the hard work to start from now. Don't breathe a word about my ideas to anybody or I'll tell Albert you've been shagging his wee girl over the desk!"

"I think you would too, but I've been told Albert is a pussycat!" Peter said, laughing as he took the offered tenner and got into a cab. As he rode up Regents Street he was thinking about Malcolm's crazy ideas. The last one was to bring a bunch of top Thai boxers over from Thailand and promote bouts in venues all over the country. What a crazy brain that man had!

CHAPTER 10

Piggin' Wigan

The next day Peter arrived at the office and was greeted by an unusually cheerful Malcolm. No mention was made of last night's conversation.

"I've got a wee job for you Peter. It's right up your street and no one else wants to do it so it's all yours."

"Gee thanks mate. What have I been let in for now?" Peter said, fearing the worst.

"Well there's a godforsaken place in the North of England called Bickershaw and a couple of chancers have decided to have a festival there a couple of weeks before the date we want to have ours. I want you to get in touch with them and arrange to go and check it out for us. You know the deal. What is the site like? How are they dealing with the opposition? Are there any good ideas worth pinching? Which contractors are they using? It's just a jolly for you but if you can learn anything it will be a bonus for us. I've ordered a car for you at eight o' clock tomorrow so I hope you will be ready."

"Oh I'll be ready. I'll just give them a ring first to see if it's alright for tomorrow. Do you have a name for somebody up there?"

"I don't, but I think Linda has. Is that right Linda?"

"I have got one name and a phone number for someone by

the name of Jeremy Beadle," and she gave him the number which he rang.

"Hi, is that Jeremy?" he said as the phone was picked up.

"Speaking," the voice answered.

"Oh hello my name is Peter Whitehead and I work for Stanley Baker's festival company. You may have heard of us?"

"Oh yes I have heard of you. What can humble little me do for your majestic company?" Jeremy asked sarcastically.

"Well I've been asked to come up tomorrow and have a look at what you're doing up there. You know to see what we can learn from you and just generally get to know you," Peter said cheerfully ignoring the sarcasm in Jeremy's tone.

"Sure why not? Maybe I can learn something from you too."

"Well we are all in this together and we will try to be as much help as we can."

"Ok then Peter so what time is your train arriving tomorrow?"

"Er… I'm being driven up actually."

"Oh, fucking la di dah. No expense spared then?"

"No it's not really like that. It's just that I've just been banned from driving and it's easier to use a driver. Where can I meet you?"

Jeremy gave him the address of the site and arranged to meet at 12 the next day.

"You will recognise me cos I'll be the poor sod with the pushbike!"

"See you tomorrow man." Peter actually liked the abrasive character and was looking forward to the next day's trip.

It was true that he had just lost his driving license and this was the first time he had been allowed a driver. He had accompanied Malcolm to several places but was really looking forward to the luxury of being driven on his own.

He was still smarting over the loss of his license and felt he had been treated really unfairly by the police and let down by the legal system. He had still held the naive idea that police did their job in a reasonably honest way and magistrates generally upheld the law. In this case Peter learnt that coppers were bent and as far as magistrates went, they were a law unto themselves.

What had happened was that a couple of months before, Bruce had needed a shower kit delivered to an address in southeast London and the easiest way was for him to use Peter and his car. The boxed shower unit was tied onto the top of the little Mini with copious amounts of string. It was a six-foot shower and hung well over the bonnet and was secured by passing the string through the open windows and tying lots of knots in order to try and stop it sliding off the roof in the absence of a roof rack. Had the car been fitted with a roof rack the shower would have been secure and legally fixed to the car.

As it was, in true Bruce fashion, it was neither secure nor legal but was the cheapest option so it would have to do.

"Whatever you do don't smash the fucking shower. I've paid for it." Were the words shouted down the street as Peter set off in the makeshift delivery van.

He managed to get to the top of the Tottenham Court Road and was sitting at a red light when there was a knock on the window. For heaven's sake, a copper, who looked all of fifteen years old, was leaning into the car.

"Excuse me sir, but would you mind pulling over? I'd like a word with you," he said. Peter budged the car over to the kerb and got out to talk to him, mentally working out if he was carrying any dope on him or in the car. He was pretty sure he was clean so felt a lot happier to talk to the cop.

"What exactly is going on here?" the constable asked.

"I've just bought this shower from a shop just down the

road and my wife is so keen to get it fitted she told me to bring it back with me straight away and her father would fit it today. What with her having the baby and all."

"Have you got a receipt for it?" he asked.

"Sure it's right here." replied Peter, wafting the delivery note under his nose.

"It says Mr Patel here."

"Yes that's right. He's my father-in-law. He's a plumber and bought the shower through his company."

"Right then let's see if it is securely fixed onto the car then," and tugged on the strings and wiggled the box and was surprised how secure the shower was and sent Peter off with a cheerful: "Mind how you go and you look after your wife and the little baby."

"I certainly will constable," and he drove off with a huge sigh of relief.

'Thank God for that' he thought and set off towards the river to deliver the stupid shower. Being a little jangled he drove towards Piccadilly Circus in an attempt to get over the river and was trying to work out the route when he noticed the traffic lights at the Circus had just turned yellow. In a split-second he decided not to slam on the brakes. Instead he throttled the Mini as fast as the little 850cc engine would allow and squeaked through just as the lights went to red. He knew he should not have jumped the yellow light but if he'd slammed on the brakes the shower might have shot off the roof onto the road.

He had just driven through the lights when what looked like a 12-year-old boy dressed in a policeman's uniform hurled himself in front of the car with his hand in the air yelling, "Stop."

Peter stamped on the brakes as hard as he could with no regard for his rooftop cargo. All he wanted to do was avoid killing the child. He screeched to a stop inches from the suicidal maniac and noticed the shower was still in position on the roof.

He jumped out of the car to see what all the excitement was about just as an older looking policeman appeared on the scene.

"It's ok," Peter said "I've just been done up the road. It's all secure and legal."

"Well that's good 'cos you're being done again so bad luck," and then he said to the boy copper,

"Tell him then."

"You just went through a yellow light," he said.

"I know," Peter replied. "I only just made it and I couldn't stop safely for fear of dumping the shower in the road."

"Shower?" the older cop said "Oh I see you've got a shower on your roof. Anyway let's get on with this then. Take down his details."

"Right then what is your address?" the boy said. Only then did Peter realise he was an actual serving constable and not a child dressed up as one. Peter started to give his address while the older man looked on.

"Now be careful how you write it down as it's a long address and you must make sure it all fits in," he coached and the penny dropped as Peter realised he was being used to teach a new recruit how to write up a traffic offence. He wasn't really bothered as he had only gone through a yellow light and that wasn't an offence. Was it?

They went through the motions of writing the ticket which was proudly served to Peter by a proud young boy who appeared to be trying to please his dad on his first day at work.

"Thank you," Peter muttered as he shoved the ticket in his pocket "Pleased to be of help to the constabulary." and he drove off for the second time thinking "What a waste of time. Nothing will come of this but I suppose they all have to learn somewhere."

He carried on with his delivery without any further interruptions and completely forgot about the ticket until later he received a summons for driving through a red traffic light! The bastards had lied about the colour of the lights so sonny boy could get his first conviction.

Having passed A level law a few years earlier Peter felt confident that when he came before the magistrate he would be able to discuss the matter in a reasonable manner and the whole thing would be forgotten as a mistake. It was particularly important to Peter as he had got enough points on his license already that three more would mean a disqualification. Surely the Magistrate would be lenient particularly considering the new job he had just started.

When the day of the hearing came Peter was still confident. He had only gone through a yellow light and that wasn't an offence.

He sat in the court awaiting his case and listened to the one before him. The man was charged with going through a red light in Piccadilly, the same day as Peter, by the same baby-faced policeman. He said he was sure he had only gone through a yellow light as he was driving carefully and trying to work out where he and his girlfriend were going.

The magistrate puffed himself up and aimed a tirade at the poor man. "I know exactly what was going on. You were so involved in a shouting match with each other you were taking no notice of the traffic lights or anything else."

"Yes I was," the unfortunate man said, "because I noticed the light wasn't red it was yellow."

"Don't start giving me those lies. I know your sort. You spend your time in the car rowing and arguing. You shout at each other and don't take a blind bit of notice about road signs or lights or these poor policemen who are just trying to do their job. It's lucky I'm here to teach you a lesson. Fined £25 and three points on your license. Next!"

The baby-faced policeman was pushed to his feet to read the charge and even before he had finished, he was told to sit down as the magistrate had heard quite enough to make his judgement.

"I know your sort. You race around London in your sporty little car with scant regard to rules and regulations. You treat the roads as a race track and have no respect for the police and the law. Well you won't find me an easy touch you young hooligan. Fined £25 and three points on your license which means you will be disqualified for three months. Do you have anything to say for yourself?"

"May God have mercy on my soul," Peter mumbled waiting for the magistrate to put on the black hat.

"What did you say?" the magistrate said.

"Nothing at all. What's the point?" Peter said clearly and walked away having lost all his faith in the police and the legal system he had once admired.

Luckily for him he had been working for a couple of months before the case was called and he was able to get settled in the job before he had his license taken away. Malcolm didn't care about Peter's car as they now had the money to use a driver as and when they needed.

In the morning his car arrived to take Peter up to Bickershaw and this was the day when he learned his most important lesson about organising a festival.

The car was a Ford. It was a huge square boat of a car. The one designed in the late sixties shaped like a brick sitting on a breeze block. A Zephyr or Zodiac or something like that. It was top of the range with leather seats and was driven by a young man called Chris who usually drove celebrities and film stars. He was a nice guy who was smartly dressed in a casual way. He had the confident air about him of someone who had been around the business for a while and knew all the angles. He knew Peter, as he had driven him with

91

Malcolm when they had a meeting in Essex, and they had got on well together.

"So they've let you out on your own today?" he said as they settled down for the long journey.

"Yeah right. I've got a big meeting with a major promoter just outside Wigan. I've been told to pick his brains."

"So what exactly do you do then?" Chris asked when they arrived at the start of the M1.

"Well I do all sorts really. Lots of paperwork. Phoning people up to arrange meetings. Soon I'll be booking hundreds of caravans and 50 Land Rovers for the site. It's a nightmare trying to find them. We don't even know where the site will be so I have to look up all the suppliers in the country from the *Yellow Pages* to be ready when we confirm where we will be having the show. Can you imagine how many caravan suppliers there are and when you try to book a lot of them, they are already booked for people's holidays. Really I work for Malcolm who came up with the idea for the festival. I generally make his ideas work."

"That's funny cos they said you were the festival director when they told me to pick you up."

"No it's a joke. It's only when someone phones up to talk about something stupid to do with the festival they call me that and put me on the phone to sort it out but there isn't really anyone who calls themself director as such."

"You should make them call you festival director then and try to get a pay rise." Chris laughed at the idea. "I bet they pay you fuck all as well."

Peter hadn't really thought about his wages because he got all his expenses paid and didn't need to use his wages much with all the dope he was selling in his spare time.

"I get by. They are quite good to me," Peter said not wanting to appear stupid in front of this cocky young man. He tried changing the subject and Chris didn't probe any more.

"Who do you most like driving?" Peter asked.

"That's easy. Richard Harris every time. I drive him all the time when he is over here. We get on well and he is easy going. Not like some of those stuck-up bastards you get in the back. They think they are so much better than you and always want to let you know. Richard is a gentleman even when he's pissed out of his mind. You wouldn't believe some of the scrapes we've got into. One time I took him to some fancy Hotel in the country where he was going to have dinner. He wanted to go in his Rolls and he also wanted to drive himself down there before he had a drink. He liked driving his Rolls and he used to make me sit up in the front with him. He didn't care how he looked most of the time and that day he was particularly scruffy as he was just meeting a friend for dinner. He turned into the drive and stopped outside the doors as the doorman ran up to the passenger door and opened it for me.

"Not him you prick, it's me you open the fucking door for," he bawled at the dismayed doorman and we both fell about laughing while Richard said he was paying me too much as I was dressed so well I outshone him. I told him it didn't take much effort to do that!

He didn't embarrass the poor man though as he was so down to earth and normal."

Peter felt comfortable with Chris and the long drive to the place near Wigan passed easily. There was paperwork that Malcolm had given him before they left which Peter had to finish and the miles passed quickly.

Chris knew a good transport cafe just off the M6 and they stopped and they each ate a hearty homemade steak and kidney pie with chips, peas and gravy washed down with mugs of sweet tea. Peter picked up the tab and kept the receipts for his expenses feeling like an important executive.

Just before 12 they arrived at the address and sure enough,

standing there was a small skinny young man leaning on his bike.

"Look at that little Jeeter! Is that who you are meeting?" Chris said unable to keep a straight face.

"I expect so. His name is Jeremy Beadle I think."

"Good luck."

Peter stepped out of the car and approached the skinny little man.

He had long dark hair that reached to his shoulders. His eyes were bulging which gave him an odd expression. He wore the compulsory loon pants but most disconcerting was when he shook Peter's hand he felt that he only had two fingers on his right hand. Jeremy seemed to take great delight in trying to disconcert people with that but Peter did not get fazed by much.

"Ah the great festival director I presume?"

"Ah the great Jeremy Beadle I presume. Who said I was festival director?"

"Some bloke called Deeley on the phone said you were. Are you not? Because I will feel cheated if they've sent me anything less."

"Oh no you've got the real festival director. You can ask my driver if you don't believe me. So tell me about this festival you're organising Jeremy. It sounds fucking terrific. What a line up. How did you wangle it?"

"Well man to man. As you are in the same line of business, it was all done by totally bullshitting everyone about everything. We haven't got a pot to piss in. We don't have any money to speak of except what we have managed to scrounge up from a few friends who really want to see the bands we are getting and it has just grown from there. The biggest help was when The Grateful Dead agreed to play. I think a lot of it had to do with the fiasco with The Stones at Altamont and them not playing there and also feeling really sorry for us. It just snowballed from there and everyone else believed we could do it and jumped on board."

"That's impressive. I absolutely love The Dead. Don't they play for four of five hours once they get on stage? I can't imagine how hard it must be to persuade everyone to wait for their money until after the show."

"You'd better believe it. I can't either. But it must be wonderful to have access to hundreds of thousands to buy whatever you like. As they are always saying about you in the papers."

"Yeah sure it's easier to be able to pay up front but it's not all plain sailing. For instance we haven't completely finalised the site yet."

"You haven't got a site yet?" Jeremy asked incredulously.

"Yes of course we have got a site but it hasn't been completely finalised yet." He lied, not wanting another 'Eavisgate' happening.

"Ah well that is where we have the upper hand because here is our magnificent site." and he swept his hand in the direction of a black muddy area of land that had once been a slag heap.

"Is that your site?"

"Yes it is and it has taken us months of wrangling to get it donated for the very reasonable price of nothing. Is there anything wrong with it?"

"At the moment it looks sort of all right but what are you going to do if it rains? Because in my personal experience of living 30 miles down the road from here, it rains almost every day."

"Don't be so pessimistic. It won't rain but if it does everyone will be up to their knees in sticky black mud but I don't have a ton of money like you, to hire a swanky site, so we just have to pray."

"Well you better start praying now cos it's just started

raining. Let's go to the pub before we start sinking. My boots are ruined already."

They walked into the nearest pub where Jeremy was greeted with a series of catcalls and jeers along with some cheerful greetings. It was obvious that there were mixed feelings about him. He didn't care what people thought about him and he always tried to be abrasive and annoying.

Peter sort of liked him as he had put together a fantastic line up for a festival with no money, albeit it was going ahead on a slag heap, but fair play to him. He had managed to persuade The Grateful Dead, Captain Beefheart, Country Joe MacDonald, Dr John The Night Tripper, The Kinks and Cheech and Chong to come and play on a promise. They were even having a tank full of water for a high-dive act in front of the stage. He wouldn't want to change places with him though.

Peter bought several pints of beer which they drank while Jeremy gave him a load of numbers for useful contractors and suppliers and then announced he was heading back to London. Jeremy made a derogatory remark about Londoners and Peter said he didn't care because he didn't come from London and he could say what he liked. He shook his deformed hand firmly and looked him straight in his googly eyes and wished him the best of luck and meant it.

Chris was waiting outside with the car and as they drove off he said, "What a funny looking bloke he is. What is he like?"

"Well he was trying to be obnoxious all the time just to get a rise out of me but he was alright really. He has got so much front to get his festival off the ground with no money at all. I just can't believe he is holding it on a slag heap. He just hopes it isn't going to rain."

"Not going to rain. What is he thinking of? It always rains. This is Wigan. It's raining now."

It certainly was raining as they headed away from the depressing town.

They hadn't gone more than halfway when Chris said, "I've been thinking about what you said about hiring those caravans and Land Rovers. I had a job for a film company once and I had to deliver a load of caravans to a location we were filming on. I must have delivered about ten of the things and as I was bringing the last spanky shining four-berth van I stuck it away from the others and put a sign on it. 'Not in Use'. Or something like that. So when I got to the location there was my very own caravan to stay in. No one has any idea how many vans there are or who has got the use of them. My advice to you is to get the hire company to choose a caravan and a Land Rover and get them to put the keys on top of the wheel and put a sign on them saying 'Not in Use' or something and then you at least have somewhere to stay and a Land Rover to use while you are on site. Believe me when I say no one gives a rat's arse about you and you have a golden opportunity to look after yourself."

"You are a star Chris. I've been sent all the way to Wigan to try to learn something about organising a festival and you come up with the best piece of advice ever."

"It's a pleasure to be of help 'my man' Just make sure you get a deluxe caravan in case you want to do a bit of entertaining while you are there," Chris added with a leer.

Arriving at the office the next day Malcolm was interested to know how the visit went.

"So what did you learn from your little trip up North?"

"Quite a lot," Peter replied. "I learnt that Jeremy Beadle is a little chancer, with no money, who has put together an amazing line-up of acts to play on the promise of future payment. I've learnt that they are gambling it won't rain 'cos the site is on an old slag heap and it will turn into a muddy quicksand very quickly. I managed to get the phone numbers of quite a few useful contractors who would be willing to hire us their equipment after that festival is finished. Also, I truly believe we will be hearing a lot more of Jeremy Beadle."

Malcolm laughed. "I remember going down to one of the first Reading Jazz and Blues Festivals to meet Harold Pendleton, who ran The Marquee and was running these festivals. They had been given the site by Reading Council who with their usual generosity let them have an abandoned landfill site. It had been topped off but it had rained for a few days before Harold arranged to meet the mayor on site. Harold and I got out of the car in our wellingtons and when the mayor stepped out of his car in his nice shiny shoes we warmly shook his hand. We were thanking him for his generosity for the donation of the wonderful site and how the festival would be a goodwill coming together of the generations and blah blah blah. As he politely listened to Harold going on and on, he was slowly sinking deeper and deeper into the mud. He couldn't believe what was happening and was too polite to interrupt the glowing bullshit Harold was spouting and when he was in the mud over his ankles we grabbed him under the arms and lifted him out and plonked him back into his car. As he drove off with his shoes and trousers covered in mud we were crying with laughter. Harold said that it would be the last official visit from that lot. It sounds like your friend Beadle has been given the same shitty end of the stick."

"He has got a really bad site in a poor location but the bands he has booked are really incredible. People will travel from anywhere to go and see them. Which reminds me. How is John getting on with booking our bands?"

"Och well, he will get it sorted don't you worry," Malcolm said shutting down the conversation.

That prick John Martin still hadn't booked a band yet.

CHAPTER 11

The middle of nowhere.

It was only a few days later when the news filtered through from the front office. A site had been found. It was signed and sealed and there was no way it would be retracted. This was the real thing and now they could start really organising the festival. There was no time to lose!

"Wow," Peter said, "how did they find a site and where is it?"

"Apparently it's in Bardney in Lincolnshire"

"Where is Lincolnshire?" Peter asked ironically.

"Don't you know anything?" Malcolm said. "It is a little north of Norfolk, of course."

"Why would anyone want to go 'a little north of Norfolk' to a festival?"

"Well. we aren't blessed with a lot of time to find a site and 'The Man With The Golden Ear' comes from Lincolnshire. I imagine he has used his influence with *Farmer's Weekly* or whatever paper he was a reporter with and secured us a site."

Just as they were discussing the new site Michael Deeley and Barry 'Golden Ear' Spikings came into the back office obviously elated and pleased with themselves that they had secured a site. Malcolm asked them some questions about the site and made a big deal about how Barry had sorted it all out himself. It sounded like a good site but the worry was that it was in one of the most inaccessible parts of the country.

"How are people going to get there?" Peter asked.

"Oh that's no problem," Barry said "Stanley says that Michael and I can use his helicopter."

"That's ok then," Peter said, wondering if these people had any idea what went on in the real world.

"So now it's full steam ahead," Michael said. "I want everything to be sorted and in place for the May Bank Holiday. Just make a list of everything we need to get in and I'll approve payment. Don't forget anything and make sure it can be delivered to the site."

"Sure will," Peter muttered as they departed to conduct some very serious film business.

The new site was at a place called Tupholme Farm near Bardney in Lincolnshire and this time there was no going back. Some bright spark coined the slogan 'The Festival They Could Not Stop' in the vain hope of getting some street cred.

Yeah man, it's Us against Them and nothing to do with Us making huge profits.

Malcolm made immediate plans to inspect the site as he was the only person in the company who had any experience in large outdoor gatherings. He had been organising major International Rallies for the World Federation of Democratic Youth and had been involved with the Reading Blues Festival and other folk festivals. Peter had been to the 1971 Pilton Free Festival and no one else had a clue about what went on at a rock festival. The company's only interest in a festival was to make as much money as they could with this idea they had been sold by Malcolm.

After ascertaining that the helicopter was not available to them, Chris and his car were ordered and they set off the next day to the wilds of Lincolnshire.

One piece of land is very much like another and once it has been fenced off it is equally suitable as a festival site. Everything has to be brought onto the site anyway so really if the access is not really restricted it is possible to hold a festival in most places. As is the case now. People hold all kinds of large festivals in their fields – pop, rock, folk, tribute, seventies, sixties, food, metal, car and even Glastonbury rumbles on every year within an almost inaccessible site.

The journey to Bardney was never ending but the excitement that the show was actually going on was what drove Malcolm and Peter on. This was going to be the Best Festival Ever. Even if it had to be held in Lincolnshire!

The site was perfectly adequate on a farm in a small village and could easily be made secure and used to put a festival on. There also didn't appear to be any evidence of many people living nearby so that was a plus. That was all they needed to know and after a quick walk around the fields and a few words with the owner they got back into the car and went to the pub for some lunch.

CHAPTER 12

You can be robbed
with a fountain pen

The money had been sorted. The boring site in Lincolnshire had been found, much of the infrastructure had been reserved in advance waiting for confirmation of where it would be needed. Unbelievably 400-plus caravans need to be reserved well in advance of the May Bank Holiday as do portable loos and all the other things. Peter had been busy locating the services that were needed to go on site and they were just waiting for the delivery address.

There was one problem that had not yet been solved and now was a pressing concern. Not one band had been booked. Not one band had provisionally agreed to perform. No one was talking to John Martin.

By now a major headline act, or two, should have been confirmed and then the other bands would follow as they would get great publicity playing with a major act. The Isle of Wight had headliners Jimi Hendrix, Bob Dylan and The Who the year before but this year no one was talking to John Martin.

It wasn't long before it was announced that John was to go to America where he would sign up some major acts for the festival. When he came back he would fill up the rest of the acts with British talent.

"Maybe we'll be lucky and his reputation won't have preceded him," Peter said bitterly.

"Don't worry. In America you can buy anything if you have the money. He'll come back with the bands," replied Malcolm.

One morning as Peter was snowed under with making calls to suppliers a couple of young men walked into the office. They were an odd couple. One was short, dark and chubby with a big nose. The other was tall and skinny with wild curly black hair. They reminded Peter of the rich kids he used to see riding around in the back of their parents' flash cars in Hendon or Golders Green looking down their noses on the rest of the world. They both had on the uniform of tee shirt and Loon pants. They smirked at Malcolm and said "Hi."

Malcolm visibly bristled and Peter could immediately see that he disliked these two intensely.

"Look what the dog has dragged in. What are you two doing here? Are you looking for a job?" Malcolm sneered.

"Not looking for a job. We've got a job. We are in charge of the stage," said the short tubby one.

"I suppose John gave you that job then?" Malcolm said. "Do you think you are up to running the stage at a major festival?" he added sarcastically.

"Well we run it pretty well at the shows we operate now. So the answer is yes."

"I know that. It's just that I don't understand why you would want to work for John when you have your own business going at the moment."

"Well you know us Malcolm we are always happy to give anyone a hand when it's needed."

"Oh aye, right. Mr Generosity is your middle name. Now fuck off and stay over in John's office. Don't come round here snooping on us. We don't need any of your assistance. Thank you."

The Odd Couple sloped off smirking and whispering

to each other and when they had left Peter said, "Who on earth were those two jeeters and why do you dislike them so much?"

"The little one with the big nose is Harvey Goldsmith and his sidekick, that skinny streak of piss, is Michael Alfandary. They think they are real hotshots. They have just started promoting shows in London and I don't trust them one sodding inch. They are up to something and it will not work out well. What the hell is John doing taking on those shysters?"

He was very agitated and Peter could not understand why he should be so upset that Harvey Goldsmith had been employed to run the stage.

Someone had to do it and it only entailed getting the bands on and off on time. They always ran late at festivals so expectations didn't run too high in that job. However Malcolm was really rattled.

"Harvey fucking Goldsmith of all the people he could have chosen he gave it to Harvey Goldsmith!"

"What can possibly go wrong? They are only doing the stage."

"That Goldsmith kid is a snake and everyone knows he would kill his grandmother to get on in the business. I don't yet know what he's up to but you can bet a pound to a pinch of shit that he's got a plan to help himself get a leg up in his poxy upcoming career."

He bustled out of the office on one of his important missions still seething from the arrival of his visitors.

John Martin's long-awaited trip drew closer and Michael Deeley and Barry Spikings were getting excited about the megastars that were going to be brought back by their superstar booker who had already told them all of the acts he was going to sign up for them.

Sly and The Family Stone were a definite maybe.

The date he was leaving for the States drew closer and the day before he was due to go Goldsmith and Alfandary sloped into Malcolm's office.

"What do you want here?" Malcolm growled at them.

"Not much. We just wanted you to know that I have to go away for a couple of weeks to stay with my sick aunt."

"Oh aye. Would that be your Aunt Fanny then?"

"No, no, my aunt Esther has broken her leg and I have to go and stay with her until she gets back on her feet."

"And why are you telling me this?" Malcolm asked.

"Oh I just didn't want you thinking I was skiving off you know."

"I don't think you're skiving off but I do think you are sneaking off. I know you are up to something you sneaky little fucker. It's people like you who give us all a bad name."

"Ah well I'll give your regards to Aunt Esther and say you are thinking of her."

"Bollocks." Malcolm said and then ignored him as they left laughing.

When they had gone Malcolm said, "I knew they were up to something and they even had the brass neck to come in and tell me. The smarmy little bastards. This is going to turn out badly for someone and it's not going to be me."

Peter knew Malcolm well enough to believe that what he was saying would be true but did not say anything.

CHAPTER 13

Love all. Serve all (Sai Baba)

Malcolm snapped out of his black mood and announced, "Come on. We're going out. I've got a meeting and you will enjoy coming along."

They hailed a cab outside and Malcolm told the driver to take them to Piccadilly. They drove up to Hyde Park Corner and Malcolm told the driver to stop outside the Hard Rock Cafe. Peter had heard about this newly opened American burger cafe but had never been there as the queues were always round the block. This time Malcolm walked to the head of the queue and said to the doorman, "Malcolm Nixon for Mr Tigrett. He's expecting us."

Off he went and when he returned he led them to a booth where a deeply tanned youngish man sat. His long hair was curly and his eyes were the most piercing shade of blue. His denim clothes looked faded and expensive and he had the super-confident aura of someone from California with a huge amount of money and not a care in the world.

He jumped to his feet and greeted them.

"Malcolm my man. Good to see you," he drawled in a soft American accent.

"Isaac! Great to see you again. This is Peter who works with me. He can't wait to try one of your real American burgers."

Peter couldn't believe what he was seeing in the cafe. The

high walls were filled with the original posters advertising gigs in America. Publicising bands like Jefferson Airplane, The Doors, Jimi Hendrix and The Allman Brothers from concerts produced by Bill Graham at the Fillmore East. There was a Gibson Les Paul, Fender Strats and Telecaster guitars stuck on the wall, all signed by guitar heroes, and every kind of rock memorabilia you could imagine. It was mind blowing for a rock fan like Peter to see such priceless artifacts displayed on the walls.

"Close your mouth Peter," Malcolm joked and Peter mumbled something about how impressive the decor was.

Isaac was such a cool guy and told the story of how he and his friend Peter Morton had the idea of opening an authentic American burger joint in London so English people could experience the taste of a real burger rather than the taste of a Wimpy. They had found a disused Rolls Royce showroom on Piccadilly and had done it out like a U.S diner and searched for authentic rock memorabilia to give it the wow factor.

Peter agreed they had given it the wow factor and was trying to work out how much it had cost to put together. Apart from the cost of leasing a huge fancy property just off Hyde Park corner.

Malcolm brought the subject back to the reason he was there.

"So the festival is confirmed now and as we discussed before we would love you to have a food concession. You can have a circus tent to turn into a restaurant and you can have as many pitches around the site as you want. We won't allow any rubbish burgers on site and hope to attract many other good food stalls as well."

"You know what Malcolm. That sounds like a brilliant idea. We are the main caterers and the whole festival gets to eat Hard Rock style. We will dress up the main tent and theme the other stalls. It sounds good to me. I won't be charging a huge amount for the food as we do not rip off our customers and after costs have been deducted my share of the profit will be donated to Sai Baba's ashram in Puttaparthi, India. You wouldn't believe the difference he makes to the lives of millions of people there."

"Whatever you do with your money is your business and I'm sure Sai Baba will be grateful. You're a good man Isaac," said Malcolm as Isaac started to make a move from the booth.

"Now I must leave you as I've got loads to do. Send a contract to me as we talked over before and I'll start making plans for the catering for your festival. Nice to meet you Peter and I've told them at the till your bill is taken care of. Have whatever you like. Take care Malcolm, we will talk soon." And he drifted off into the crowd.

"What a guy!" Peter said "I have never met anyone with so much charisma. Are all Americans like him?"

"Oh no not at all. Mr Tigrett is a one of a kind. He is a typical super wealthy California dude. He has shitloads of money and donates a huge amount of it to an Indian guru who is building a heart hospital for the poor in the middle of India. Isaac swears Sai Baba is the real deal and he is helping him as much as he can along with the millions of other devotees around the world."

"How do you know all this?" Peter asked.

"Cos he told me last time I spoke to him. Stupid!… Now you order up your fantasy burger meal and pretend you are in San Francisco. It has all been paid for by Isaac. I'm not eating as I've got to run. I have another meeting in half an hour so I'll just have coffee."

When the waitress arrived Peter ordered a chocolate ice cream shake and a cheeseburger with everything. Whatever that was.

Malcolm just had a coffee and when the burger arrived Peter could not believe his eyes. A huge burger sat in the middle of a giant plate. It looked nothing like any burger Peter had ever seen before. It appeared to be at least a foot high. The giant bun barely held the burger which oozed melted cheese that ran down the sides. There was a large slice of dill pickle, which was new to Peter, onions, tomatoes, mayo and American mustard all served with a large salad which was slathered with a pink salad dressing called "One Thousand Islands" and the crunchiest golden chips, called fries, served with a bottle of ketchup and a huge napkin.

"Have you ever seen anything like that in a Wimpy?" Malcolm asked, taking great delight in the pleasure Peter unashamedly showed as he greedily sucked on the straws in his chocolate shake.

"I can quite honestly say I have never seen or tasted anything like this in my life. Have you really arranged for this to be served at the festival?"

"Well it won't be quite as fancy as this… but yes Isaac is bringing the Hard Rock to Bardney."

"How can you sit there not eating all this amazing food?"

"Because every time I have met with Isaac to work out this deal I have eaten a full meal and to be honest my trousers are a wee bit tight," Malcolm laughed. "Anyway you enjoy the meal and do try the chocolate brownie with ice cream before you leave and I'll see you in the morning."

With that he scurried off to another meeting leaving Peter dreaming of California as he ate the heavenly meal.

He pictured himself driving a classic black 1956 Pontiac Star Chief car along the Pacific Highway with a California chick sitting beside him and eight ounces of pure cocaine in his bag. They would be toking on a single skin sensimilla joint before pulling into a burger bar. After the meal they would drink a beer, watching the sun go down on Fisherman's Wharf, then spend the night in a motel before flying up to Lake Tahoe to spend a week skiing.

Obviously that was not specifically what he was imagining. He would never have been able in his wildest dreams to imagine it but that was exactly what he was going to be doing five years down the line.

"Are you ready for some dessert, sir?"

Peter almost jumped out of his seat and came out of his reverie as the waitress brought him back to earth with a jolt.

"Yes please I'll have the chocolate brownie."

"A la mode?"

"Oui, d'accord" Peter replied wondering why she was speaking French to him.

"That is with ice cream, sir."

"Great thank you." When it arrived Peter realised why Americans were so fat. If they ate like this every day, it was no wonder! He now had an idea in his mind and it had the seeds of a dream about getting to the States somehow and Living the Dream.

The girl at the till waved him away when Peter approached, saying that it was all taken care of by Mr Tigrett, so he put 50p in the tip jar, thanked her profusely and went home to Shepherd's Bush to tell everyone about the amazing meal he had just been 'comped' at The Hard Rock.

CHAPTER 14

Starry eyed and laughing

John and Nick were both impressed that he had met the owner of the hottest new restaurant in London and were doubly impressed when Peter told them he had jumped the queue, been given a free meal and the Hard Rock was doing the catering at the festival.

"You should have seen Isaac," Peter said, "he is the coolest guy I have ever seen. I've never met anyone with so much confidence, charisma and money. He just gives off such a strong aura and is super successful."

"I can't believe the Hard Rock is the main caterer at your festival," Nick said "I can't even get near the bloody door for the long queues."

"Nor could I," Peter said "And the best bit is that he's giving away his profits to an Indian guru to help him build a heart hospital in the middle of India."

"He could give some to me to help me get on in the BBC."

"Me too," chipped in John. "I could use a few quid as well."

"Ya Bollix! You've already got so much you don't know what to do with it you tight-fisted bastard," Peter said half joking at John's legendary caution with his money.

They all agreed it was time to go to the pub and walked down to the Shepherd's Bush roundabout and went to the pub which was nestled next to the spanky new 'Shepherd's

Bush Hilton' as they liked to call it. John found an excuse to be last through the door so he would not have to buy the first round. This meant if they stayed for two drinks he wouldn't have to buy one and if they stayed for four or five he wouldn't have to pay for two rounds. It had become a standing joke with Nick and Peter to see if they could ever get John to the bar first. This involved dawdling on the walk there or at the last minute not going through the door first but they had never succeeded. John was the best. He absolutely never ever bought the first round.

"Look there they are. The Three Tops," Nick said and waved to the three old West Indian guys who were sitting at their usual table smacking down their dominos with a loud crack.

They had arrived just as the band started to play. They were a guy and a girl who called themselves Starry Eyed and Laughing which Peter thought was a cool name as it came from a Dylan song. The music they played was pretty good. Some Dylan, some Paul Simon and some old rock and roll tunes. The singer was a pretty blonde girl who had a good voice and a really strong lisp. The highlight of their show was when they played The Crystals number 'Then He Kissed Me'. After she sang about the stars shining bright the whole audience joined in the chorus and sang along at the top of their voices, "And then he KIFFED me."

After they had finished that song there were the usual calls for them to sing 'Fwieght Twain'. The band loved the attention and never realised the silliness that was going on. The combination of a few joints and a few pints of beer made for a mellow evening and three pints of beer only cost 42p or not even ten bob in real money. After a few pints they walked home and John went on upstairs while Nick and Peter stopped at Nick's flat on the first floor to smoke some of Peter's amazing Zero Zero Moroccan hash.

They sat on the cushions on the floor and told each other about their work as they shared a joint.

"I had an audition for *Blue Peter* last week you know," Nick said.

"Wow you would be brilliant on that show." He meant it as Nick looked the epitome of a kid's television presenter. He was tall and skinny with wavy, longish, blond hair. He had a very slight Northern accent. He was quick thinking and was used to interviewing all the famous people who he persuaded to appear for free on his radio show. But most of all he was driven by a burning ambition to get on in the Beeb.

"So what happened at the interview?"

"It was a bit weird really. We were all in the studio and I got on well with everyone and just chatted and I told them about my radio show and the stars I had persuaded to come on it and everything and then Biddy Baxter, the producer, set up a piece to camera. It involved me holding a squirrel and adlibbing to camera, all about this squirrel. They gave me a handful of parrot food and said to make sure, at all cost, the squirrel didn't run up my arm.

"I got the squirrel in my hand and started improvising about red and grey squirrels and how this red squirrel liked parrot food. I said I didn't know why it was called parrot food and then the little fucker escaped and ran up my arm and sat on my shoulder."

"Oh shit, what did you do?"

"What could I do? I said deadpan to camera 'Now I know why it's called parrot food.'"

"And they gave you the job on the spot. Right?"

"No they didn't. I can't believe it. I blew my chance. I heard later they didn't want me."

"Oh man that is such a bummer. You know that apart from the fact you don't have a serious speech impediment you would be a perfect *Blue Peter* presenter."

"Yeah I thought so too but it's not to be. So anyway, how's life treating you in the grand world of rock and roll?"

"Well it's still good although there is so much to do I don't get much time to do anything for myself anymore. It was so good just to go to the pub and be stupid."

"Well we are all good at being stupid I suppose."

"Yeah well I need some sleep as it's another early start tomorrow."

As he climbed the stairs to his own flat he felt sorry for Nick and how unfair it was that he hadn't got a chance to work on *Blue Peter*. He would have been perfect and they couldn't see it.

Biddy Bastard Baxter

CHAPTER 15

Don't ask me, I might just tell you the truth

The day arrived when John Martin had got back from America. Everyone was waiting with bated breath and dragged themselves away from fighting off the people who were still trying to put a stop to the festival, to convene in the Front Office to hear about his trip.

Michael and Barry were sitting at the monster 18-seater table as Peter and Malcolm joined them. John Martin was not there and was still in his office conducting some Very Important Business that couldn't be put off!

While they waited for him Michael said they had taken on a design company to come up with a name and a logo for the festival. The company had suggested: "The Great Western Express" for the name of the festival and the logo was the front view of an American style steam train on a bright yellow background. The layout would be done around the bands as they were confirmed.

Peter was decidedly underwhelmed and thought the mock up poster was naff and not at all Rock and Roll but as usual did not make a comment.

"So you've given the go ahead to this have ye?" Malcolm asked.

"Yes I have," said Barry Spikings a little abruptly.

"Good, good. That's one thing out of the way then. When

do we hear about the bands then? Ah here comes John now. How was everything across The Pond then?"

To which John just grunted his usual ignorant grunt.

"I'm sure we will be delighted with the progress John has made during the three weeks he's been away. Won't we John?" said Barry.

"Well It's a little early to have all the bands sorted but I do have some fantastic acts signed up and lots more waiting to confirm."

"Come on John. Don't keep us in suspense. Did you sign up Sly and The Family Stone?" Barry asked as he tried to be hip and happening.

"Well no they couldn't fit a trip to England in their busy touring schedule but I have confirmed and signed our headline act for the festival. It's…Joe Cocker."

Peter couldn't believe his ears.

"Did you say Joe Cocker is the headline act?" he asked.

"Yes I fucking did. And what does it have to do with you? I'm the fucking booker for this festival not you."

"Alright John calm down. Peter is just a little surprised that Joe is headlining considering he's only had a couple of minor hits and stories of his not turning up to shows and his alcohol and substance abuse make him a bit risky." Malcolm added, "He's not the greatest draw is he?"

Spikings said nothing. He obviously knew nothing of Joe Cocker's legendary problems and wasn't really interested but asked who else John had got.

"I've got The Beach Boys and Sha Na Na."

"Is that The Beach Boys who haven't had a hit since 1966 and who the fuck is Sha Na Na?" Peter asked.

"Shut up you little shit. Who do you think you are?"

"I'm the only person here who has ever been to a festival. That's who I am." Peter answered. Detesting the booker even more. Couldn't anyone else see what a useless twat the man was. He had an open chequebook and couldn't even sign up one decent act.

"Well I'm the booker and it's down to me to get the acts. It's not easy to persuade bands to come to England in May for an outdoor festival."

"No I'm sure it isn't but Jeremy Beadle got The Grateful Dead and some of the biggest acts in America for no up front money, on just the promise of a future payment, for a festival on a slag heap, just three weeks before ours so it can't be that hard," Peter continued.

"Well it was hard. I had to give Joe Cocker 60 first class return air tickets for him and his band on top of his hefty fee. The same for The Beach Boys and Sha Na Na have 27 members in the band so they got 50 first class and 40 cabin class tickets. If I hadn't given them those tickets they wouldn't have come."

"So remind me again. Who is Sha Na Na?" Malcolm asked.

"They are a Doo Wop band. They played Woodstock and they are going to be big in the States," John said, and with that he strode out of the room back to his office to continue with his important business.

"What a dick!" Peter muttered to Malcolm who shushed him.

"Well I think we have made a very good start with those acts," said Spikings and Michael agreed with him a little hesitantly.

"I suppose it will work when we get the rest of the line up in place. Anyway, I'm sure we all have a lot to do."

When Peter and Malcolm had got back to their office Peter was fuming.

"Junkie Joe 'With a Little Help From My Friends' Cocker with 60 first class air tickets to headline what we are calling The Great Western 'Experience', not even 'Festival', in

Bardney, Lincolnshire is pathetic. I'm ashamed to be associated with the shambles John 'I'm the fucking booker' Martin is turning this show into. No one in England will talk to him and he goes to the States and gets a junkie, a sixties surf band and a doo wop band that played Woodstock. That is supposed to draw thousands of people to the wilderness of Lincolnshire in May. I really don't think so. The Isle of Wight had Hendrix, Dylan, The Who and Jethro Tull as the headliners and loads of other big acts and the attraction was huge and crowds of people went and the promoters made a fortune, one way or another but they had Bob Dylan for one thing. Deeley and Spikings have not got a clue about what the festival crowd wants or where and when they will go to get it. It's not enough just to put on any old show, call it an Experience and expect people to turn up to it."

"My, my, that was quite a speech and I know for a fact Michael and Barry don't want to listen to your opinions so I would keep them to yourself if I were you. I have got so much money riding on this festival that I don't care if they put Engelbert Humperdinck at the top of the bill. The only important thing is that the festival happens. So please don't rock the boat, just go along with it and I will see you right after it's all over."

"Alright Malcolm. Whatever it is you are doing is fine by me. I'm working for you and not them so just carry on and I won't say a word out of place until you finish what you have started."

"Good man. Now let's get back to work

CHAPTER 16

How long does it take to understand there is no sense in trying

Have you ever had a really good simple idea and not been able to get it off the ground for lack of money and enlisted the help of someone else to finance the venture?

If you have, you will know how quickly the person you enlisted will think the idea was so simple anyone could have thought of it.

In fact they could have thought of it themselves.

If they could have thought of it and they were now working on the idea, it should have been them who thought of it.

They financed the idea and so really it is their idea and they don't really need to include the person who originally came up with the idea in the first place. It is also a bit embarrassing to have the originator of the idea around as they can't claim the idea as their own.

Does that sound familiar?

Well, that is what started to happen to Malcolm. With the idea in motion, the money in place, the site secured and three bands booked, Barry Spikings saw the possibilities of raising his profile from hick reporter to rock festival promoter. The original idea was so simple anyone could have come up with it and now everything was in motion it was time he took the reins. He persuaded Michael Deeley that he was the best person to oversee all the arrangements by bringing in professional people who could make all the arrangements just like Michael did when producing his films.

When a company makes a film, a production manager is used to book transport, catering, caravans, lighting, etc. and all the practical services that are needed in the process of shooting the film. However in the film business all the catering, transport, caravans, and lighting is readily available from established dedicated companies who can be contacted and employed to supply everything needed to complete the film. This can be achieved with three or four phone calls, by an assistant, and doesn't take a lot to do as the infrastructure is generally already set up.

A production manager, who probably worked on *The Italian Job*, was brought in with great fanfare. He was pushed into Malcolm's office and pushed straight back out. Michael went in to see what was going on and was informed there was no room for another person in the office as he could well see. Another desk space was found somewhere else and the production manager started to try to organise some transport. He contacted the film transport suppliers who did not have the right vehicles for a festival. Then he contacted the film caravan people who wouldn't supply their vans for a festival. The caterers couldn't supply that amount of food and had film work. The production manager had hit a brick wall and was desperately trying to find someone to whom he could delegate this work.

Not wishing to be beaten he phoned a caravan company close to Lincolnshire and was told that all of their caravans had been booked on that date, as did the Land Rover hire companies. It appeared that you couldn't buy a festival out of a box.

The reason they were booked was because Peter had reserved them as soon as a site was found. Booking these vans was not easy as they were usually returned trashed and not paid for at the end of the festival.

Weeks ago, Peter had made a list of the largest caravan companies in the Midlands and when the site was confirmed he rang one of them and the conversation went something like this.

"Hello my name is Peter Whitehead. Do you rent caravans?"

"Yes we do. When would you like it?"

"For two weeks over the May Bank Holiday please. I want more than one if possible."

"How many do you want?"

"How many have you got?"

"What do you want them for?"

"We want them for VIP accommodation at our festival in Lincolnshire."

"Sorry we don't rent them for pop festivals."

"Oh. Why not?"

"Because we never get paid for them and mainly because they always get trashed."

"What would you say if we paid for them up front when we booked them and also put down a security deposit decided by you in case there is any damage, and also paid for you to deliver them to the site and then pick them up."

"I'd say where do you want them delivered?"

"That's great. Let me know how many you've got and the total cost for the hire, delivery and returnable deposit. I'll wait for your call and we can send you a cheque."

"Right. I'll get back to you today."

"Alright. Just one thing. I want one really nice caravan left on site for me personally. The keys are to be left in the gas bottle compartment and a sign in the window saying "Out of Order" it will be paid for with the others but the paperwork is to be left in the van and not given to the site office. Is that ok?"

"Sure thing Peter. We can also leave you an envelope with a finder's fee for this large order if you want. We can just add it to the delivery cost and no one will know."

"That would be great. So let's keep this little arrangement to ourselves shall we? Do you have the phone numbers of any other friendly caravan hirers I can contact?"

"Sure. I will contact them first to make all the arrangements for you and give you their numbers this afternoon when I give you the bill. It's been a pleasure to do business with you Peter."

All the arrangements had been made when Peter talked later that day with various other caravan suppliers. Only one van was reserved personally for Peter, as was one very special 1965 aluminium body Land Rover which was singled out of the many that had been ordered. It was to be set aside for the personal use of Peter with the keys left under the driver's seat and a note on the windscreen saying 'Non Runner'!

The words of Chris the driver echoed in his head as he sorted out a few home comforts for himself and if a few companies wanted to pay him a finder's fee he was delighted someone appreciated his worth.

Rumour had it that Stanley was borrowing a huge 50-foot-long vintage Showman's Trailer from the circus owner Billy Smart so he had somewhere luxurious to stay and entertain his close friends. Peter only wanted one little four berther!

Peter didn't feel very secure in his job and just hoped Malcolm had enough influence to be able to stop the festival being hijacked from under him.

He said goodbye to Linda and told Malcolm he wasn't available over the weekend as he would be busy. Malcolm shrugged and said, "Oh aye I'm sure you will have your hands full. I'll try not to disturb you whatever it is you are up to."

CHAPTER 17

Dealer boots

All the time Peter had been working on the festival he had also been cultivating his dealer friends and contacts. It had been quite impressive to be known to be working as a promoter of a major pop festival and Peter had used the position to gain respect and trust among the dope dealers he had been buying from and selling to. It was so important to gain trust from the people you were working with.

Malcolm also expected total dedication to the job, sometimes working seven days a week, but had been flexible about Peter taking days off when he wanted.

The days he took off were carefully chosen to coincide with selling pounds of hash among the group of dealers he had garnered and he had built up a profitable little business that paid him much more money than he made working for Malcolm.

The chance meeting that had made the most impact on Peter's dope selling business had been his introduction to Christine Bradley who lived on the other side of Shepherd's Bush Green in W14. She was affectionately known as 'Lady Bradley' by a certain group of her friends.

Christine was a bit older than Peter and owned her house in Redan Street, which was pretty impressive for a start. She worked as an assistant for a fashion photographer called

Manfred Vogelsänger who had taken the pictures for the cover of The Rolling Stones album *Beggar's Banquet*. She was completely independent and almost didn't need to work as her grandfather had left her all his money in a trust fund many years ago.

He had drawn up the trust long ago in order to let her live a very comfortable life from the benefits of the huge sum of money he had left her. As she was 'only a woman' the trust had been made ironclad so she couldn't access the money directly or be swindled out of the fortune by anyone. For this reason he had allowed her no direct access to the capital. He had allowed for inflation and a sum of £4500 was set aside to buy a house. It was a huge sum then and would have bought a magnificent property. No one could have foreseen how house prices could have escalated so much over the years. This amount was all she was allowed. If she bought a house and astutely sold it for more money she was not allowed to keep the excess profit and it went back into the trust and she only had another £4500 to start again. She could do this as often as she liked.

The house she had bought was in a lovely little street off Blythe Road. It had cost the measly sum of £4500 for the simple reason a flyover was planned to go over it in five years' time and the whole area was to be flattened. Of course this was of no interest to Christine as she just got another £4500 to buy again. However plans change and the flyover idea was dropped and the value of all the houses in that area skyrocketed and the area became known as West Kensington. The downside was that if she sold her house for the hundreds of thousands it was now worth, the profits would be locked back into the trust, and she would only get back the original stake and that would buy nothing around there. Her caring grandfather, had also left an allowance to be paid annually to allow his sole heir to live in luxury. He stretched his imagination and came up with the princely sum of £30 per week. A fortune in those days but not enough to get by on in the seventies which explained why she worked for Manfred.

In fairness the trust was not set up to deny Christine any money. It was just that he wanted to protect the money from gold digging suitors who would steal it from a 'silly young girl'. He also could not imagine how much inflation would grow. Christine spent hours with the executors while both of them tried to work out a way of extracting some money from the vast capital but there was absolutely no way around the watertight conditions. She had become resigned to the unbelievable fact that all the money would go to the government on her death. Ironically this was probably the very last thing her grandfather would have wanted to happen. It was probably this fact and the knowledge that all her money was sitting there and she was not able to access it that made Christine a little crazy.

This arrangement was unknown to Peter as he first visited her house and smoked joints and drank coffee and talked about music and photography and dope.

Dope, it transpired, was pretty high on the list of interests for both of them. Christine's unique position had turned into an unlikely asset for her and her friends, some of whom turned out to be drug smugglers.

Having a permanent base and having no need to get involved in the financial aspect of smuggling gave the opportunity for Christine to provide a safe house, where no large amounts of dope came, but where meetings could be held, plans could be made, people connected to each other without the fear of phones being tapped and a safe neutral place where everyone could meet, relax and discuss strategy. The house became an informal control centre, with people always coming and going, and Christine was always rewarded with choice lumps of hash from the special stash smugglers always brought back with them, and sometimes an amount of cash if a deal went particularly well. The amount of smuggling was not huge but a few friends setting up trips to Morocco, Amsterdam and occasionally Afghanistan on a fairly regular basis.

Peter's rock and roll credentials and the fact that he was always able to come up with really good dope meant he was introduced into this group and gradually became an honorary member of the club. Soon he was being given kilos to sell because Christine wanted him to become the main distributor.

In 1972 Peter believed that selling drugs, although illegal, was not immoral. This attitude did not mean he openly advertised the fact that he was selling drugs, in fact the opposite was true, great care was always taken so no obvious clues were given about the illicit trade that was going on.

As many people as possible should be 'turned on' and all the people involved in smuggling and selling dope were thought of as outlaws living on the other side of the law but doing good for society. Good hash was a great thing for changing people's viewpoints. It was less damaging than alcohol. It broadened your mind and made you more relaxed but the other thing was it made you a ton of money. Viva La Revolution.

This idealistic way of looking at things was enjoyed by quite a few likeminded spirits but was still by no means the consensus of opinion of most of the general public.

Peter was fascinated with all the stories about smuggling trips and the dangers involved all through the trips but at that time had no wish to get involved in any other way than to sell the hash when it got back in London.

It was ridiculously easy for Peter to change from being a buyer to being a supplier. He was already buying several pounds of dope at a time from a few dealers who were selling him some dope and also selling larger amounts to other buyers. When Peter was offered dope from the smugglers he could just offer it to his suppliers, who already knew and trusted him and he became the supplier. They had other buyers who would buy large amounts from them and everyone wanted to buy as close to the source as they could because the price was better. As he was offering it at the best price, directly from the source, all his one-time sellers wanted to buy as much as he had. Immediately Peter became a wholesaler with the added advantage that he didn't have to pay up front for the gear which made life so much easier for him to move larger quantities.

Smugglers hang out with other smugglers and they also started to hang out with Peter who then became their choice of seller when they landed their gear in this country. The amounts coming in were not huge but they were starting to get regular and from different countries.

It was causing a bit of a dilemma for Peter as selling dope was taking up more and more of his time and he was not going into the office as often as he should. One noticeable thing about Peter at that time was his appearance. It had become obvious to Peter that it was time to revamp his image and he took a wad of money from his stash and went to the King's Road in search of some specific items.

First he bought several pairs of prewashed Levi 501 jeans. Then he bought a selection of denim jackets and shirts. His favourite was a skinny overshirt restyled from old jeans with the back pockets stitched onto the front. He thought it looked really cool with all the fading and wear, chunky stitching and original back pockets making it obvious that it was a reworked pair of jeans. There was one more item he needed to buy to complete the look. Next door to the Chelsea Pharmacy was a shop that specialised in American stuff. Hats, biker jackets, cowboy jackets and cowboy boots.

The objects of Peter's desire were the boots. Cowboy boots were the essential wear for any self-respecting dealer. They were not to be too flashy. Not too pointy toed and not with a Cuban heel either. They had to look plain and sturdy and reach halfway up the calf and be loose fitting. These specific requirements were because the boots were one of the most important pieces of equipment when doing drug deals. On any occasion when it was necessary to carry a large amount of money, it went into the boots. Every time you did a deal you either walked in with a lot of money or you walked out with a lot of money. There was no reason to carry any sort of bag because you could get up to £5000 in the boots and why would you want to carry a bag? The money was safe, secure and very close to your body at all times. If at any time it was necessary to take away a sample of the gear, it went into the boots. Up to a couple of pounds went into the boots with no trouble and not noticeable as it would be if it was in a bag. It was very important to choose the right sort of boot and Peter spent half an hour trying on all shapes and colour boots until he finally decided on two pairs that were suitable for his purpose. One pair went into the bag full of denim and he strode out of the shop into the King's Road in the others.

Now he felt the part. Now he was ready to start doing some real business.

CHAPTER 18

Easy money.

Work was finished for the week, plans had been made to sell ten pounds of hash on Saturday afternoon, Gill had arranged to buy a couple of weight for a friend who was in the music business and turned up at midday. She hadn't seen anything of Peter for about a month but they had kept in touch by phone. She knew his job kept him busy but she also knew that he was getting plugged into some really good contacts and wanted to get involved as well.

The doorbell rang and Peter looked out of the window and saw Gill looking up.

"Catch." he called out and dropped the keys three floors down, in a matchbox. As usual Gill did her thing of flailing around pretending to try to catch the keys but always getting nowhere near the hurtling projectile. Watching her doing that routine always made him laugh. He slipped the lock and went back to the living room and waited for Gill to climb the three stories. She arrived in the flat slightly out of breath and came through to where Peter was rolling a joint with a sample of what he was selling that day.

"My God, look at you all dressed up looking like a dope dealer," she said.

"Oh these old things. They were at the back of my wardrobe and I thought I'd put them on for a change."

"Yeah, right! But they do look really good on you. You look ready for business. Is that a sample you've got there? Let me try it."

"Sure is. It's a really nice lump of Moroccan. It's much better than the usual commercial but it's not Zero Zero. It's very nice and the price is really good as well."

"Yeah, I know the price is good and I appreciate you cutting me in on the deal. I know you can move ten easily so you don't need my two."

"I've missed seeing you and thought it would be fun to mix a bit of business with a bit of pleasure. If you know what I mean."

"No I don't know what you mean," she said smiling.

"Well I thought that when we've finished with the dope we can nip out for a bite to eat and come back here and try this."

"And what is this?" she asked.

"It's two tabs of Purple Haze. Pure LSD. All the way from The United States of America courtesy of a very good new friend of mine. Are you in?"

"I'm in but I have to go home first as soon as we've moved the dope."

"That's no problem, you can drive my car. Can you sit with my buyers in Nick's flat while I look after the seller up here?"

"I knew there would be a reason why you wanted me here."

"That's not the only reason I want you here. Honest."

"I know that's true as well." But she was smiling and Peter knew that things would be fine with them.

The two buyers arrived at three o'clock and Gill showed them into Nick's living room in his first floor flat. He was out, doing his radio show, and had allowed Peter to use his flat with Gill looking after them. She was brilliant. Very business-like.

She gave them a sample of the dope to smoke, made them a cup of coffee and counted out their money while they waited for the sellers to arrive upstairs with the bag. It was very important to keep the buyers and sellers apart, because if they met it would be easy for them to cut out the middleman. It wasn't until very strong bonds had been made with both sides that all the business could be done in one room and even then most sellers wanted to stay anonymous for safety's sake, particularly if they were also the smugglers. The fewer people who knew each other the less chance of being grassed up, in exchange for leniency, in the event of a bust.

At ten past three the seller rang the doorbell and was shown into the living room where a set of grocer's scales sat on the table. His name was Ron and they had only recently met. This was the first time Peter had bought from him and he was plugged into a firm who were going to be bringing in a constant supply of Moroccan hash on sailing boats as soon as the weather improved in the Bay of Biscay. The goods were examined and then weighed. Eight pounds were weighed out and Peter put them in a carrier bag and nipped down to Nick's flat and exchanged the bag for the cash. The buyers had tried the dope already and handed over the money and were shown out immediately saying they must do this again soon. Peter removed £400 from the cash and stuffed it into his boot, to keep for himself, and took the rest back upstairs with Gill's money. He had only been five minutes and when he got back in he handed over the cash, which was quickly counted, and Ron went on his way back to Wimbledon after saying that he would be in touch soon when he had some more to sell and also to be sure to contact him as soon as Peter had something to sell. He had already been laying the foundations of his new position.

Gill came back up the stairs and said, "So where is my gear then?"

"It's right here under the cushion and I've got an extra ounce for you as a bonus for being a star!"

"Well thank you sir for being so generous. Let's spark it up and then make a move back to mine. I'll only be a few minutes and then we can do whatever we want."

They drove over to Olympia where Gill was now living in a two bed Mansion flat which she was sharing with Eric. He was just her lodger and was easy to get along with. Peter had liked him from when he first met him in Hendon and was glad they had both managed to get away from that dump and was a little bit jealous of their flat. One day he would get himself a cool place to live that wasn't over a fried chicken shop. But his flat was really good for now. It was large, anonymous, cheap and close enough to the Tube and was perfect with Nick's flat being conveniently downstairs and the constant stream of strange looking people who were constantly coming and going into the shop below provided great cover for people to enter the side door to his stairs unnoticed.

"Do you want to come in?" she asked.

"Yeah I do. Is Eric in?"

"Yes he is and for some unknown reason he's hoping to see you."

Gill squeezed the little Mini into a parking space right outside the flat, which was at the end of a cul-de-sac, called Avondale Road, just south of Olympia, and went up to the first floor flat where Eric was making a cup of tea.

"Hi, man," he said with a big grin on his face, "It's good to see you again. I hear you are doing really well for yourself. Do you want a cuppa?"

"Yes please I'd love one. I suppose I haven't done too badly since the time you all found me a job from the *Evening Standard*."

"That was so funny! I can't believe what you turned that

stupid job into. What a complete surprise. And you seem to be doing well in the other business as well."

"Yeah, it all seems to be picking up at the same time. Who knows where it will end."

They sat down with a cup of tea and Peter rolled a joint and gave it to Eric and very soon Gill came back in after having dropped off the two pounds of dope to her buyer who handily lived in a nearby flat.

"That's done then. Now the music business has enough smoke to last a week or so and I've made a nice few quid thanks to your generous pricing," Gill said.

"Good for you! Now what do you want to do?"

"I want to go down to the King's Road and buy a denim jacket from the shop you got that shirt and then get something to eat and then go back to your flat. But first I have to shower and change. You boys can amuse yourselves for a short while."

Eric was interested in what Peter did when he was working for the festival company and was told that it was not really very interesting at the moment but really involved organising things for his boss and there was no contact with anything that had to do with rock and roll. In fact he was beginning to get a little bored with the work and not liking the direction the festival was taking. Before long Gill came back. She had changed and looked stunning. Her faded jeans were tight as was her white tee shirt and her lovely boobs strained against the cotton.

"My, my, you do scrub up well," Peter said.

"Well, I do have to try to keep up with you."

"Oh no you don't have to do that. Come on, let's go eat."

The Mini's big bore exhaust rasped as they drove up the King's Road and it looked for all the world to be a trendy lowered Cooper S, like all the other rich kids' Minis, that were driving around. It looked like such a stylish car and

Gill really looked the part behind the wheel as she expertly nipped in and out of the traffic. So trendy and the couple inside were feeling great having made a pocket full of easy money and were now off to spend some of it.

They went to the shop that sold the denims and Gill bought a short bomber jacket made from remodelled jeans and when she slipped it on Peter thought she had the cutest ass he had ever seen.

"How does it look?" she asked.

"I haven't got the words," he said laughing as she spun around and wiggled her cute skinny bum at him. "Oh you know me so well."

"Like putty in my hands. I guess as you helped me make the money it cost, you also get to handle the goods," she joked.

"O.K. you hussy but first let's go and eat. There's a place I've seen that I want to try. It's a creperie called Asterix, like the comic. Shall we go there?"

"Sure. Let's go," and off they went to eat galettes.

Sure enough Asterix was a little French-owned creperie that also sold savoury galettes the likes of which had never been tasted before on the King's Road. They ordered galettes stuffed with asparagus and cheese, drank red wine and followed that with sweet crepes filled with chocolate ganache. The food was lovely and the owner, who was making the crepes on a huge hotplate, was being very friendly to the pair of them. Peter had a great idea and suggested the owner bring his hotplates up to the festival and supply fast food to the huge captive crowd that would be there. He was sure Malcolm would think it a great idea and the owner said he would be interested in doing it. It was tentatively arranged with the details to be worked out later. At least the food would be good at the festival, even if the music was shite!

As they drove back to Shepherd's Bush, Gill asked, "Can

you really just arrange for that man to sell his food at the festival?"

"Yes I can just tell Malcolm I want Asterix there and he will sort it. He trusts my judgement and I think it will work really well alongside the Hard Rock burgers."

"You've got the Hard Rock doing the food?"

"Yes. The food will be amazing. I just hope we get some decent bands to come along. That's one area where I don't have any influence."

"You've got the Hard Rock doing the food? That is amazing. How did that happen?"

"Well Malcolm knew the owners and worked out a deal with them."

"That's amazing. I hope you are making good contacts for when this is over."

"Oh sure. If you ever need to hire a caravan in Lincolnshire come to me. I'm 'The Man'."

"Oh Peter I love the way you don't take yourself seriously… You know I don't want us to get back together, don't you?"

"Sure I know. We don't have to do anything now. We both have plans and are busy in other directions. I've got so much good business coming up when some smugglers get back here and I have to finish all the festival stuff. I really have my hands full now."

"That's good 'cos I don't want to get involved right now what with college and my dad and everything. We can hang out and do business and whatever. In fact, I want you to meet a friend of mine who sells a lot of dope to some quite important people in the music business. He is a pain in the arse because he just keeps trying to get me into bed but he wants more dope than I can supply him and he pays top dollar. You can sell to him if you give me a small cut."

"Sure. We can do that. Now let's go up and see if John is home."

On the way upstairs they stopped in Nick's flat. He had returned from broadcasting his radio show and Peter handed him half an ounce of Moroccan hash and thanked him for the use of his flat.

"It's really no bother and you don't have to give me all that much. Really," Nick said.

"Of course I do as I couldn't have done it without using your place. So thanks a lot mate, and enjoy the blow."

"Sure will and see you both later maybe."

Upstairs in the top flat John had returned and was in his room with his girlfriend Susie. They came out and warmly greeted Gill and asked what they had been up to today. Gill said: "Not much. We went to the King's Road to buy a jacket and ate crepes and are going to drop some acid later."

"Isn't that dangerous?" asked Susie who had never even smoked a joint in her life.

"I suppose it is but it depends on where you got it from."

"And I bet you got it from Peter," Susie said.

"That's right. It's where all the good stuff comes from," Gill replied.

"Are you going to open that bottle of wine?" John piped up, as soon as he noticed the bottles in Peter's hands, and soon a bottle was open and four glasses filled. John rarely bought decent wine or any luxuries into the flat, because he was such a mingebag, but he was happy to help drink their bottles.

"Did everything go alright today?" he asked.

"Yes, sweet as a nut thanks. I appreciate you letting me use the flat for a bit of business and here's some rent up front and a little bit for you to use as you wish." Peter fished in his boots and pulled out £100 and handed it over to John. Susie's eyes widened as she saw the money and said to John, "I hope you are going to give me some of that," and both Peter and Gill smiled as John tried to think of a way of keeping all the money for himself. Peter had deliberately handed over the cash in front of Susie so he could see how John would get out of sharing it.

"I'm sure you will. Won't you John. Have you seen the jacket Peter bought me today in the King's Road?" Gill said, elaborating the joke a little more and watching John squirm.

"Of course I'll give you some, Susie, but this money is mainly to be used to pay the rent Peter owes me. We all know how erratic his payments are."

With that he shoved the money into his pocket and changing the subject said, "Are you really going to take acid tonight? I would be too scared that it would send me mad or something."

"You'd be too scared it would cost you a tenner is the truth." Susie added and they all laughed and drank some more wine.

Peter and Gill went out into the kitchen and he poured a glass of water and offered her one of the Purple Haze tabs.

"Are you sure?" he asked.

"Absolutely. I've heard so much about Purple Haze tabs and I really want to try them. I'd rather be out in the countryside but it doesn't matter. You will look after me, won't you?"

"Of course I will, you mean a lot to me."

They both swallowed the tabs and he kissed her and slowly ran his hands over her breasts saying,

"You know you have got the most beautiful sexy body and you drive me wild every time I see you."

"What I know is you are obsessed with my boobs and will do anything to feel them."

"That is the truth. Guilty as charged."

"Well that may have to wait a bit until this acid kicks in and we can try it then."

"I love the sound of that idea."

Then they started the waiting to see what the trip would be like. Would anything happen? Would it blow their mind? They would know in less than an hour.

CHAPTER 19

It's alright, I'm only dreaming.

They went back to John's room and finished the bottle of wine and when the first flashes of the acid started they went off to Peter's room to enjoy the trip.

"I think this is going to be a good one," Peter said as the psychedelic waves started crashing in his brain.

"I think you're right. Hold tight, this could be a bumpy trip," Gill said as they started giggling uncontrollably. Later they heard a knocking on the door and John came in.

"Sorry guys but Malcolm is on the phone for you."

"Tell him I'm busy and can't talk to him," Peter said.

"I've already tried that but he insisted that I make you come to the phone. It is really important."

"Oh shit! I don't know if I can hold it together to talk to him right now," Peter said and Gill thought it was the funniest thing ever.

"Stop laughing. What am I going to do? I think he is going to fire me. What a bummer. Oh well here goes." He took a deep breath and tried to clear his head and stumbled off to the phone leaving Gill and John having hysterics.

If you have taken acid you will understand the problem Peter was about to experience. If you haven't just imagine you have totally taken leave of your senses and have to pretend you are perfectly sane and that wouldn't even come near it. This was Purple Haze in his brain.

"Er, hello Malcolm," he said.

"Where the hell have you been? I've been waiting on the end of this phone for ages."

"Sorry I was a bit tied up."

"What do you mean 'tied up'? Oh never mind I don't want to know."

"No, I don't mean tied up like that I mean involved in something."

"Why are you talking funny?"

"I'm a bit pissed. We are having a bit of a celebration here."

"Pissed my arse. You're out of your mind on Waccy Baccy if I know you."

"Yeah, sort of," Peter managed to say.

"Well it's up to you if you want to get stoned out of your mind. I don't care what you do when you're not at work."

"Well thanks for that. It means a lot to me. Really it does. So what is the big problem that makes you call me on Saturday night?"

Suddenly the trip stepped up a gear and Peter understood the meaning of the words, "The chimes of freedom flashing."

Malcolm started off on a seemingly endless story about what was going on at the office between Michael, Barry and him. How there was a power struggle and Barry wanted to take over and how things were going to change from now on.

Peter was hanging on for dear life to normality. He was trying to take all this office politics stuff seriously and also not to say anything that would give the game away. After what seemed like an hour he just came out with it. He was bored with this pretence and wanted to get it over and done with.

"So you have rung me to tell me I'm fired, right?" he finally came out with.

"Fired? What? Fired. You? No not fired, you stupid wanker. I've persuaded them to make you festival director. What do you think of them apples?"

"I don't believe you, that's what I think. The only thing on Barry's mind right now is how to get hold of a position or someway to make himself important and now Festival Director is a step up for him. It's not as grand as he really wants but he has no respect right now and is desperate to make a name for himself. He needs to prove to Michael that he is not just a hick junior reporter and this is his first opportunity."

"You are so erudite but so wrong. Go back to puffing on your weed and you will see on Monday that things have changed."

"Ok, Malcolm. Will do," Peter said, "And thanks for what you have done for me."

"Yes, well that's alright. But I haven't done it just for you." And he continued chatting on and on about the power struggles and importance of controlling the reins and how he needed this festival to succeed until Peter just quietly put down the phone wondering how long it would take Malcolm to notice.

Gill was waiting for him in the bedroom and asked if he had been fired.

"I don't know what has happened. Malcolm has just not stopped talking at me and I can't really remember much about what he said. I think he said something about making me festival director in amongst all his waffle but I don't know if I imagined it. Anyway, how are you liking the trip? It's pretty full on isn't it? I really thought I was gonna blow it with Malcolm but at the moment I couldn't care less what happens to me. Let's go and see what we can get up to outside."

"What a good idea. This flat looks a bit cheesy right now and I need some room to expand my head," Gill said as they started down the staircase to explore the outside world and all its psychedelic wonders.

There is nothing more boring than listening to someone describing an acid trip.

If you've done acid you know. If you haven't, no number of descriptions will get anywhere near what it's like, and all you will get is the equivalent of the New Orleans trip scene in *Easy Rider* and that is not good.

Nevertheless the stoned couple spent the next eight hours exploring all the delights LSD had to offer and had what is called 'A Good Trip' and when they woke up the next afternoon, tangled in bed, they felt hungover, exhausted and confused about what they had done. They both had vague memories of where they had been and what they had done and an overwhelming memory of the dazzling colours and momentous conclusions they had experienced throughout the night.

"Did your boss phone you last night?" Gill asked as they were sitting eating some breakfast at about four in the afternoon.

"Oh God I seem to have some recollection of listening to him banging on for hours," Peter half remembered.

"Didn't he say you were going to be made festival director or something?"

"I do have a vague recollection of him saying something about that but I don't think it could be true."

"So what are you going to do about it then."

"I'm not going to do anything about it. I can't remember clearly what was said and I don't want to ask him if I imagined it when I was tripping. Surely they will tell me about it soon enough."

"I guess you're right. For the organisers of a rock festival, though, they do seem like a bunch of flat-faced fuckers. Apart from Malcolm of course. He seems sweet."

"Malcolm is certainly not sweet but he is marginally less likely to cut my throat, to get what he wants, than those other wankers."

"It's been fun but I have to get home and wash off all this crud I seem to have picked up last night. Were we really crawling around The Green at midnight?"

"Yes we were. But strangely enough we weren't the only ones. That was weird. Come on, I'll get you a taxi home."

CHAPTER 20

I'm not the one you need

Monday morning arrived too soon and Peter felt really ragged. It was with trepidation that he entered the office building on the Embankment and by the time he got to his office he felt sick. As he entered he could see something momentous had happened. Malcolm was shouting at the top of his voice to nobody in particular but when Peter stepped in, he caught it full on.

"That snidey little prick Harvey Goldsmith has really turned us over. I knew he was up to something and nobody would listen to me. Why doesn't anybody listen to me?"

"I'm listening, Malcolm. What has happened?"

"This is what has happened. Look at this." He thrust a copy of *Melody Maker* into Peter's hand and sat into his chair with a thump.

Peter looked at the page and saw a full-page advert for something called The Crystal Palace Garden Party. It was a concert scheduled for June 3rd, organised by John Smith for whom Harvey Goldsmith and Michael Alfandary worked.

The headline acts were Joe Cocker, The Beach Boys and Sha Na Na. It was to happen in South London two weeks after they headlined the festival in Bardney.

Any interest those acts would have had to draw people to a festival all the way up in Lincolnshire would certainly be affected by the opportunity of seeing them for a quid in London.

"What's going on? How did he do it?" Peter asked.

"That snake Harvey Goldsmith went with John to the States and signed up the bands, after they had signed for us, is what happened."

"But how could he sign them? They had just been signed for our festival."

"Well the problem is John didn't make them sign an exclusivity agreement."

"So that fuckwit paid huge fees, paid for hundreds of first-class flights and accommodation, to get them over here, but didn't sign them exclusively and Harvey Goldsmith has paid them nuppence to play in London two weeks after our festival because all their air fares and expenses are paid for by us? So now no one needs to travel for six hours to go to Bardney to see them?"

"Yes that's it in a nutshell. But we have to look on the bright side. He now has confirmed bookings for Nazareth, Stone the Crows and Lindisfarne," Malcolm said with considerable irony.

"Well we are stuffed. You can kiss goodbye to any chance of this poxy festival doing any good. John Martin has to be the worst booker ever and I can't believe he has kept his job. This whole thing has become a joke. No one has a clue how to run a festival and we are a laughing stock."

At this point Michael Deeley came bursting into the office followed by his trusty shadow Barry.

"What is going on?" Michael yelled.

"What are you talking about?" Malcolm asked with a straight face.

"Where is John?" Deeley said.

"I have no idea. He doesn't deign to speak to me." Malcolm said.

145

"Have you seen this?" He waved the paper at both of them.

"Yes we have a copy here. I was just showing it to Peter before you came storming in."

"Well we are banjaxed. Completely fucked. What are we going to do now?" Michael wailed.

"Well it's not all bad," Peter chipped in. "Apparently John has signed up Nazareth, Stone the Crows and Lindisfarne."

"Ooh I like 'Fog On The Tyne'," said Barry only to be cut short with an icy stare from Michael.

"He's taking the piss. So who do you suggest we get then Peter?"

"Don't ask me. I've been told in no uncertain terms, 'You're not the fucking booker'. Get John to sort it out and good luck with that." And he started to busy himself with some very important business until those two had left.

Malcolm was obviously very upset by the proceedings but still did not blame John for the mistake. Instead he cursed Harvey Goldsmith and put all the blame on him.

Peter took the opportunity of a lull in the storm to ask Malcolm a question, "I was a bit pissed on Saturday night," he began.

"Yes I realised that when I spoke to you."

"Well I can't really remember what you said. Was it anything important?"

"No not really. I just wanted to have a bit of a chat with you. You know, just a moan really."

"Oh, right then," Peter said, thinking 'I did dream all that'. "In that case I don't think I can spend so much time here anymore."

"What are you saying? Are you walking out on me?"

"No I'm not walking out on you I just can't spend so much time here. I've got other things that I have to spend more time on. Barry seems to have delegated the day to day running of affairs and there is not so much for me to do anymore. He doesn't really want to involve me in things so I thought I could come in if and when you needed me. You can call me and I'll try to get in to help."

"Right then. Let's go out now. We will be back later, Linda, if anyone wants me. Come on, let's go," Malcolm said, hustling Peter out of the door.

"Alright I'm coming."

They went down in the lift and flagged a passing taxi and crossed the river and drove into Soho. This was a part of London that Malcolm felt at home in. It was a vibrant, if not cheesy, place full of people trying to make their way up The Ladder. The rents had taken a dive, as Soho had fallen out of favour but it was slap bang in the centre of London. So many new start-up companies based themselves there amongst the strip clubs, sex shops, coffee bars, delis, music shops and all the call girls and rent boys. In Soho you could feel the air buzzing with excitement. The taxi stopped outside The Blue Posts in Berwick Street and they squeezed through the throng of customers availing themselves of an a la carte liquid lunch. Malcolm seemed to know most of them. Writers, journalists, A&R men from up and coming record companies based around the corner in Wardour Street, hustlers, pimps, dealers, musicians and a perceptible number of lowlifes. All of them busily networking and drinking, saying 'Hi' and continually scoping the room. At the bar Malcolm ordered their drinks and found himself standing next to a scruffy young man dressed in full on Hippy Gear.

"Malcolm!" he exclaimed, "Long time no see. Where have you been?"

"Felix you old Hippy. How have you been? Peter meet Felix Dennis, the next huge name in publishing," Malcolm said leaving Peter unsure whether to believe him, as he didn't often tell untruths, but he could never be sure and had learnt not to dismiss people based on their appearance.

"Nice to meet you Felix," Peter said and then had a light-bulb moment. "Oh my God, you're Felix Dennis from *Oz* magazine."

Oz magazine was an alternative magazine of the 1960s that had given over its last publication to a bunch of school kids and allowed them to publish an issue filled with whatever they wanted. Whatever they wanted turned out to be as shocking as you would expect from a bunch of uncensored school kids. The newspapers were horrified with the generally obscene nature of the kids' publication and Richard Neville, Jim Anderson and Felix Dennis were taken to court and charged with publishing pornographic material. There was a huge trial at the Old Bailey and John Mortimer had defended the three men. It caused a huge divide of opinion among the Establishment and the rest of the country ending with the three being found guilty and sent to prison for fifteen months and fined £12,000 with recommended deportation for the two Australians. The judge said that he would only send Felix Dennis to jail for nine months as he appeared to be "a bit stupid and was led astray by the others." After spending the night in Wandsworth Prison psychiatric ward, where they had their heads shaved, they appeared back at court, the next day, on appeal where the judge was found to have grossly misled the jury along with many other major miscarriages of justice. Their sentences were overturned, the fine reduced to £50, the deportation recommendations lifted and the three men walked free out of court, laughing and wearing long, extravagant wigs.

The three men had become heroes of the counterculture and even though they had essentially lost their case, they had kicked the Establishment squarely in the nuts in the opinion of the younger generation.

"I really admire what you, Richard and Jim did," Peter said lamely.

"Oh you know, we just thought the magazine was getting a bit boring and old hat and thought it would be funny to see what a bunch of kids wanted to say. We never thought it would start such a shitstorm. Although I think It's really funny how it turned out."

"So what are you doing now, Felix?" Malcolm asked.

"Well being called stupid by the judge made me realise I had the capacity to become a publisher. I've got a little office round the corner and I'm selling colour posters of all the new pop stars for young girls to put on their bedroom walls. It's just starting to pick up in a big way. At the moment I've just signed the rights for a Swedish tennis player who will win Wimbledon sometime in the future. Nobody has heard of him yet but when he wins I've got two rooms stacked high with posters of him that will make me a fortune."

"So what's his name then?" Malcolm asked.

"Bjorn Borg," Felix answered.

"Never heard of him." said Malcolm.

"Exactly. Nor has anyone else but I am convinced he will win Wimbledon sometime in the future and I have got sole rights on him!"

"Good luck with that Felix," Malcolm said laughing as he grabbed an empty table and motioned Peter over with him.

"What do you think of that idea then Malcolm?"

"It's impossible to say. He is as crazy as a fox and if the Swede wins he'll clean up. But who knows? Anyway that's enough about Felix I want to hear what is going on in your pea brain. What is it you want to do? And why?"

"You don't want to know what I think about the festival in case I rock the boat with Michael and Barry so why should I explain anything to you?"

"I want to know what is wrong with you. I want to know what you think is happening. I want your input because I am so close to the whole thing I can lose sight of it. This thing means so much to me and I don't want to lose it. Speak to me."

"I will tell you what I think about what is happening now, because I don't care anymore, I didn't want to upset anyone by disagreeing with them. I needed the work and the money and was quite happy to go along with everything because it didn't matter what I thought. The only thing that was important was that you make your big idea work so you could make enough money to set yourself up for the next big thing. Whatever that is. Right now I couldn't care less. Feel free to stop me if I'm boring you," Peter said, taking a deep pull on his pint of lager.

"Just stop behaving like a prima donna and say your piece." Malcolm said abruptly.

"Ok then. Here goes. This whole festival thing is turning into a piece of shit. Your idea has been shanghaied and is starting to fall apart on all levels. Starting with the site. Although there are some people who will be prepared to travel all the way to Lincolnshire for a festival, quite a large number will not, so you are effectively dismissing a large number of your audience.

"I know we had a problem getting a site but Barry Spikings ploughed in with this one because I think it was important for him to be seen as a success in his hometown. No longer the hack reporter for *Farmer's Weekly* with a Golden Ear for his efforts. Local boy makes good and so on and he can show off on television with his famous new friends. If we had held out a bit longer we could have found a better site. Again the problem comes around to Spikings. He is so out of his depth it's not even funny. He doesn't have a clue about putting on a festival but he has waded in and has taken control and is using this as a step up whatever ladder he is trying to climb, trying to do everything when he actually knows nothing at all."

"Alright. I hear you. What else?" Malcolm said, catching the eye of the barman and miming for two more drinks to be sent over.

"The next thing is the choice of bands. I know you won't hear a bad word said about John, but it's not just me who is concerned. The fact that he couldn't book a band in this country is not a problem but to go to the States and come back with Joe Cocker as the main headline act is pathetic. Then for it to transpire that he paid for all the first-class airfares for him and The Beach Boys and Sha Na Na only for Harvey Goldsmith to sign them for nothing to play a gig in London two weeks after our festival is ludicrous. If there is anyone who wants to go and see Cocker they will just nip down to Crystal Palace and see him there for a pound. Again a large segment of the audience has been removed. The bands that John is now filling the line up with are so weak they have hardly any draw at all. At best they are doing the Student Union circuit at about £75 a night. Bands like Nazareth, Stone the Crows, Status Quo, Lindisfarne, Groundhogs, Propeller, Locomotiv G.T, Focus and so on don't have the draw like Bob Dylan, Jimi Hendrix and The Who did at the Isle of Wight. The bands John has booked are so piss poor that hardly anyone will be prepared to come and see them. I know it isn't much of a guide but no one I know is remotely interested even in a free ticket to go and see this show as my guest. There is absolutely no interest at all. I can't even give away a sodding ticket to my girlfriend!"

"And your point is?" Malcolm said as he gave the barman money for the drinks he brought over.

"My point is, that even if there aren't any more problems than this, there will not be enough people going to this festival. The whole show has been taken over by Spikings who appears to be Michael's shadow. All he wants to do is please his boss. He is so keen to make a name for himself it's frightening. The organisation has been farmed out like a film production to contractors who don't have a clue about what a pop festival needs. It's like the television reporter watching someone performing brain surgery and saying 'Can I have a go?' because the surgeon is making it look so easy. They don't want any input or have any communication with either of us anymore and now think they are cool because they have stopped wearing a shirt and tie and they both now wear roll neck jumpers under their tweed jackets. They still look like twats and have started to grow their hair so it is almost touching their ears!

"Rock and Roll!!… necks.

"Whenever a problem occurs you can see either one on the television promising it will be sorted out with 'The best that money can buy' and that will alienate our audience. Nobody goes to a festival and says, 'Ooh look at that lovely security fence. It is the finest one I've ever seen!'

"They come over as too Establishment and thoroughly unlikeable and Spikings now tries to get his face on TV as often as he can. Every time they show their faces on the telly they lose more punters because they are so smug."

"What I don't understand is why you are so worked up about all of this?" Malcolm asked. He was starting to lose interest in this conversation and his mind as usual was off and running onto more important matters.

"It's not so much a problem for me, as it is for you, as I see it. The way things are going the whole festival is going to be a complete clusterfuck. It will turn out to be another disaster with a very low attendance. When that happens, our friends Deeley and Spikings will look for ways to appropriate the small amount of money that will be sloshing around, for themselves. In order to cover their asses there will have to be someone to blame. Looking around I can only see one person who fits that bill and that is you. When the money goes missing and you get blamed, who will the financiers come looking for? You. That's who." Suddenly Malcolm's attention was focused again.

"You're serious, aren't you?" Malcolm said disbelievingly. "And what do you intend to do now, as if I didn't already know."

"Well I have got a little bit involved in the marketing side of an import company where the people are 100% honest with each other and are trying to change this rotten society, in any small way they can."

Malcolm laughed and said, "It sounds like a very noble venture and I hope for your sake the returns reflect the risks involved."

"Well the returns are very high and the risks are, at the moment, very low, so I don't really want to associate with those asshole wannabe promoters anymore."

"How nice to be able to be so choosy."

"I just can't believe how this is all turning out. Stanley is cool. He just wants to stick his fingers up to society, to really be the 'Villain' he plays in his films and do something mildly illegal that makes him a bit of money. Good luck to him because he had the guts to front his own money at the beginning. He can get his girlfriend involved and it can all be one gigantic party for all his ex-gangster friends. He can fly in his helicopter to the festival and stay in his huge trailer. Afterwards if it goes wrong I can see Deeley and Spikings tricking him into some scheme or other. Eventually he will be the victim because he really is not the sharpest knife in the box. The big winner will be Spikings because I don't believe there is anything he would not do, or anyone he would not walk over, to make it big. In a few years' time he will have amassed a small fortune and left a trail of casualties behind him. The only hope I have is that his karma will repay him for whatever things he does as he ascends to the dizzy heights he so desires."

"Don't hold back for my sake," Malcolm growled. "Tell it like it is. I hope to God you are wrong but I don't think you are. I didn't think you could see that far into the future. Don't you worry about me. I have protected myself in a way that nobody can screw me over. Anyway, good luck with your new venture and let's get ourselves back to the office so we can tidy up your affairs for now."

They squeezed their way back out of the still crowded pub and Malcolm seemed to know most of them by name and had a brief conversation with a few as they passed by. As they stepped out onto the pavement Peter remarked that Malcolm was well known in that pub. To which he replied, "Aye well you meet the same people as you rise up as ye do when you are falling back doon."

"Where did you get that? Out of a Christmas cracker?… Taxi!" and off they went out of the madness that was Soho in the seventies.

It was only a brief time Peter spent back at the office as it had been decided in the taxi coming back that there would be no mention of the fact that he wanted to stop working on the festival. Linda was told that he was going off to do some freelance work on another venture Malcolm had, and would only be coming in now and then to help out when needed. Linda was sad to hear that as she had forged a strong loyalty to her two bosses and fiercely defended them from the other secretaries, who worked for Deeley and Spikings, in the day-to-day power struggles coming from the front office. She also still had a bit of a crush on Peter, although she had not really forgiven him for turning her down, so she was pleased to hear that he would be coming back now and again.

Peter rode the lift down to the Embankment, after he

had picked up a large wad of expenses from the front office, thinking about how much he had changed in the short time he had been working there. It was a different person that was leaving now. He had been a naive boy from the country when he had arrived and had been forced to adapt very quickly to the cutthroat way business was conducted. He had learnt so much about how to make money for himself. How to survive in a dog-eat-dog situation. When to speak up and when to shut up. Now, though, he was making good money for himself and he felt strong and confident, ready to take on the world and make a change. Make some real money and not have to listen to the crap those 'straights' back upstairs had to say. He did not want to cut himself off completely from the festival as he wanted to go and see if it worked or not and find out what the outcome would be. Anyway he had a caravan and a Land Rover waiting for him up there and possibly a little money as well and it would be a shame to waste them after all the hard work he had put in sorting them! It felt like a huge weight had been lifted from his shoulders. He was now only answerable to himself. Now responsible for his own destiny. With a feeling of golden euphoria he headed back to his tacky flat over the Kentucky Fried Chicken takeaway in Shepherd's Bush knowing that this was the start of a whole new era for him.

CHAPTER 21

It's good to touch the green green grass

Climbing the stairs Peter looked at the peeling, baby-shit-coloured woodchip wallpaper and the ratty carpet and thought maybe this flat wasn't the best he could do but it was ok for now. When he had made some serious money he would get a stash pad where he could do some business and keep the dope away from where he lived. There was no point in making it too easy for the cops if you were busted.

Then thinking of being busted he started wondering where Ian, and his Irish friend, Niall, were now. They were a pair of smugglers, introduced to Peter by Christine, who had agreed to let Peter sell their dope when they got back. They had set out in an old Austin Westminster, chosen for its low price and extremely roomy heating ducts inside the engine compartment, to drive to Morocco. If nothing had gone wrong they should be back any day now with at least 50 kilos of primo Moroccan hash tucked inside the heater. This was a desperate shit or bust run to raise funds for some more serious runs in the future and was typical of the way Ian worked and was the reason why he was ironically called 'The Boy Wonder' as very few of his magnificent ventures ever came off. This run was completely kamikaze but relied on the fact that the border controls were not at all sophisticated in their methods of detecting dope hidden in cars. It was possible to blag your way through the occasional border like this but if you did get away with it once, use the money wisely on a decent conversion to hide the dope, and don't push your luck with another chancy run.

They should also be bringing some really nice Zero Zero to be shared among friends who could not be expected to smoke the commercial gear. That was just for selling. The best stuff was always purchased from the grower as a way of showing off how they could bring back some of the finest smoking hash that was available. These brave out-laws scoured the world for the best dope they could find. Each trip to more exotic locations brought better and more exotic hash being paid for by the commercial quality that was brought back to sell. There were so many wonderful places where it was possible to easily visit and pick up choice varieties of hashish that had been produced there for eons.

The Northern Provinces of Afghanistan around The Hindu Kush, Kashmir where they press the pollen between their palms, the North West Frontier in Pakistan around Chitral, The Baalbek Valley in Lebanon and not forgetting Nepal for the magnificent Temple Balls. All lovely peaceful places where the wandering Hippy could visit, as if on vaca-tion and freely buy any amount of Righteous hashish for a very reasonable price and find inventive ways to smuggle it back to England. Surely this would never change?

So Peter pulled off his favourite boots and made a joint from the Thai grass that Barry from Brentford had given as a sample of the 5000 Thai Sticks he wanted Peter to move. He was waiting for approval on the quality before the wholesale price of £2 a stick could be agreed. This was the first big deal Peter had been offered since he had been working his way up the ladder and a feeling of excitement rushed through him as he thought of the money he could make. The sticks were made up of prime buds of grass, tied to six-inch-long fine slivers of bamboo. Everything had been steamed and pressed flat so they could all be rolled tightly into the centre of a few bolts of silk material before being sent back here.

Thai Sticks were a dynamite smoke and very highly thought of on the London scene as they were so strong and spacey. Peter was delighted to have been given the chance to be the first person to receive them and to sell them. Although they finally achieved a high price per stick on the open market, they arrived in compacted sticky blocks that had to be steamed apart so the sticks could be presented properly and sold individually. This was the reason it was called a Thai Stick and commanded a higher price than loose grass. At least £5 a stick when they were sold by the hundred. At the time, for some reason, Thai grass was being sold for a really low price in Thailand. Barry couldn't be arsed to do the separating so offered a low bulk price that allowed Peter to sell them on with a profit of 50p a stick after he had steamed them apart. Not only did he get to make that profit, as the separating was so messy and bits broke off and not every stick survived the process, five hundred sticks were thrown in for free to make up for the breakage. All the bits that fell off the sticks were collected in a separate bag to be shown off to and shared with Peter's new smuggler friends and dealers, as a sign of the quality of the gear Peter was capable of finding and selling.

The grass was outstanding quality and laid Peter out for an hour before he could get up and contact Barry to say it was on and they could meet up in the pub later that night to arrange the deal that had been simmering on the backburner for a couple of weeks, since in fact, when the bundle had left Thailand. All of Peter's buyers were eagerly awaiting the shipment and all 5000 sticks had been easily placed. All that was needed was for Barry to drop off the bag and the buyers had to be phoned to get round to the flat to collect some of the best weed to arrive in London for ages and Peter's reputation would rise another notch as would his stash of money. He had been keeping most of his profits to build up an amount of cash large enough to put down as a sizable deposit on any large deals done in the future or enough to buy smaller amounts outright. The money made from the Thai Sticks would add to his stash and give him a fairly large working capital so people would not have to worry about 'fronting' most of the dope for a couple of days, which made it much easier to sell.

Setting off to the pub later that evening he still felt the effects of the grass and by the time he reached the Tube station he felt an overpowering desire for something sweet to satisfy his cravings. He crossed the road and went into the brightly lit Donut Diner and bought a couple of unbelievably sweet and sticky chocolate doughnuts to satisfy 'The Munchies'. This was the sweet craving people get from smoking good gear and it reassured him he was getting something good to sell. He ate the doughnuts as he went down the subway under the roundabout and had finished them by the time he got up on the Holland Park side. As he was coming up the steps, he was stopped by a confused looking couple who asked, in a broad New York accent.

"Excuse me but can you tell me where the Subway is?" Peter was still a bit stoned and was confused by the question.

"This is the Subway right here by the big blue sign that says 'Subway'."

"Yes, I can see that," the man replied. "We have been following the signs for the Subway and have been under the road, and up again four times. Now we are back where we started and there is still no sign of any trains."

Peter realised what was happening and started to laugh. He explained: "In England a Subway is an underpass and the Underground is what you call the Subway and it's just over there. Look can you see the red and blue Underground sign." The couple also thought it was funny that they had been following the signs that only took them under the road and said "Thank you so much, we might have been going around all night if you hadn't translated the language into American for us!" They went off to the Underground and Peter walked the short distance to the pub laughing at the thought of the couple going round and round under the roundabout all night looking for the trains.

Barry was leaning against the bar and raised a hand in greeting. Peter walked over saying "Hi" in passing to The Three Tops, who were involved in a furious argument over their dominos game, and ordered a pint of lager at the bar.

"I'll get that," Barry said and motioned Peter over to a quiet table in the corner where another man was sitting nursing his pint.

"This is Mark. He's my partner. He's a bit of a nutter but he's ok really."

"Nice to meet you Mark," Peter said warily as Mark did look a bit of a nutter but it may just have been the Thai grass he had been smoking.

"Did you like the sample then?" Barry asked in a lowered tone.

"Yeah, I thought it was brilliant. I can't believe they don't appreciate that quality over there in Thailand." Peter remarked.

"Neither can I but they are all a bunch of idiots out there so they don't know any better." Mark growled over his glass.

"Well that isn't entirely true but it doesn't matter. We have got the product here. Can you move it?" Barry asked.

"Sure I can. I've got it all placed for tomorrow. I can give you a grand now and settle up tomorrow evening. Is that alright?" Peter said to Barry who looked at Mark and waited for him to nod approval.

"That's fine then. We'll drop you back at your flat and swap bags. Drink up then. Let's get this done."

They finished their drinks and left the pub together. Barry's car was parked just outside and they all jumped in to drive round The Green to Peter's flat. They pulled up in the side street just past the door and Peter fished in his boots for the bundle of money he had counted out before he left.

"Here. Take this." He said discreetly passing the package through the gap between the front seats.

"Right, that's nine you owe us tomorrow." Barry said. "It's in the boot. Come on, I'll give it to you."

"Don't get any ideas about keeping it." Mark said quietly but with a certain amount of menace.

"Why would I do that? I thought we were going to do a lot of business together."

"I just don't want you to get any ideas. That's all," Mark said.

"Come on Peter let's get the bag." As they climbed out of the car and opened the boot. Inside was a Puma sports bag that looked pretty full and Barry passed it to Peter.

"We'll come round here tomorrow evening to pick up the money and we have something we want to talk to you about. See you tomorrow. Don't worry about Mark, He's ok."

He got back in the car and they drove off leaving Peter standing by the road with £12,500 worth of drugs in a sports bag. It was the largest amount he had been given to sell and by tomorrow would have made £2500 profit with more regular shipments coming in a few weeks. He let himself in the door and hid the bag in a cupboard outside his front door. There was no one in the flat so he turned on the gas ring and set up the huge food steamer John's girlfriend occasionally used when she made a meal there. The water was bubbling away as Peter nipped out of the door and brought in the bag and opened it on the kitchen worktop. When he opened the bag he was hit by the powerful smell of very strong grass and he smiled to himself as he loaded the bundles of 100 sticks into the pan ten at a time so the steam could separate them. It was a slow painstaking process and could not be hurried. The sticks had to be steamed enough so they would plump back up to their original size and not get damaged as they were being peeled apart. Luckily Peter was feeling patient and carefully deconstructed the solid blocks of grass into beautiful single bamboo skewers with plump buds tied on with a single wrap of cotton thread. They had returned to almost how they had looked originally before they were compressed. He looked at the piles of 100s laid carefully on the worktop and thought they were one of the most beautiful things he had ever seen.

A natural plant that when smoked it sent you off to another place where everything was peace and love.

Why was this organic plant so hated and hunted by the Establishment? Why was it illegal to smoke this plant but not tobacco which was addictive? He didn't care though. He was an outlaw and his duty was to get as much of this lovely weed to the people who would appreciate how good it was and then it would be legalised. In the meantime it was illegal and dangerous to be caught selling it so the product had a high value and there was a profit to be made.

The bundles of 100 sticks were put into polythene bags and counted into packs of 1000. They were going to be sold in units of 1000 tomorrow and were counted back into the bag. By careful steaming Peter had managed to separate 5300 individual sticks so he had gained an extra 300 sticks which he could easily sell for £5 each, to friends, making another £1,500 and he had a large bag of loose buds that had fallen off the sticks which he would share with his friends round at Christine's house. He put the bag back into the cupboard and poured himself a drink and sat down and thought 'This is hard work.'

He wasn't serious though as he was going to make over £3500 tomorrow and also learn what Barry had in mind. Maybe it was another run that he wanted him to distribute or another deal to be sold. He would find out tomorrow.

A few phone calls were made to let everyone know that it was still on for tomorrow. Ron was coming from Wimbledon and was bringing Lucien with him as he also wanted some of the sticks. Ernst and Dave wanted more than they originally ordered but were told it had all been sold. Michael, who was known as Eddie Merckx, would be forgoing riding his namesake's bicycle and coming from the East End by tube. He also wanted more but was happy when he was told there would be more coming soon. Michael was Canadian and different from the others and he always looked at the overall picture. He didn't wear denim and boots to look like a dealer but tried to be as unnoticeable as possible. Sometimes he arrived on his bike, wearing cycling shorts, looking nothing like a dope dealer. This had the effect of unnerving the other dealers who he met but it was not long before most people were following his example. Ditch the denim but keep the boots. Keep your head down, don't stand out from the crowd and don't get noticed. Peter was spending time hanging out with Michael and they had started to get quite friendly aside from the dope selling.

Everyone was told to get there from one o'clock and they could pick up 1000 sticks each.

The next day the buyers started arriving just after one. Ron and Luce were first and were blown away by the quality of the gear. There had not been a lot of Thai grass in London although it was well known for being excellent blow. They left with the promise of buying more when it next came and Ron said he was also waiting for something to arrive and would be in touch soon with news. They drove off in Ron's lovely maroon 3.4 Jaguar that he had just recently bought.

The doorbell rang and Peter leaned out of the window to see Ernst and Dave waiting to catch the keys. They had arrived in Dave's huge white Camaro muscle car that was parked just down the street sticking out like a sore thumb in Shepherd's Bush.

Dave was well over six feet tall and had really long straight hair that reached halfway down his back. He was wearing a denim jacket, shirt and jeans and looked like the lead guitarist from a rock band. The keys were dropped down just as Michael arrived round the corner. They already knew each other and all came up together. Peter liked Michael and was fascinated by his attitude and intelligence. He was the only person Peter knew who lived in Bethnal Green. Michael was living rent free in a council approved squat in a lovely Georgian terraced house by Victoria Park even though he had enough money to rent a place anywhere he wished in London. He had given the house a cut price makeover consisting of knocking the plaster off the walls to expose the bare brick and stripping the paint off all of the woodwork and floorboards exposing all the natural wood which he had waxed to an antique shine. It had cost virtually nothing and the old house looked a million dollars. The council was waiting until the area was developed for the new Yuppies to take over in about ten years from then. It seemed wrong to Peter, who had never even visited the East End, and he could not believe anyone would want to live there. They sat around enjoying the amazing grass and exchanged cash for the dope. It was a very relaxed deal among friends who were just moving a little bit of 'draw'. No big deal. Just getting stoned and hanging out.

"You know how much I love my Camaro?" Dave said after his and Ernst's 2000 sticks had been put away.

"Everyone knows how much you love your Camaro, Dave," Peter said.

"Well I've got a bit of a problem. See I only like big American cars and won't drive anything else and Ernst here has just taken a foreign car as part payment for some drugs we sold. We know you are pretty keen on cars and wondered if you wanted to take it off us. We'll give you a good deal just to get shot of it."

"I don't know, man, I've got that piece of shit Mini and don't get my license back for a month so I'm not really in the market for another car," Peter said, with an affected air of disinterest, but his mind was turning over.

"Not getting your license back for a month wouldn't be a problem as it needs some work doing to it at the moment. Think of it as ordering a Morgan while you are waiting on remand to go to trial. It will be waiting for you when you get out in five years if you go down and you have something to look forward to, or you can cancel it if you get off," Ernst helpfully added.

"Yeah, I don't quite see how that helps me, but anyway what is it?"

"It's a crappy old Porsche," Dave said disdainfully.

"It's not so bad," Ernst said as he was the one who had to get rid of it.

"What type of Porsche is it and what needs doing to it?" Peter asked. Now he was interested.

"It's a Porsche 356 I think. It's a 1960 model and it's got tax and MOT for a few months but it's quite rusty and the engine runs a little rough."

"Wow that's cool," Michael said. "That's the car James Dean was killed in."

"Great, Thanks for that Michael," said Ernst. "I'm trying to get rid of the bleeding car and that isn't helping."

"How much do you want for it?" Peter asked, trying to sound disinterested.

"I just want it off our drive, It's such an embarrassment having it next to the Camaro, so you can have it for what it stands us in, £300."

"Take it," said Michael. "You can do it up and have a really cool car."

"I'm interested," Peter said. "I'll give you 100 sticks and you can sell them for £500 and make a profit."

"Done," said Dave without a moment's hesitation.

"Whoa, wait a minute I haven't even seen it yet. If it's a heap of crap I don't want it. When can I look at it?"

"Right now. It's outside. Ernst drove it over cos we knew you'd take it. Let's go have a look."

They went down to the street and there it was. A white 1960 Porsche 356. The sills were a little rusty and the paint was a bit shabby and the engine ran a little lumpy but it was a Porsche 356! It had tax and MOT for four months and Peter said, "Done. I'll take it. Let's go back up and do the paperwork and I'll pay you."

So they climbed back up the three flights and Peter was paying for the car with 100 of the extra Thai Sticks he had got for free from the 5000 bag, and all he had to do now was to find someone to fix it up.

They signed over the log book and Thai Sticks were exchanged. The key with a very old leather Porsche fob was passed over and everyone thought they had done a great deal. What a momentous day. A load of money, a bag of dope and a Porsche. How much better could life get?

Dave and Ernst roared off down the street in the Camaro leaving Michael in the flat with Peter. "That was a sweet deal," Michael said when they sat back down. "This dope is Righteous and a good price too. Are you getting more soon because I can move loads of this so you don't even have to involve anyone else if you don't want to? I've also got my Land Rover coming back from Afghanistan with 50 keys of top-quality Afghani, worth a fortune, which you can sell half of, if you want. It's come through the worst bit and is now just coming through Europe."

"That sounds great. Maybe I'll need to sell something to pay for all the work that needs doing on that old car," Peter said, laughing.

"Yeah right! I can imagine how much you made on this deal and I bet that car didn't cost you a penny. Good luck to you I say. I really like the way you work and I have a lot of projects planned and I want to get you involved in them. Are you interested?"

"Of course I'm interested. Do you still want to buy from me?"

"Of course I do. Buy from you. Sell to you. 'Same Same, No Difference'. Very soon my stash of money is going to be big enough to buy 50 keys outright. We could keep back a large part to sell on at a higher price after we have wholesaled some of it. We would be in a position to buy most of the small runs being brought into London. Apart from the tons that Breadhead Howard Marks brings in and nobody has enough money to buy that much. What a greedy bastard he is. He is starting to give us small time smugglers a bad name. Anyway, I think we could work together really well."

"Ok then, it's a deal."

Michael then disappeared down the street to do whatever he had in mind leaving Peter to tidy the flat before John got home.

He had made £2500 cash, 200 Thai Sticks worth £1000 and a Porsche. Not too shabby for a day's work. Not bad for a hick from the sticks and certainly better than working for the festival company.

Barry phoned a bit later and said he was on his way over if that was alright and could be there in 15 minutes. They climbed the stairs and Peter met them at the door of his flat.

"Hey man. These stairs are a killer, aren't they?" Peter said as they paused to catch their breath.

"I don't care as long as you've got my money." Mark said.

"I sure have. Here it is." and pointed to the bundle of money that was on the table.

"Come on in and you can count it," Peter said amicably. He felt pleased with himself as he had counted the money himself and sorted it out. All the Queen's heads were facing up on the right-hand side and the notes were in £100 wraps with one of the notes folded over the top of each bundle to keep it together. This was the accepted way of keeping money as it made it easy to count and kept it neat. It was easy to take out a few hundred without losing count. Barry and Mark split the stash and each counted it with ease as Peter rolled a three-skin joint.

"That's right." Barry said as they split the pile of money up and carefully stuffed it into their boots. Peter gave them each a bottle of Pilsner Urquell lager and they all relaxed with a smoke and a beer after all the business was finished.

"Have you seen that old Porsche parked in your street?" Barry asked.

"Yes. It's mine. I just bought it off a friend today."

"Isn't that the one James Dean died in."

"Well not that one, but I think it was a similar model. Maybe the Speedster."

"What you gonna do with it then?" Mark asked.

"I thought I could do it up a bit and then use it occasionally and sell it."

"Nice," said Barry "Where are you going to get it sorted then?"

"I don't have a clue as I only got it today."

"You should take it to Billy and Steve in Chiswick. They would do it and they won't charge you the earth if you say you're mates with me. Steve is a diamond geezer. He's a brilliant mechanic and he's the most honest bloke I've ever met. Billy is a little gobshite. He kind of runs the garage and tries to rip off everyone who comes through the door. You just have to try to deal with Steve and don't let Billy get too involved. I mean watch him like a hawk!" Barry said. "They could do the bodywork, tune the engine and take it next door for a quick respray. I'm sure it wouldn't cost much at all. Here's their address and tell Billy to do a good job or Marky will be down for a little visit."

Mark laughed and said, "I'd love to give that little shit a dig. He deserves it and one day he will really get it."

"That's great. Thanks. I'll go down there tomorrow and see what they say."

"So that's your toys sorted, now we have something we want to talk about," Barry said. "We're just starting another little number from Morocco and you seem to have a few good buyers and we want you to move it for us."

"I'm interested for sure. It depends on the price that it comes to me. How often it comes and how many kilos?" Peter was very interested.

"Well it's like this. We know a huge number of crazy Ossies who are living here for the moment, working in bars, who would rather have the money to be able to go surfing somewhere else in the world. We can give them that opportunity and have started them on the path. This is how it works. We give them some money and they individually go to a bloke in Notting Hill who rents out a dozen or so VW campervans. They each book one a month from now until the end of the summer. They say they are going to Spain to a surf beach to meet up with their friends and catch some waves. Then they can fill up the van with as many of them as want to go, stick their surfboards on top, and drive like crazy to Malaga. While they travel down they make the inside of the van, particularly the fridge and cooker, as disgusting as only an Ossie surfer can and head across into Morocco where they are met by our man. He only needs the van for an hour and then they can head off to wherever they like for three weeks. They can drop their mates off in Agadir or wherever and then the van comes back to Spain with a couple of lairy surfers in a stinking bus complaining about 'Pussy Waves' and lousy food. When they go through Customs, they will sometimes get holes drilled all over the sills of the van as The Man looks for the conversion. The Customs won't find anything and the boys drive straight back to England. When they go through Customs here with their sills looking like colanders they won't even get a tug as they have been thoroughly searched before and it's a waste of time to do it again. We take the van to Billy and Steve who fill the holes with P38 and spray paint the filler so you can't see the damage. We pull the gear out for you to sell and back goes the van, after a quick valet, clean and tidy, to the owner. They get paid and meantime another van is heading down to sunny Morocco. Every four weeks at the moment a van will bring back 50 kilos or so. If you want you can put up a grand to help pay up front for some of the van hire, which we have to book now before someone else rents them, and you get the gear at a cheaper price as you are in at the beginning and you risk your money at the start. What do you say? Do you want some time to think about it?"

"The only thing I need to know is where is the conversion?" Peter said.

"That's the beauty of this simple little plan. Inside the crusty, smelly and dirty van is a crusty, smelly fridge and cooker. These are fitted into the wooden cabinets and are insulated with four inch thick, fridge sized, blocks of Styrofoam. If you undo the front of the cooker and fridge you can slide out the insulation and you have a four-inch gap all around the appliance. You can fill up these gaps with the hash and glue a two-inch deep dummy Styrofoam liner onto the front of the gap and it looks just like new. Nobody wants to touch the cooker, because it is so filthy, and nobody yet knows about the insulation. We don't even have to weld up a conversion. We just pull the insulation out over here before they go and stick in the dummy front so it looks kosher. When they get back we slide out the dope, replace the insulation panels and pay for someone to valet the inside of the van. Billy and Steve are only repairing damaged bodywork so everything is completely legal for them. Not that they give a shit."

"It sounds good to me. I'll give you a grand now and you can give me one kilo from every van. I get to move all the gear that comes back as well," Peter tried.

"That is a done deal My Friend. Once the first van gets back and we have more money we can send them over more often, if we want to." Barry said and Peter got up and went out and pulled ten wraps from his well-hidden money stash and gave them to Barry.

"It's a pleasure to do business with you, Peter. We have to get moving as we have loads to do. We are ready to go again with the sticks and there will be twice as many this time. The van will be off to Morocco soon and will be back in about four weeks so you will have plenty to do. See you soon." And with that they left.

Peter wasn't concerned that he had just handed over £1000 pounds as he had just made much more from Barry who was more interested in the smooth running of his scams than stealing £1000 and upsetting the supply chain. It was not that he completely trusted Barry, it was just this deal was a no brainer. It was better business to use other people's money to set up more runs to make more money than to just go around ripping people off. That is just how it was.

It would not be like that forever and soon the whole smuggling business would take on a whole new darker dimension. However in 1972 things were simpler. There was honour among the outlaws and everyone helped each other out. After all, it was only money!

Peter could hardly believe what had happened. He now was the sole supplier of the Thai Sticks and also of the regular monthly run to Morocco, in which he was an investor, from which he got a kilo of hash each time it landed and the opportunity to sell the dope which he got at a cheaper price. He certainly didn't need to rely on Great Western Festivals any more.

He had decided he would go to the festival anyway. He would stock up with some good food and wine to put in his caravan. There was a Land Rover to get around the site and he didn't have to do any work if he didn't want to. The only downer was that the music was going to be so dreadful. There wasn't a band on the bill he would cross London to see so he just had to make his own amusements. Having a large bag of assorted dope was a good start and would liven up most dire situations. He could also come back any time he wanted to. How bad could it be?

CHAPTER 22

Never say no to a Gypsy, he'll put a Bokh on ya!

Waking up around ten the next day Peter again ran through the last couple of days' events to make sure he wasn't still asleep and dreaming. Once that had been ascertained he started on his mission to get his new car sorted. He got into the Porsche and started to familiarise himself with the controls which was pretty easy as it was just like a Volkswagen Beetle. He started the engine and had to nurse it along as it appeared to be running intermittently on one carburettor. By driving down the back streets he could get to Billy and Steve's garage in Chiswick without travelling very far on the main roads. This was necessary as he was still banned from driving. Soon he arrived at Woodstock Road which was a typical suburban Chiswick street full of expensive houses. He continued to what looked like the end of the street, but was in fact a sharp left-hand bend in the road, where the houses ended and a row of lock up garages started. The first was a bodywork and spray shop and next to it was a pair of garages with the doors open and a car was being worked on amongst a scene of complete chaos. There were tools all over the floor, empty cans of oil, full cans of oil, oily rags, air filters, oil filters, spark plugs, brake shoes and all the rubbish involved with repairing cars just thrown on the floor. It looked like heaven to Peter who loved to be involved with all aspects of working on cars. He was completely useless at the actual repairing but had spent a fair bit of time hanging out in a friend's garage in Somerset and had a basic knowledge of cars and was pretty good at diagnosing their faults. He pulled up in a space outside the lockup and as he was getting out a little man with a ratty beard, which made him look like a ferret, came over.

"Smokey Pete, I presume?" he said grinning. "Barry said you would be down today with a 356."

"That's good, I thought maybe you were telepathetic." Peter said. "You must be Billy." Just then a body slid out from under the car in the garage. Wearing overalls covered in oil, steel toe cap boots and a huge grin emerged a tall, long-haired guy who had the look of a Gypsy John Entwistle about him.

"I'm Steve Wilkins," he said "Isn't that the car James Dean crashed in?"

"Well no, not this actual car. I think his was a write-off." Peter said, laughing.

Steve thought that was funny and said, "I hope you are a better driver than him cos that thing don't look too special. It's one of those German pieces of shit. I bleedin' hate working on them. Did you get it off Barry from Brentford?"

"No I didn't but he told me you might be able to fix it up for me."

Billy jumped in at this point and said, "Don't listen to Steve, he hates working on every car that comes in here."

"No I don't. I love working on Jags and Yanks. Give me an American V8 and I'm as happy as a pig in shit."

"But unfortunately we don't get to see many of those as they are not the cars of choice in this neck of the woods." Billy countered.

"Well do you think you can do mine?" Peter asked.

"Of course we can," Billy jumped in. "Let's have a look at

it. The bottom of the doors are starting to rust and the sills have got holes in them. We can fill them and get it sprayed next door. Do you want us to just clag it up and make it look good cheaply, or do you want us to strip it back and spend a lot of time on it?"

"I don't want a bare metal rebuild but just get it looking good so I can drive it around for a while."

"The engine sounds lumpy. I think only one carb is working," Steve offered.

"How do you know that?" Billy said.

"I've got ears haven't I? I heard it pull up. If you were a mechanic you would have heard it too."

"I'm as good a mechanic as you. I was just busy doing something else."

"Yeah, yeah," said Steve "I can go over the car and also I know a bloke who is a wizard with Porsche engines. He could sort it and make it go just as good as when James Dean first had it."

"That would be fantastic. Roughly how much do you think it will cost?" Peter asked. Again Billy jumped in sucking the air through his teeth audibly in the time honoured manner of someone about to give a large quote.

Steve however answered first.

"You're a mate of Barry from Brentford and he puts a lot of work our way and pays us well for it. As you are in the same line of business we will give you a good deal. No receipts and payment in cash of course. Even if we have to completely rebuild the engine I reckon we can do it for under £200."

Peter was as surprised as Billy who muttered about working for nothing. Steve was having none of it and said, "You won't forget Barry works with Mark. Will you Billy?"

Billy blanched visibly and said, "I'm not scared of Mark."

"Well you should be you twat." Steve said laughing.

"Anyway I am going down to the caff for my breakfast and you can use your superior mechanical skills on the clutch in my lovely little Allegro. Are you coming Pete?" With that they went off leaving Billy floundering on his own.

They arrived at the cafe and both ordered breakfast and coffee and sat in the window watching the people walking up and down The Avenue. Steve was telling really funny self deprecating stories and then started talking about the customers who came to the garage and how Billy blatantly ripped them off. So much so they were losing their trade. Nobody liked being taken for a mug and they went elsewhere. Billy was angry about the situation and had said he was leaving the garage at the end of the month. Steve advised Peter to hold off paying Billy for the work on his car as he didn't want him to be able to walk off with all the cash.

"Don't worry mate, I will only be giving it to you." And after a leisurely breakfast and a long conversation they went back to see how far Billy had got. Which wasn't very far.

Peter left the car with them and they said they would make a start the next day. He said he would come down and hang out if that was alright and Steve said it was fine: "Just don't forget the coffee and doughhnuts."

He walked on down to The Avenue and jumped onto a passing bus hoping it would take him back to the Bush. What an odd pair of guys Billy and Steve were. If it was Billy doing the work he would not have left the car but Steve was something else. He had told Peter that he came from Gypsy stock. The last of the Ronanes who were apparently Gypsy royalty. He had worked with horse folk in Shepherd's Bush since he was twelve and then learnt to be a mechanic. He grew up in Acton with Roger Daltrey and John Entwistle who later went on to form The Who. He still remained good friends with Entwistle who lent him his fancy Monteverdi car and invited him to stay in his 'Country Home' in Gloucestershire but Steve wasn't impressed with all that money and stuff and just used to go round occasionally to his house, just off the North Circular, and have 'a good drink' from his well-stocked bar. Steve was not impressed by large amounts of money and had absolutely no ambitions to be rich or famous. He didn't touch any sort of drugs, he had never smoked a joint and had no interest in trying, but he had no objection to helping his friends in their efforts to bring the stuff into the country. In his own way he was even more of an outlaw! All of this set off ideas in Peter's brain and he really wanted to get to know Steve better.

There were a few smallish deals that were arranged for the next few days and they went off easily adding some more money to Peter's stash. The hash was a few kilos of some commercial Moroccan that Ron had got hold of and it was quickly moved on to Dave and Ernst who were interested to hear about the progress of the Porsche. Between selling the hash Peter nipped down to the garage to hang out with Steve. He enjoyed listening to his stories and loved his absurd sense of humour.

After a few days Peter turned up at the garage to see that the paintwork on the Porsche had been sanded back and had exposed all the rust in the sills and a considerable amount of filler in the wings.

"That doesn't look too bad," Peter said inspecting the bodywork.

"I was going to crumple up some tinfoil to shove in the sills before using P38 to fill the holes," Billy announced proudly.

"No, I don't want that. Grind the rust out and tack weld a layer of sheet metal on before you start filling. Maybe that will last a bit longer. I don't want the shonky option, thank you," Peter said.

"I told you so, Billy," Steve said. "It may be a piece of shit but it's HIS piece of shit."

"Alright, I was just trying to save you a bit of money."

"Well as it happens the motor doesn't stand me in a penny so I've got a bit of leeway to get it done up. I have no idea what it's worth but I do like it and want to use it when it's done."

"That's cushty. Leave it to me. I'll make sure the little twat doesn't do a bodge job. Come on, let's go for a coffee."

They sat in the cafe drinking their coffee and Steve said, "Why don't you come down to the Cross Keys in St Peter's Square after work and meet a few of the lads. We always go down there after five and have a few jars and maybe sort out any business that needs doing."

"Right I'll see you down there tonight after five." and he stepped out of the cafe and got on the bus.

It was a ragtag bunch that he met when he entered the Keys later that night. There was a mixture of music executives and musicians from Island Records, which was just around the corner, local residents from St Peter's Square including Patrick Moore and Magnus Pyke and a large group of scruffy looking blokes who appeared to be trying to drink the bar dry. Steve was leaning on the bar talking to a tall man with curly blond hair.

"Pete, this is my mate George, we call him George the Jag cos he's got hundreds of them."

"Good to meet you George," said Peter.

"Likewise Peter. What are you drinking?"

"A pint of Bitter thanks." And then a few of Steve's friends who happened to be in the pub that night introduced themselves.

'Soapy' Don't call me Soapy, Roy and Big Tony who both worked for George. Eddie Brightsparks the brilliant auto electrician, Chris Coleman the King of Jaguar parts in West

London. Johnnie Briggs the car salesman, Alan the Postie and Phil 'Mike' Hunt who sold Snap On tools and was 'not to be trusted'.

Over the next few weeks Peter saw a lot of different people who came to the pub at night, specifically to meet up with one of the guys, to pay for the use of their specialist and individual skills. The Keys was like a one stop shop where you could get most of the things you needed. It was not necessarily illegal, though some of it could be, but the range of services that could be obtained for friends was both varied and far reaching.

George owned a large scrapyard just by the roundabout in Brentford and was now extremely cautious about over-stepping the law. The yard was full of carcasses of cars and pretty much any spare part could be obtained, if you had the ability to remove it or the money to pay Big Tony to do it. If you have ever seen an episode of *The Sweeney* where the villains end up crashing their Jag getaway car in a large dilapidated warehouse both of them would probably have belonged to George and used by the television company for a suitable fee. He mainly stored damaged cars for insurance companies, at a high daily rate, and broke hundreds of cars and sold the parts. He also had a large collection of old Jaguars for sale or for hire to the movies and television companies.

The whole group was a unique bunch. They were all doing well in their lines of business. Some of them would never dream of breaking the law, some occasionally broke the law, and one or two made a living from breaking the law. Nobody cared what each other did but would fero-ciously defend them if it became necessary. In a way it was like the Freemasons but smaller and with more drinking.

Everyone seemed very keen to buy a round and Peter had to force his way to the bar to get a 'Shout' and by seven everyone had bought a round so everyone had drunk ten pints. Some people left to get their dinner, some stayed and a few more friends came a bit later.

Peter was feeling a bit pissed and sat at a table with Steve.

"Are you alright?" Steve asked. "Cos I want to ask you something."

"Ask away."

"Well it's like this. Billy has been ripping off so many customers nobody wants to use the garage any more. Also a few people have threatened him with a hiding and he is about to bail out. Leaving me in the shit so to speak. I've still got plenty of work, everyone here puts punters my way, it's just I don't want to be responsible for the lockup on my own. I am useless with money, I don't like asking people to pay for the work I do for them, and I've never got a tanner to my name. If I have to pay the rent and buy parts I might not have the money at hand to pay for them and I would lose the lockup."

"How much is the rent?" Peter asked.

"It's ten quid a month."

"Ok. How about if I guarantee you the rent each month and I will front you the money for spares or anything if you ever need it. I will become your partner in name only. I won't be working with you much but I will be there to help if you need me. I can make sure you get paid for the work you do, for a start. I won't be taking any money out of the business, that is all yours. But I will be getting you a lot of well-paying customers and there will be a lot more money coming in to you. How does that sound?"

"What do you get out of the deal then?" Steve wanted to know.

"I get a real working front. A cash business I can own that will do very well and I can say accounts for some of the money I'm making. I will run some money through it to account for some of my cash. Also we get to look after my cars and all the cars my dealer friends have, including a big Camaro and a couple of Jags. We give them a first-class service that they will pay well for and if they need a repair done quickly you will drop everything to sort them out first. You don't have to do any conversions for the smugglers, but you can if you want to, and you can charge them as much as you like. I might use the lock up occasionally to unload a vehicle but it won't be very often and I don't want anything illegal going on in the premises. I want it to be clean and I want it well known that it's clean. What do you think?"

"I think we've got a deal but I have to get approval from my missus Pam first." Steve said on his way to the bar for more drinks. Peter went over to George and outlined the plan he had offered Steve and asked if he had any objections. George said that it sounded like a good deal for both of them and he would send Big Tony round to have a word with Billy about getting out now and not doing anything to harm the business like nicking all the tools. He seemed very pleased that Steve should have dropped into a sweet little deal like that and told him as much. He also said that Steve's wife Pam would have to give the ok or the deal wouldn't happen but he didn't think that would be a problem.

"Listen to what he tries to tell you and stop doing work for nothing when those wankers come round with their piece of junk cars they want fixing for free." George told Steve. Knowing that it would never happen.

It wasn't long before Peter remembered that Lady Bradley had told him he had to get round to her house tonight and he ducked out after arranging to see Steve in the next few days to finalise anything that needed sorting. He waved to his new friends and stumbled out of the pub into the cold night air.

CHAPTER 23

All aboard 'The Marrakesh Express'

Christine opened the door of her house in Redan Street with a look of relief on her face. She smiled when she saw Peter and ushered him into the living room where Ian, with his long curly hair, dark beard, booming loud voice and overbearing manner, was lounging on the cushions. He spoke at 100 miles an hour very loudly.

"Hello man. Good to see you again. I've heard lots of good things about you. Here try this. It may be the best piece of Moroccan you've ever smoked. Tell me what you think. Is it? You wouldn't believe what I've just been through to get this stuff back to London. Niall is still over there sitting in a poxy jail on a stupid jumped up charge and I have to get back over there to buy him out from a greedy crooked bastard of a police commissioner. We haven't got any time to waste. We have got to get the money together for this run and..."

"Slow down Ian," Christine interrupted the flow. "Peter looks like he needs a cup of coffee before he falls over and you can't sell anything now as it's too late. Just chill out for a moment and tell Peter all about your run."

"Sorry man. I am just on such a rush and I need to sort out Niall really quickly."

"That's fine we can get started tomorrow. How much have you got?" Peter asked.

"I've got 50 keys of really good Rocky and one key of Zero Zero to split with friends."

"Is it out of the car yet?" Peter wanted to know.

"No but it's easy to remove and I can do it in the morning," Ian answered helpfully. "I need to make £300 a key and I want it yesterday."

"That's no problem. I can move most of it tomorrow and I'll buy what is left over so you are free to go back and get Niall out."

This was how The Boy Wonder got his Nickname. Everything had to be done immediately or sooner. Nothing was ever straightforward and every disaster was never his fault. Quite often what sounded like a good deal turned into a complete nightmare. He was very demanding but had some good contacts so it was difficult to refuse his deals.

Christine went out to make a cup of black coffee for Peter, and Ian started with the tale of woe.

"Everything started so well. The car drove like a dream and we got through France in record time. As we got near the border Niall said that he wanted to go up to Andorra as it was Duty Free and we could buy a load of cheap booze and fill up with cheap petrol. As we were going past so close we decided to give it a go. Why not? As we were going up the mountains we stopped and bought some snow chains. We're not completely stupid, are we? There was not a speck of snow anywhere in sight as we started the ascent. The higher we got the colder it got but the heater was large, as we knew, and worked very well and we were both warm. We did think maybe we should have brought some winter clothes but we were going to Morocco for fuck's sake. Anyway, the car was running beautifully, pulling like a train up the mountains and then we arrived at the snow line. We pulled over and fitted the snow chains and set off again with about four cars following us up the narrow road. The higher we got the worse the weather was getting but we were not far from Andorra by then. A light flurry of snow turned into a storm which turned into a blizzard but the chains gripped well and we powered on up the mountain. A few kilometres later after a particularly steep climb we rounded a sharp bend and there was a lorry that had skidded on the snow and was jammed sideways across the track with the front buried in a drift. As we braked to avoid sliding into it, the cars behind saw it too late and ran into the back of each other, ending up in a tangle blocking the way down. We were now sandwiched between two accidents. We couldn't go up and we couldn't go down. We were running low on petrol as we were going to fill up with Duty Free petrol in Andorra and we had no warm clothing to get out of the car, into the howling blizzard, to try to free the obstructions. We put on all of our tee shirts and ran up to the lorry, which hadn't even got any chains on and the stupid driver just sat in the cab shrugging his shoulders. We shouted for him to dig the truck out so we could get through but he wasn't interested. We immediately started to freeze and had to run back to the car and try to warm up. The heater was coping very well considering the outside temperature but the big engine was using petrol at an alarming rate and we soon would have none left. Some of the drivers from the tangle below us came up and motioned to us to get out and help push the lorry out but we were so cold we couldn't. They got angry but they didn't understand us and at that point we thought we were going to freeze to death in the poxy mountains in a place we never even really wanted to go to! I admit that I lost my rag and blamed Niall for being such a cheapskate but I had agreed it was a good idea so I suppose I was partly to blame."

"And that is the closest Niall will get to an apology," Christine said laughing.

"That's not true. Anyway let me try that grass you've got there. It smells Righteous."

There was a brief pause in the narrative which was fascinating Peter but Christine seemed less impressed as if she had heard tales like this many times before. Anyone who spent time with The Boy Wonder became used to this sort of story.

"We were running out of petrol and locked in the car so the angry drivers, who were beating on our windows, couldn't pull us out into the storm and we could see no happy ending and really thought we were going to run out of petrol and die in the cold snow. Then some huge bright lights started approaching from the road above us and a massive snow plough came down the hill and when it met the lorry it just shoved the rear end back down the slope into the side of the road, with its giant blade, and came past leaving us a newly ploughed path up the mountain. We just slammed the car in gear and drove through the gap and continued up the freshly cleared road to the nearest town. To this day I don't know what it's called. We checked into a Hotel. Warmed up in the bar and the next day bought some cheap booze and petrol and scooted back down the mountain as fast as we could go. I never want to see Andorra again in my life!"

"That's some story. So it all went smoothly after that." Peter joked which sent Ian off again completing the tale but this time it got a little sketchy in parts.

"I have never been so happy to see the sunny plains of Spain and we just hammered on through and into Morocco only stopping for a little food and sleep. We were taking loads of speed to keep us going and eventually we were really wired and uptight after so much driving. We met up with our contact with no bother and bought some really nice gear with some Zero Zero as well and stashed it safely in the heater system. The poor old heater had saved our lives once and we wouldn't be needing it any more, hopefully. By now the pressure and all the speed had got to us and we were really paranoid about every car we saw twice and people looking at us in cafes and on the street. Our long hair made us pretty noticeable and different and we had attracted quite a lot of attention which was beginning to grate on us. We were making our way back to Tangier and stopped in a cafe as we were coming down from the mountains. Some of the locals were taking the piss out of us and I couldn't take it anymore so I told Niall to get ready to run and I jumped up and twatted the ringleader full in the face and ran out of the door before he hit the floor. Niall tripped over his chair and they all jumped on him pinning him to the floor. I sat in the car waiting for him to run out and then realised he wasn't coming so I drove off as fast as I could before they captured me as well as the dope. I knew it would be a bullshit charge which we could buy off for £50 or so and it was better for both of us not to be caught so I could get him out and be on our way. However when I later managed to find out what had happened, it transpired that I had punched some local off-duty policeman and he wanted £500 to drop the matter. I obviously didn't have that much money left but I promised it would be paid as soon as possible and I hightailed it home as quickly as possible breezing through all the borders in my very expensive short hair wig. Here I am now and I need my £15,000 to get Niall out and bring back another 50 keys."

"You are mental Ian," was Christine's response to this story. "How can you think about doing another run with Niall in jail?"

"Well I've got to go back there to pay the bribe, and get him out, so I might as well pick up some more dope and make some money on the trip."

"The Boy Wonder rides again," was all Peter could come up with, and that sounded extremely funny, after smoking all that fine hash.

Peter walked home with Ian's tale ringing in his ears. He was sure he didn't want to get involved in running borders. It was all a bit too dangerous for him. If it meant doing it with people like Ian he definitely was not interested in the slightest. The man was a lunatic and could start a fight with himself.

The next day he got on the phone to all his buyers and said the dope was here and it was a rush job and had to be completed that day as a friend needed to be bought out of jail in Morocco, tout suite and the tooter the sweeter. There was a fair bit of complaining and moaning about how short notice it was to get the money together but most of them said they would be there before the end of the afternoon. The possibility of acquiring a few ounces of really high-quality Moroccan hash for their personal use certainly sweetened the deal. Dave and Ernst said that they could do 20 keys that day and would take anything that was left over tomorrow. Ron wanted ten as did Lucien and Michael got the last ten kilos. Peter would clear up anything that was left over.

Ian delivered the gear in two suitcases just after lunch and they weighed out the packages on the greengrocer's scales and bagged them up ready to go. A kilo of the Zero Zero was also left to be shared out at £20 an ounce as a treat for the buyers. There was enough for them to pass on some to their special customers at a cheap price as a special bonus. Ian left and it was arranged that he would get his money later that day.

As the afternoon wore on, a small procession of bags and suitcases entered and left the flat unnoticed as they mingled with the many customers from the Chicken Shop below

and drifted off on their way. The large pile of dope trans-
formed into a smaller pile of money and then Peter took his
cut and hid it in his stash and sorted what was left into 150
neat bundles of £100. He also made up a separate bundle
for the kilo of 'personal' everyone had bought. He needed
a bag to carry the cash and so he put it in the bottom of a
large shopping bag and put a load of veg on top. That would
look like a normal bag of shopping as he walked through
Shepherd's Bush to deliver it to Ian.

Normally the money wouldn't go to Christine's house but
this was an emergency and when Peter arrived he handed it
over and Ian said something about paying back his backers
and getting back to Morocco. He blew out of the house, like
a whirlwind, thanking Christine and Peter who were left
amazed at what had just happened. Christine handed over
an eight ounce lump of Zero Zero and said it was a gift, left
for him, by Ian and said she had been given some as well.
Peter told her he had already bought eight ounces of it for
personal use but all donations were welcome.

Peter said he wanted to take Christine out for dinner as
a way of saying thank you and the two of them walked
round the corner to Blythe Road and celebrated the future
release of Niall with a couple of bottles of red wine and
steak and frites in a cute little French Bistro without really
making much of a dent in the £2500 he had made that
day. They walked back to Christine's house and he didn't
go back inside but walked on home. He felt exhausted by
the sheer speed at which everything had happened that day.
He just hoped not every smuggler was as crazy as Ian but
he realised they lived under extreme pressure and were not
normal people.

A few days had passed before Peter managed to get down
to the garage again to see Steve. Billy had already left after
a quiet word from Big Tony and he had cleared out the till

saying he was owed the money for the work he had done on the Porsche. Steve said that he was happy to have Peter as a partner and was glad to see the back of Billy who had become a liability. Steve could not fully grasp why Peter wanted to be involved in the garage if he wasn't taking any money out of it. So he explained.

"It's like this. You have an established business that has no record of turnover or profits. Your outgoings are minimal so in the completely unlikely event of you not making any money for a month it will only cost me a tenner and a few tins of beans to keep you alive. The garage will start picking up a lot of new cash rich customers from me, who either need their cars fixing, disposing of or replacing so you get much busier and start making good money. My money comes from a source that I can't legally declare and if the garage is doing well I can say I own a garage which is doing ok and it looks less like I'm involved in anything illegal. It's a front for me and a way of making some good money for you, for the first time. I love cars and all things to do with them so I will enjoy spending time here and we can get this place up and buzzing. I don't want to do any dope dealing business here. There can't be any suspicion of dealing or smoking going on here, not that you do, but it is important that this is just a repair shop 95% of the time. I will make sure your flaky old customers are weaned away by charging them for the work you do and replace them with customers who pay well. If I ever take any money off a customer, I will give it directly to Pam as it seems you don't. How much did Billy take?"

"Oh I don't know. He looked after all the money. I guess it was £100."

"Right here's £150. Give £50 to Pam and do whatever you want to do with the rest. But for fuck's sake don't give it to some conman, with a sob story, like you usually do."

"No I don't, usually, but sometimes these people I know are having a hard time and I help them out."

"All you help them do is buy more drink. I'm surprised Fuller's Brewery hasn't offered to give you some shares for all your charitable work."

"Anyway," Steve said, changing the subject. "I've taken the engine out of your Porsche. It was only about four bolts holding it in! It took me five minutes. I can't understand how it doesn't just fall out into the road. Anyway, I've had a good look at it and it seems to be alright. For a rusty old German piece of crap. The carbs are shot through but I got in touch with George and he says he's got a spanking pair of carbs that might have come off James Dean's actual car… Not really, I just made that up. But he says these are 'the bollocks' and you can pick them up at the Keys tonight. Come and look at the bodywork. All the filling is done. I can take it next door for Black Roy to finish it off and he can give it a respray if you want."

"I do want, and can he do it the same colour as it is now? It looks like Porsche Ivory but however close he can get to it will do. I can see all the clagging Billy has done but they can sand it down next door. I think it will look amazing when it's finished."

Steve grudgingly agreed and said: "Well it's lucky you didn't pay any money for it, that's all I can say. I just don't understand why you didn't buy a proper car." Which made them both laugh.

Peter stayed for a while and said he was getting headed notepaper and receipt books just in case Steve ever wrote anything down and said, "What do you want to call the garage?"

"Carsey Cars," was the immediate answer.

"Very funny but Billy has gone now. What about Woodstock Motors?"

"Yeah, that sounds very classy and a bit rock and roll don't it?"

"Ok. Woodstock Motors it is. Directors Steven Wilkins and Peter Whitehead. How posh is that? I'll get the headings done so we can at least look legit. I'll see you down the pub later."

After sorting out the letterheads with the printer he went to a cafe in Chiswick and had something to eat to soak up the huge amounts of alcohol that were going to be consumed so early in the evening a bit later. He really liked George and his mates for being so unpretentious and normal. They were self-assured, financially successful, funny and didn't give a shit about what anyone thought about them. Although they came to the pub every night dressed in their grubby work clothes, they were confident enough to have no problem about looking scruffy or out of place in a pub that was in an upcoming posh area. Also they were not interested in how you conducted your business. If you were a friend that was reason enough for you to be accepted. Everyone knew that Peter had something to do with dope, they called him Smokey Pete, but no one had tried to find out what exactly he did. None of them had any interest in smoking any sort of drug, but if he had found a way to make good money out of drugs, good luck to him. As long as it was just hash. Just be straight with Steve and don't try to cheat him in any way!

True to his word George was waiting in the pub with a heavy-duty polythene bag by his feet.

"That is a genuine pair of reconditioned Zenith carbs for your 356. They are a bitch to set up and balance but Steve knows a guy who can do them for you. Make sure you use him or you will have no end of trouble with the idling and the balance. Don't try to cut corners by letting Steve try to do it."

"Thanks George." Peter said "Steve has already told me

about his Porsche guy and we are getting him in to set up the carbs and tweak the engine. How much do I owe you?"

"Give me £20 as you are on the firm now." and Peter passed over a note to him while he ordered up a round of drinks.

"That car you've got is a bit special, you know. In a few years it will be a classic and worth a lot of money but right now it is a well-designed car that drives pretty well and is simple to work on. My advice is to hang onto it for as long as you can and watch it's value go up. Put it into storage, if you don't want to use it but don't get rid, is my advice."

"I don't know about hanging on to it but I do want to drive it for a bit, As soon as I get my license back. Of course."

"Yes of course. We wouldn't want to be caught driving without a license would we?" and they laughed at the very thought of it.

Steve took the carbs and put them in the boot of his car so he wouldn't forget them and the normal everyday drinking started.

Everyone seemed really pleased that Billy had gone, although he had never come to the pub, and they welcomed Peter into the group. They joked about how he would get on with Pam when he met her and Steve said that it wouldn't be a problem and she would be there for the Sunday lunch session. This was when Steve Benbow's band played at the Keys. Sometimes wives and girlfriends came down, sometimes they weren't interested in talking about boring old cars and stayed at home. Peter was interested in seeing the band because the guitar player was an old time Legend and he wanted to see if he was as good as people had said he was. His name was Denny Wright and he used to play guitar with Lonnie Donegan in the Skiffle days. Apparently guitar players of a certain age learnt their licks from either him or Hank Marvin.

After a few drinks Peter said that he was going and he would see them on Sunday. He made his way back to the flat and began to be a little excited about driving his Porsche when it had been sprayed and tuned up. He was getting his license back next week and would have to decide what to do with the Mini. Even if he put a real Cooper engine in it the car was so uncomfortable to drive. He would probably just get shot of it and buy something that was less noticeable, like a Renault or a Peugeot. Something that was reliable and ordinary looking, for when he had to drive around with kilos of dope or money in the car, that didn't attract attention from the police. He would have no trouble getting rid of the Mini or buying another car now he had a garage and all those contacts. He really liked the idea of helping to run the garage with Steve. It was putting a bit of normality into his life in a crazy sort of way. Another bonus was that Peter had paid for Steve to take over the traders insurance policy that allowed the named policy holders to drive any car related to the garage. Peter's name had been put on the policy, as had his two cars, and now any car he owned or drove would be covered by the insurance policy. He would tell all of his dealer mates that they could get a special service to have their cars looked after and maintained by Woodstock Motors. If they broke down in the middle of a deal, Steve would get to them and get them out of trouble. They would have priority access to the garage and be repaired first and sent on their way. If they wanted to buy a car, one would be found and if they had to get rid of one it would be disposed of with no trace. This service would be useful because most dealers didn't register their cars in their name and in the event of a tug by the police the cars needed to be got rid of immediately. All of this service would come at a premium price but that wouldn't matter to them. The garage would get busier with well paying customers who would also recommend their friends and Steve would start to make some real money at last, not doing anything illegal, just working on cars and giving personal attention to Peter's cars. He would still give most of it away before he got home, as he always did, but Peter would make sure Pam at least got hold of some of it. She needed to be kept sweet at all costs!

CHAPTER 24

Gotta keep on keeping on

Malcolm had phoned and asked if Peter was going to show his face at the office, so the journey was made to Alembic House. He was not too excited about going in as he had a million other things that were more interesting to do but he felt he still owed Malcolm.

"Ah the prodigal returns," Malcolm joked as Peter entered the office.

"Do you know what prodigal means? It means spending money wastefully and extravagantly. So I suppose you are right, though you didn't know it," Peter said laughing at Malcolm's look of surprise.

"What have you been doing that is so much more important than coming in here, as if I didn't know."

"I've been very busy with my new business venture, actually. I've become a part owner of a garage repair workshop with attached spray unit in the leafy suburb of Chiswick. We are rebuilding classic cars and will be selling them on to our wealthy neighbours," Peter said, embellishing the truth somewhat.

"And which classic cars are you at present restoring? If it's not too rude a question."

"Not at all. We have almost finished fully restoring a classic 1960 Porsche 356."

"Oh really," Malcolm said "I know very little about cars but I do know that was the car James Dean was killed in."

"Very good Malcolm. You can buy it if you like. Oh no, I forgot you don't drive."

"Well when you have completed your own answer to Jim Gregory's Motordome maybe you can do a bit of work for me. If you are not too busy."

Malcolm proceeded to launch into the full details of how the festival was progressing. It was not a happy tale and Malcolm was feeling considerably distressed by the way things were going.

Michael Deeley and Barry Spikings had been spending a lot of time appeasing the 'powers that be' to make sure they didn't carry out their threats and shut down the festival. Although the Night Assemblies Bill had been shelved, the right-wing government hadn't given up on the idea of trying to close down pop festivals. Deeley was fully immersed in throwing money at all and sundry. A deposit of £10,000 had been lodged with the local vicar, for some unknown reason. Seven hundred extra police had been ordered along with a huge number of security men to keep the riots to a minimum, probably. The high point of the affair was that Deeley, Spikings and John Martin had been bound over in some way so that if there was any trouble at the festival they could face imprisonment. Spikings had gone on television and announced this to the general public, hoping to appear as a Rock and Roll crusader, acting as if he was risking his liberty for the freedom of the kids. Actually he was just doing whatever was needed to keep the Money Machine on the rails. If John Martin had to go to jail, it was only what he deserved, for his pathetic choice of bands, according to Peter. It was a risky move to announce the situation publicly because, if the festival goers felt short changed in any way by the company, they could easily organise a mini-riot just to throw a spanner in the works and have the pleasure of seeing The Fat Cats thrown in prison.

Meantime all the sitework had been developing at a steady speed and most of the infrastructure had been put on site. Far from being the 'best money could buy' it was turning out to be just the same stuff all the other festivals had used and delivered to Bardney after a quick wipe down. The only difference was that it had all been paid for up front, at an inflated price, to the delight of the owners of the loos, tents and the stage builders and fence constructors to name a few.

The fence was a piece of work! Twelve feet high with spotlights, yes! spotlights, mounted along the length. It probably would be the most effective security fence of that time and nobody would be able to escape from inside the festival without building a tunnel.

There was a brief interlude when Linda announced that someone was on the phone asking for Peter.

He picked the phone up and cautiously put it to his ear.

"Hello mate. How are you doing? It's Jeremy. Jeremy Beadle you know. Am I speaking to the festival director?"

"No, you certainly aren't. But I can get the call transferred to him if you like."

"No thanks. Not if it's that Spikings bloke. It's you I want to speak to."

"It's always a pleasure to hear from you Jeremy. How did your festival do? I haven't heard much about it yet," Peter lied.

"I'm not surprised as it only ended a few days ago. Well it was kind of mixed. In some ways it was fantastic. The Dead played for four hours and the people who had bothered to stay really enjoyed the set. All the other bands were brilliant, and it was really worth going to all the trouble to get them over here. However, I do wish that John Martin had paid for their airfares for me."

"I hear a 'but' coming," Peter said, waiting to hear the rest.

"Well one of the problems was that it started raining from the very beginning of the show and as you know the site was a little boggy. The longer it rained the deeper the mud got until it was knee deep and it was almost impossible to move around the site. Loads of people didn't pay to get in and loads of people bailed out as they couldn't stand the conditions. The killer was when the high diver attempted his dive in front of the stage and on impact the water tank split and a tidal wave of water gushed over the first hundred yards of people who were in front of the stage. That amount of water can put a downer on even the most enthusiastic festival goers," Jeremy said laughing at the horror of it.

"So apart from that, how was the show, Mrs Lincoln?" Peter joked.

"That is the last time I try to put on a festival of my own. But I was wondering if you had a job for me?"

"Wait a moment, Jeremy." Peter was nearly crying with laughter as he covered the mouthpiece with his hand and asked Malcolm, "Do you want to give Jeremy Beadle a job on this festival?"

Malcolm laughed and said, "He can fuck right off."

Peter uncovered the mouthpiece and said, "He said 'You can fuck right off' Jeremy." He was laughing out loud now.

"Alright, I'll take that as a no then, shall I?" He was also laughing on the other end of the phone.

"Well good luck with whatever you do Jeremy."

"Yes, I think I'll try to get into television somehow. Thanks for nothing you old tosser." And he hung up. Malcolm was still laughing and said that Jeremy Beadle was a real character and he was sure to get himself onto television sometime soon as he would be perfect for it.

There wasn't really any work for Peter to do so Malcolm

decided they would go out. Linda had plenty to do and the pair of them went off to find a pub for some lunch. They once again headed for Soho, which appeared to be a favourite of Malcolm and this time went into a building with no signs or name on it and it turned out to be a private member's club. Again Malcolm was greeted warmly by most of the clientele though he didn't spend much time talking to them. Peter didn't recognise anyone but thought they were mostly writers and journalists. They ordered drinks and sat at a table and Malcolm asked Peter if it was actually true that he had got a garage.

"Yes it is true and it feels really good to be working with honest hardworking villains, who would always be there to mind your back rather than stab you in it."

"That's good then as I always worried about your involvement in the drug scene. There always seems to be so much risk involved in that game."

"I know there is a risk but I would rather do that than have to take on the Money Men after their money has been stolen."

"I think you have got a little confused about who is financing this venture and you don't have to worry about me." Malcolm finished his vodka and tonic and went to the bar for more. He was always generous about buying drinks. When he sat down, he started on a new matter.

"You know how all the services and structures on the site are being sorted by production managers?" Malcolm asked. "Well I am having serious reservations about the quality of all the stuff going on site. The one thing that is indestructible is the fence. It would last for 50 years. Everything else is so shonky. The site doesn't look real. It looks like a film set and has no substance to it. The stage is only built from scaffold poles and doesn't look like it would survive the smallest puff of wind. There are tents all over the site which also look great but appear to be very fragile. We all know how the weather can affect a festival but this is all style and no substance. They have been going on television and saying they are buying the best money can buy but they only use the cheapest option now and I don't think it will work."

"Well that's great isn't it? The worst ever line-up of bands in the most inaccessible part of the country with shonky facilities all surrounded by a fortified mega fence. What could possibly go wrong?" Peter was now getting into his stride and had no loyalty to the company any more. They had made it perfectly clear that they were the ones in charge of everything and they knew best. Let's see about that shall we?

"You know what I like most about you Peter. It's your optimism and happy disposition. The ability to see the best in people and always to look on the bright side. Never looking at the worst-case scenario and never one to say 'I told you so'."

"That's one of the reasons you used to pay me such a huge wage, ha ha. My unfettered optimism and happy personality. Nothing to do with the fact that I used to work seven days a week with no questions asked."

"You are lucky it wasn't me charging you money for all the business acumen I taught you."

"'Ya Bollix' as they say in Ireland." And they ordered a handmade pork pie with pickled onions and mustard and Peter bought more drinks.

"I guess you won't be coming into the office any more then?" Malcolm asked.

"No, but I do want to go to the festival just to see what a disaster it turns out to be. Can you get me an All Areas Pass and I will meet up with you there?"

"It's already done." He handed Peter a laminated Access All Areas pass in the name of Peter Whitehead. The red pass featured the stupid train logo and it would get him through the entrance gate and anywhere else on site.

Peter shoved the pass into his pocket and said that he had to go now and Malcolm said he would see him at the festival next week. He wished him good luck with his new business and they went off in different directions from the Colony Club.

CHAPTER 25

To live outside the law, you must be honest

It was Friday afternoon when Peter got a phone call from Steve.

"Wotcher mate, what are you up to? Can you come down here?" Steve asked.

"Funny you should ask. I was just getting ready to come and see you. I've been a bit busy and wanted to see you so I'll be there in 15 minutes."

He was out of the door and down the road immediately and was hoping Steve hadn't got a problem that needed sorting on a Friday night. Never mind it wouldn't be impossible as he knew a few of his friends had taken their cars to be serviced and sorted and they were really happy with the work Steve had done.

When he arrived at the garage, the doors were shut and Steve was standing outside, smoking a Hamlet cigar that he called a 'toof', with Black Roy and the other guys from the paint shop next door.

"What's up?" Peter asked "You haven't all gone out on strike have you, cos I think you will find you all work for yourselves."

"No nothing like that. We've got something we need you to take a look at inside."

Steve opened the garage doors and inside, pushed to

the back was a dust sheet covering something that looked remarkably Porsche shaped.

"Now comes the big reveal," and Steve pulled off the sheet.

Peter couldn't believe his eyes. It looked like a new car. The bodywork had been repaired and made to look brand new. The new spray job was superb. The car gleamed in its new Ivory white paint. All of the chrome bits, the bumpers, light surrounds, hubcaps and mirrors had been cut back, polished and shone like new. Inside the seats, carpets and headlining had been valeted and glistened.

"That is unbelievable. It doesn't even look like the piece of shit car I brought in here. It looks brand new. No it looks better than brand new cos it looks like it's had some use and it's got character." Peter was truly amazed.

"Do you like the number plates?" Roy asked and Peter noticed there was a new plate on the front. It read 'P38'. Everyone fell about laughing. "Personalised number plates. We thought P for Porsche or P for Peter but mostly P38 for all the cans of body filler Billy shoved in this car!"

Steve pulled off the mock plate they had made up and Peter started the car. It sounded so good. The new carbs had been tuned and balanced and it didn't sound like a lumpy old Beetle any more. He said he just wanted to take it round the block and was absolutely delighted with how it drove. This really was a classic car. It was so much fun to drive with great handling and a nippy little well-tuned engine, but best of all it just looked so good.

He parked it up outside the garage and thanked all the lads from next door for all their hard work and asked how much he owed them.

"You don't owe us anything. Steve has settled up with us already. We enjoyed working on it. It's a really cool car," and they went back next door to carry on with their body work.

"Thanks, Man. I can't believe the job you've done on this car. I love it. Tell me how much I owe you."

"Well I had to pay Black Roy for all the bodywork, spraying and valeting. I sorted the engine myself but the carbs and tuning was done by my mate Terry. Billy has already been paid by you so it's not much and I've already paid them. I've had some of your mates down to fix their motors. That long haired bloke brought his Camaro down for a full service and I renewed his brakes. He gave me £200. Another geezer brought a red Jag that needed a lot of suspension work and he gave me £150 and I sorted a Triumph for Lucien and he gave me £100 so I've got loads of money."

"That's good you're making money but take this hundred or I will just give it to Pam on Sunday."

"You can do that if you want. She couldn't believe it when I gave her 50 quid and told her you gave it to me. So you give her that and I'll keep the rest."

"Just try to keep a few quid as a float for spares and stuff and make sure everyone pays you." The chances of either of those things happening was about zero. "Is it alright to leave the car in the garage til Monday when I get my license back? It can go outside during the day but it's best to lock it away at night."

"Course it can. It's far too nice to leave out round here. Drive it in now and we can go down The Keys. I can't wait to tell George how much money I made this week."

When they got to the pub Steve immediately told George how much he'd made and George laughed and said, "That's great. Now try to hang on to a bit of it. You don't need to spend it all in one go tonight."

"I can't believe his attitude to money," Peter said. "I've got to give a ton to Pam for what he did on my car as he won't take it off me."

"He's never been any different. We all try to put money

his way and he just gives it away. It does drive his missus mad though. That's why she is so suspicious of anyone new coming on the scene because he just doesn't care about money. It does sound like you are getting some good punters through the door now and they appear to be top payers as well."

"Yes well, it's a match made in heaven. Steve is a brilliant mechanic. I know some people with a bit of cash who need special treatment and I can help him to hang on to a bit of his money. Anyway, thanks for the carbs, they are brilliant. The car is finished and it's looking good. Thankfully Billy didn't have too much to do with it."

"I heard it was finished and even Steve said it looks The Business now. Don't forget. Hang onto it for as long as you can. One day it will be worth good money."

Steve was in a good mood as he was flush with money and tried to buy every round. Nobody let him do that and even he managed not to spend it all that night.

Everyone was starting to see what a good little business Steve and 'Smokey Pete' had started. More drink than usual was consumed because it was Friday night, though none of the other punters dared to get involved with the huge rounds that kept getting bought as more and more people joined the group. Eventually Peter made his way home after agreeing to be back for the Sunday lunch session when he would finally meet up with Pam!

It had been a standing joke for days about how long it would take for Pam to 'deck' him. Although he didn't believe she would, he had heard some terrifying stories about what Pam had done or said to people who had crossed 'Her Steve'.

He spent Saturday just hanging out around the flat doing some chores and a bit of shopping and then went to his hiding place where he kept his stash of money. He pulled out the sports bag and took it into his bedroom and tossed it on the bed. The money inside had grown considerably as Peter had not really spent much but had just kept adding in the profits to try to build up a decent amount so he could pay outright for dope and sell it on at a later time, in smaller amounts, for more money. This was also the idea Michael had suggested but he had a larger stash to work with. If they combined their buying capacity, and their customers, they would be able to control a much more lucrative share of the market. Michael had phoned in the afternoon and asked if he wanted to come out on Monday for lunch at Jimmie's in Kensington and then go on to a sale where he could invest some of his ill-gotten gains for the future. Peter said he was interested in hearing about the idea and would meet him on Monday and would bring some money, so he pulled out £500 to take on Monday for whatever Michael had in mind.

Sunday lunch at The Cross Keys was a whole different affair to the evening sessions as Peter discovered when he walked in at around one o'clock. The usual team was there but they looked so different. Gone were the oily clothes, dirty hair and hands and they were all cleaned up and dressed in smart casual clothes. George looked even more like Roger Daltrey who, as rumour had it, he had stood in for on a drunk driving charge, but George never mentioned that. Most of the wives had come as well and they all were all dressed up and seemed very friendly but were also ready to watch a showdown. Peter was introduced to everyone and he took the opportunity to get a round in.

Steve was at the back of the room laughing and joking with Steve Benbow, whose group was playing there. As he spotted him he noticed a short, stocky lady, with long dark brown hair, fixing him with a fierce icy stare. She nodded at him and pushed through the people and made a beeline for Peter. This was obviously what everyone had come to see.

Was she going to tear into him and throw him out of the pub and the partnership? Or would she accept Peter into the group as a friend? Peter took a pull on his pint and waited for the trouble to start. She looked fierce and he would have taken on most of the blokes in the pub rather than her. He had heard of one or two episodes of how protective she was when it came to Steve. As she approached Peter smiled and said, "You must be Pam?"

"And you must be Peter Wanky Whitehead!"

Peter laughed at the name and replied,

"Well I am but only my very close friends get to call me that."

"Well I call you that and I'm not your close friend." She said but there was a glimmer of a smile on her chiselled face. "Steve hasn't stopped talking about you and what you are going to do for the garage and the dope you sell and the money you have given him. Thanks for the 50, by the way. I couldn't believe it when he give it me. He told me you had said he had to do it. So what's your game? Why are you getting involved in the poxy garage that Billy robbed into the ground?"

They sat down at a table and Peter told her about using the garage as a front but also building up the business by getting his friends to become paying customers. Letting Steve keep the money but being there to help with business matters. Not needing to take any money out but making sure Steve took money from his punters.

"If you can teach that soapy fucker to hang onto his money you deserve a medal. I've been trying for years but he gives it away as soon as he gets it."

"Well he's had a good first week with his new customers and he wouldn't take any money for the work he did on my Porsche so I said I would give it to you… If you want it."

"Course I want it. He never gives me a penny. I just don't want you getting him into trouble."

"He doesn't need any help from me to get into trouble."

"That's so true." She said and started to laugh.

"So here's the money he earned doing my Porsche. He wouldn't take it off me so I'm giving it to you," He passed over an envelope and continued: "I think Steve is a brilliant mechanic and a really good bloke. I can put a lot of good work our way. Work that is legal, although the customers are not 100% legit, but the garage won't be used for anything that could get Steve into trouble. I don't know what he gets up to now but I would prefer he stopped doing anything hookey as it might bring trouble down on my head. He can earn enough money legally if he sticks with me and I guarantee we will have enough excitement going on to keep him interested."

"Thanks again for the money. I think I believe what you are saying but if you are lying, I swear I'll tear your head off," and she was only half joking.

"Come on, I need a drink." and they went back to the bar and bought another drink. Steve was standing there and said, "I told you he was a diamond geezer didn't I?"

"Yeah well he's ok I s'pose. He'll do, until he stops giving me money!"

"That ain't gonna be for a long time, is it Pete?"

"I hope not. Anyway, now I want to go and listen to Denny play. I've been told he's The Business and I want to listen to him." He walked away so Pam could tell Steve what she thought.

Denny was 'The Business' playing beautifully free flowing guitar riffs to Benbow's singing and rhythm guitar on quirky, humorous jazzy songs. He sometimes played a lead riff while he was having a long, involved conversation with a friend, without missing a single note. He was a legend and the whole pub enjoyed his playing and came every Sunday to listen to him and Benbow and sing along, drunkenly with the band, to classics like 'Ghost Riders in the Sky' and 'Mule Train'. It wasn't rock and roll but he liked it as did everyone in the jam packed pub. Benbow kept up a string of corny gags and funny stories between songs and mostly the music was drowned out by the crowd in the pub who were talking and laughing while occasionally singing along to the music. Steve came over to the table where Peter was sitting and put his pint down and pulled up a chair.

"I don't know what you said to Pam but she thinks you are the best thing since sliced bread! Usually she thinks all of my friends are absolute wankers and she won't even speak to them but you apparently are a good bloke and I have to listen to what you say from now on! What have you done to her?"

"I just told her the truth and it makes sense for both of us. So if you listen to her as well as me you can start to make some money."

"Funny you should say that cos I got a visit from California Bob last week and he asked me if I could hide a kilo of stuff in a car he was shipping back to the States. I asked if he wanted it cheap and he said he hadn't got a lot of money so I told him to go away for half an hour and I would do it for him. The dope was all sealed up in plastic so I loosened the battery terminals, lifted up the battery, stuffed the gear underneath, whacked the battery back on top and did up the bolts. You couldn't see a thing! I was dead chuffed. He was delighted when he came back and gave me £200. Do you want some of it?"

"No, I don't want any of it. I don't even know California Bob and I had nothing to do with it. Keep the money and maybe buy a car off George to do up to sell to one of my mates. That would be so simple for you and would make good money. I can tell you what ones would be good cars to buy and would also be good work horses for my mates," Peter said.

"Alright," Steve said. "George has always got some really tidy motors going through the yard that really are too good for scrapping but he hasn't got the time or the inclination to do them up so he either breaks or crushes them."

"That's great. We should ask him to let us know when something nice comes in that just needs a clutch or gearbox or something that he has got the part for that you can fix and we can turn it over quickly for a good profit. We might even be able to rent them out as disposables for a short time for good money. They just have to be plain and ordinary as well as being reliable. Let's give it a go."

"I'll catch him now before he gets too pissed and see what he's got in the yard."

"Good thinking. Nothing too flashy to start with but we can go on to more interesting things later on, when my punters have made so much money from all the dope I am selling them, and they want fancy motors to swan around in. May be we can even interest them in some renovated classics!"

The session was not as raucous as the evening sessions as the wives kept their men a little calmer. But only a little as they also had a large capacity for drink. It was no wonder the landlord, 'One Leg Mac' Mackenzie, loved them as they spent an absolute fortune over his bar every day.

Eventually Peter left them to it and made his way over to Christine's house to drink black coffee and sober up. They talked about Michael and his idea about an investment and they couldn't work out what he had in mind. Peter hoped it didn't have anything to do with oriental carpets but they did know that it could turn out to be interesting as Michael was a very smart cookie. He was always buying things like oriental rugs and tucking bits of money away as a kind of pension scheme or investment. He had been impressed by Peter's partnership with Steve which he thought was a brilliant move on all levels.

"How's your little car coming along?" Christine asked as Peter was on his way out of the door.

"It's fantastic. They finished it on Friday and I get my license back tomorrow so I'll drive over and show it to you. I can't believe how good it looks."

"I'll look forward to that and do listen to Michael. He can make a lot of sense but don't do anything that you are not 100% sure about," Christine advised as he left.

CHAPTER 26

... But I know what I do like

Just before ten o'clock on Monday morning Peter was pulling up to the lockup in his little Mini. Steve popped his head out of the doors and started to laugh.

"What the fuck is that? It looks like a Cooper S but it sounds like a Morris 1000 with a hole in the manifold."

"Yes I know. I got it cheap from a guy who had it modified so he could race it, but he didn't get as far as the engine. I am fed up with it now. It drives like it is on rails and there isn't a corner in this country you need to slow down for, but the engine is only a standard 850."

"What are you going to do with it?"

"I've no idea. I don't want to spend money putting the right engine in it cos it's not a real Cooper and I'm no boy racer. When I was driving Malcolm all over the country they paid me by the mile and it paid for the car many times over so I thought maybe we could use it as a courtesy car for a while. You can use it if you want and we can sell it a bit later. It's too noticeable for me to want to drive it around when I'm working, especially at night. I don't really want to use the Porsche much either. Did George say he had anything interesting?"

"He said you can have as many boring motors as you want. Renaults, Peugeots, Citroens, any of that sort of crap." Steve pulled a face of disgust at the mere mention of those cars. "I'll ask George if he's interested in swapping your Mini for something. I bet he's got a Cooper engine that he could put in and make it a tidy little motor."

"That's great if he wants to do that. I just want to see the back of it. Can you ask him to ring you with the first decent motor that comes along? I need a working car. Not too smart, not too shabby. Completely unnoticeable and ordinary from the outside."

"Right-ho. I'll get onto that straight away."

"I'll take the Porsche now as I'm meeting Michael for lunch and I want to let him see it. Let me know what car George is offering before you get it or I might end up with a Jensen Interceptor or something. I fancy a Renault 16 if he has got one but anything like that would be great."

"You should be so lucky to get a Jensen but I'm sure his yard is full of crappy Renaults."

Peter pulled away in the Porsche loving the sound of the well-tuned flat four engine. The car drove beautifully, the engine sang its way through the gears, as he made his way through Notting Hill and down Church Street. When he got to the bottom he saw the red brick wall that was the front of Jimmie's Wine Bar. There was an empty parking space just outside the entrance to the courtyard and he nipped into the space and fed some money into the meter. He hadn't been to Jimmie's before but had heard about the crazy retired guardsman, who it was named after, who ran it in his own inimitable way. Inside the door was a gloomy brick vault with a mismatch of tables and chairs scattered around. Along the length of the side wall was a large charcoal grill from which radiated a roaring heat and the delicious smell of the crispy steaks cooking on it. Michael was sitting at a table, as far away from the fire as possible, with a girl whose blonde hair fell in natural curls onto her shoulders. She had her back to Peter. They appeared to be deep in conversation but as Peter got closer Michael looked up and smiled.

"Peter. Good to see you. This is Susan, my girlfriend, who is also known as 'The Babe'. Susan meet Peter. Peter meet Susan."

For a moment Peter couldn't speak. He was just overwhelmed by her. She was the loveliest girl he had seen. Ever! She was absolutely stunningly beautiful. Her golden hair hung in natural ringlets over her face. Her eyes were the lightest shade of emerald green with tiny flecks of gold in them. She had traced a fine line of kohl across her eyelids, to accentuate their loveliness, and this appeared to be the only scrap of makeup she wore. She appeared to glow like a movie star and was simply exquisite. She wore a black jersey dress with casual ease and it clung to her gorgeous tanned body making it even more desirable.

It was apparent that all the other men in the bar had noticed her as well as they couldn't take their eyes off her.

"Peter," she repeated. "I will call you 'Peter Bear'," and she put her arms around him and kissed him lightly on the cheek and then hugged him tightly. It felt as though a static shock arced between them as she pressed herself against him and she just said, "My, oh my," in his ear.

They sat down at the table and Peter tried to get his spinning head back together and he tried to continue as if he thought Michael's girlfriend was just another ordinary person. It became obvious that Jimmie had been smitten as well, as he kept coming to the table offering Susan all kinds of free snacks and offers of tasters of wine.

"You've picked up a fan there," Michael said as Jimmie went off to get a special bottle of wine for the table.

"He's a real sweetheart, isn't he?" Susan said.

"Oh yes he's a sweetheart alright. I wonder what wine

he'll come back with. Do you like wine Peter?" Michael asked.

"Sure I do. I spent a few months in '69 living in Paris with a French girl whose father was a wine merchant. He thought that as I was English I knew all about wine and he tried out lots of really good wine on me. After a while I began to appreciate it and learned a little bit about vintages."

"I love Paris," Susan said. "Where were you staying?"

"It was a little atelier in the quatorzieme district."

"Ooh, Le Montparnasse. That was a cool place to stay. It does sound very romantic."

Just then Jimmy came up and asked what they were going to eat. Both Michael and Peter opted for rare steak from the grill with chips, salad and some bread. Susan screwed up her pretty nose and said that was disgusting and she was a vegetarian. She said she would have a salad with bread and the stinkiest piece of cheese he'd got, a good bottle of red wine and she would nick a few of their chips.

Jimmie's wine really was good and went beautifully with the charred but rare steaks that were served. Peter said they were the best he had eaten in this country and Michael agreed. Susan said her cheese was really stinky and lovely but why is it that vegetarians are always ignored and the two men laughed at the possibility of a vegetarian restaurant opening in London any time soon.

"So where are we going then?" Peter asked.

"We are taking you to my favourite place in London," said Susan. "Sotheby's Saleroom. They are having a sale of Modern and Pop Art prints this afternoon and Michael wants to buy some pictures as an investment."

"Isn't Sotheby's very expensive?" Peter asked.

"No not at all." Michael said. "That is the beauty of it. There are hundreds of new artists who put their limited edition prints on the market every year. Some of them will become famous in a few years and their pictures will be worth a lot of money. If you buy them now you can get them for next to nothing and they can only become more valuable."

"That sounds great but what if the prints don't go up in value?"

"Well that's part of the fun of it. It's art. You have to choose something that you actually like and can also afford. If you really like it you can put it on your wall and enjoy it for years so it doesn't matter what it's worth. It is unlikely anything you buy today will go down in value, so it's a good way of protecting some of the money that we have, instead of continually reinvesting it in dope which is always risky. I try to put some money into things that have a value but I want to enjoy them too. They must be portable and attractive like rugs and art. Who knows when you may need to cash in some assets."

"Don't worry, babe," Susan said across the table. "I will help you choose some really great art. Trust me." And looking deep into those green eyes, how could he not trust her? Michael then lowered his voice and said, "My Land Rover is due back at the end of this week. Can I use your lock up to break into the wooden roof rack and get the dope out? If Steve wants to help me I will see him right as he would be a great help. It seems like you will be away then so when you get back I want you to trickle out 25 keys, in small amounts, to as many small dealers as we know, at a high price so we can make top dollar for this high quality dope. I can move the other 25 keys quickly to get my money back straight away but I want to maximise the earnings on this one. It's getting much harder to do this sort of run and people have to be prepared to pay well for Primo Afghani."

Jimmie came back with a 'One Day Only' offer especially for Susan, but he included them as well. He had some cases of half bottles of Chateau Margaux 1962 that he didn't want in his cellar for very long, 'wink wink', and did they want them at £24 for a case of six. Both Michael and Susan said yes immediately, closely followed by Peter who said he wanted two cases as he believed it was a superb year and would be perfect to take up to the festival that weekend.

"I've heard all about this festival you are promoting. Is it this weekend?" Susan wanted to know.

"Yes, although it's not me promoting it. I'm not looking forward to going but I spent so long working on it I want to see if it works. I have a strong feeling that it is all going to go tits up, but I have a caravan and Land Rover waiting for me on site and I have got a goody-bag of dope so how bad can it be?"

"It might be quite bad if that huge storm that is coming in from America hasn't blown itself out by the time it hits land this weekend," Susan chipped in, "but they do say it will have calmed down by then so I am sure you will be alright in your fancy caravan. Do make sure you take a hamper full of nice food so you don't have to go out if you don't want to and you might find someone you can share your goodies with while you are there, you never know babe." Susan delivered the line with a coy look that more than emphasised her meaning.

"Getting a hamper is a great idea... Now let's leave the wine in my car and get a cab to Sotheby's. We can sort it out later," Peter suggested. They settled the bill and Jimmie air kissed Susan, but she didn't hug him, and they carried the four dinky little half cases out through the courtyard.

The Porsche was sitting by the kerb and when Peter put his key in the door Susan's green eyes flickered and she started squealing.

"Oh my God. Oh my God. Is this yours? Do you really own this car? Michael you stinker why didn't you tell me?

You little shit! I can't believe it. I don't like cars, but this is the one car I love. A Porsche 356. I fucking love it. I want you to promise you will sell it to me when you have finished with it. Will you? Please. Can I have a go in it? Please, Please."

Michael stood there laughing. He had known how much she would love that car and had been hoping Peter would drive it there today. It made him feel so good to see the pleasure it gave Susan.

"Let's just leave it here with the wine and get a cab because we will be bringing some pictures back and there is no room for all of us to fit in," Michael suggested.

Peter agreed but said that she could drive it soon, and that was a promise, and he stuffed some more money into the meter.

"In that case I will choose you some lovely pictures that will eventually be worth a fortune," she promised.

They stashed the cases in the front boot compartment of the car and walked the few paces down to Kensington High Street where they hailed a cab which took them to New Bond Street and dropped them outside Sotheby's. The saleroom was a magnificent old building and had a distinct air of opulence about it. Peter was beginning to feel intimidated by the whole affair. Susan spotted his concern and said,

"Don't worry about a thing. This is purely for fun. You have to let go of all your preconceived ideas and look for something that either touches you or something you really like. Try to find something that you would like to keep for years. Something that would always give you pleasure hanging on your wall. It can be anything, and you will see many varied and crazy kinds of artwork inside. Just relax and go with the flow."

"You're right. This is for fun and if I don't see anything I like I will just enjoy the outing," Peter said.

"Right. I am going to get our numbers from over there so we can all bid on something if we want. I've got an account here and it's easier for you just to register with that." Off she went to the desk and started charming the man who was allocating auction numbers.

"How come she's got an account here?" Peter asked Michael.

"Because she comes here quite a lot. She doesn't always buy but we attend a lot of sales here. Her account was set up so she doesn't have to register every time we come and also it means I don't have to declare my purchases and I can pay in cash. It just goes down as a sale through Susan's account."

"But isn't that a problem for her?" Peter asked.

Michael laughed at the idea.

"Not at all. A few prints being bought through her account would hardly show up as anything more than petty cash. She is loaded. Her grandfather invented and patented some kind of agricultural hedge cutter and made a fortune out of it. He gave a lot of it away to Susan's father and to Susan, to avoid death duties, but he still has millions. They are his only relatives and both are in line to cop the lot when Grampy dies."

At that moment Susan arrived back with the auction numbers and catalogues and they each took one.

"I don't think I want to buy anything to take back today, as my flat is like a building site. Tony Reggie is knocking the plaster off the corners of my walls at the moment so he can make them all perfectly straight for me. Everything's covered in dust," Susan announced.

"I was just telling Peter how we can pay cash for the pictures and use your account."

"Of course you can. We don't want the taxman sniffing around you, do we? Now let's head downstairs and see what is coming up for sale. Stick with me Peter and we will see what we can find for you."

They went down the stairs to the saleroom and entered a room that was crammed full of all kinds of artwork, both framed and unframed. Everything was displayed either on the walls or piled on the many tables around the room. It was much less formal than Peter expected as he had only seen auction sales of Old Masters on the television. The more valuable prints were on the wall and everything else was available to pick up and look at. They were all numbered and corresponded to a listing in the catalogue which named the piece, the artist and the estimated sale price. The first few prints Peter looked at were by Andy Warhol and were estimated at several thousand pounds, and some by David Hockney for several hundred. There was a little Hockney pencil sketch print of a French shop and cafe that Susan told Michael was the one she had always wanted. Peter kept looking and saw a couple of prints depicting two pairs of cowboy boots. They were black outlines of fancy, tooled boots, one pair on a gold background, the other pair on a silver background. The estimate was £10 to £20 so Peter marked them in his catalogue as he really wanted them. Susan came over and he showed her the boots and she said they were a good choice for a start as they suited him perfectly. They saw various prints signed by artists with names that meant nothing to Peter. Pieces by someone called Man Ray seemed to be getting good money so were walked over. Two prints caught Peter's eye and he looked them up and found they were estimated at £40 to £60 each. He really liked them and showed them to Susan. Both of the prints were from a limited edition of 125 and signed by the artist who was an American called Ed Ruscha. One of the prints had a vibrant blue background with the letters 'O O O' that appeared to have been written with chrystal clear water. The letters glistened on the top of the blue colour. The other print was a pale yellow background with the word 'RAW' printed in brown in a stylised way. Susan said they looked good and if he liked them he should take a punt.

The sale started and Peter got the boots prints for £20 for the pair. He was delighted and loved the idea of hanging a pair of gold and silver cowboy boots on the wall. The Ruscha prints got knocked down to him for £50 each and he also bought a little pair of prints by James Rosenquist of Marlon Brando's hat and Clark Gable's hat, each on a hat peg sticking out of the world, and an oddball Jim Dine print called The Wolfman. He bought them without seeing them previously but they seemed cheap at £30 for the pair and £20 for the Dine so he just bid as they came up for sale. Michael bought the Hockney for £250 and a few other prints that he liked and they settled up with cash and they took the prints away with them straight away.

Michael said he would go back to Susan's flat with her and they both got out of the cab in Cadogan Gardens where her fourth-floor flat was located. It was just behind Sloane Square and just off the King's Road in a very smart street opposite a private garden. Peter said he wouldn't come in as he had to get his car before the meter ran out and he went back to Kensington High Street with his new acquisitions feeling really chuffed with himself. He promised to bring the cases of Margaux round in the next couple of days and Susan had said she would go round the corner with him to Sloane Street and choose a lovely box of food prepared by the fancy Delicatessen she used and they would put it all in a hamper for him to take up to the festival. She teased him about preparing a proper little love nest to keep him occupied during the boring festival. He said he wouldn't be bored as he had plenty of Thai grass left to keep him amused

CHAPTER 27

Yippee aye A... Yippie aye O!...

He drove the Porsche home from Kensington with the prints sitting on the back seat. He felt that he had now stepped up to a whole new level. Somehow spending time with Michael and Susan had opened his eyes to a new world that really was accessible to him. It was not like the world Michael Deeley and Stanley Baker inhabited but a more real existence that was not so far from his reach and felt much more exciting and vibrant. Susan had given him such a confidence boost just by flirting with him and asking for his opinion about things like the wine and giving him the confidence to have an opinion and to pass on some of his knowledge. Michael had such a different twist on things and was prepared to work with Peter as an equal, to grow their dealing into something much bigger. Everything became so much clearer and he had now gained a lot more confidence so he could focus his mind on the direction he was about to take. He carried the prints up the stairs to the empty flat and had them hanging on the wall in his bedroom before John got back from work.

There were now just three days before the festival started and Peter had been in touch with Chris the driver and arranged to meet him on Friday to get a lift up to the site in Bardney. Chris was being employed to be there in case he

222

was needed to drive anyone around but had told Peter that he was not very excited by the thought of sitting around in a poxy field for three days as a taxi service, and would probably go on the missing list on Sunday, if Peter wanted to come back to London with him then. He had told them he couldn't go back up there until Friday, due to work commitments on Thursday, so he wasn't taking anyone else up there and would pick up Peter wherever he wanted in London. It was arranged that they would meet outside Sloane Square Tube station giving Peter the opportunity of stocking up from the deli round the corner from Susan's flat.

On Wednesday afternoon he went down to Chiswick to see what Steve was up to. He always looked forward to going to the garage to hear Steve's stories, opinions, jokes and blatant lies about the world in general. When he got there the 'Brightsparks' van was parked by the doors and Steve and Eddie had their heads under the bonnet of a maroon Renault 16.

"I see you've managed to find the engine between the pair of you," Peter called from the doorway. "It looks like it's costing someone a fortune if Brightsparks is on the job."

Eddie 'Brightsparks' was an auto electrician and a really good one and therefore didn't work cheaply. His job was to isolate electrical faults on cars and fix them. This sounds simple but in fact the complex wiring system on a car is sealed inside the chassis and consists of hundreds of yards of wiring, called a loom, that eventually deteriorates and shorts out at random. Then the engine system also has a variety of electrical functions that have a million different ways of breaking down. Even if the fault could be located it was usually virtually impossible to access the wire to fix it. Eddy Brightsparks could usually manage to fix the fault somehow but always with a lot of huffing and swearing and saying how it was not possible to fix without putting in a new loom. He was a genius and was always called in to repair all aspects of the electrics that no other mechanic would even attempt, after the basic fix had been tried and had failed. He was called in when all else had failed and the job was deemed impossible to fix.

A job like that involved a lot of pressure combined with frustration and Eddie was considered to be 'A little bit mental'. In a good way though.

"Yes, it is costing someone some money and that some-one is you," Eddie called out from under the bonnet.

"Yes, he's right. This is your motor, if you want it. Isn't this what you said you wanted? A poxy piece of French crap that doesn't even run!"

"Just what I ordered. But I feel a bit nervous now I know the Brightsparks meter is running. How long has he been here?"

"Not long and it's an easy fix. We have nearly finished. It turned out the alternator was being shorted out elsewhere and I was just gonna put another one in when Eddie was passing and dropped in. He just checked over the wiring and spotted the fault straight away," Steve explained. "He said he would test it to see if anything else was wrong."

"Yeah I'm just doing you a favour but you can still buy me a drink tonight if you like."

"Course I will Eddy. Thanks for the help. Wilkins idea of sorting the electrics is the same as how he fixes a faulty Morris 1000 fuel pump. Whack it with a lump hammer."

"Oi. I resemble that remark," Steve said as he tightened up the last bolt. "Good as new and twice the price. Start her up Pete and let's see what she's got."

He jumped into the car and fired it up. It started first time and the alternator light on the dashboard went out and the engine sounded really sporty.

"The lights gone off so it must be working. That is the

joy of having a professional electrician working beside you," Peter said.

He looked at the interior of the car and saw it was in really good condition. No tears or splits anywhere. It seemed as though someone had really looked after it before it was scrapped. The body was in good shape as well with only a few little marks on the paintwork which was a little dull.

"What's the story, then?" Peter asked.

"Well I told George that you were looking for a Renault 16 and he said he had just got one in. The owner had been having huge problems with it cutting out all the time. It didn't charge and he changed the alternator and that didn't help. George didn't think it was a big problem but didn't know what it was. He said he would swap the Mini for it as his son wanted one to play around with as a project so we swapped cars and Clever Bollocks here found the fault," Steve explained.

"Yes I did," said Eddie. "It was the usual thing. A loose connection on the woofle valve. It happens all the time but no one thinks to look at it."

"Ah I can now see why your services are in such great demand at such a high price, Eddie. Will you be at the pub tonight so I can settle your bill in full?"

"I certainly will and it will be two drinks, not one!" Eddie said as he made his way out of the door. "Now I've got to go and do some proper work for real money."

"He always was a greedy bastard," Steve called after him and Eddie drove off in the Brightsparks van waving a finger out of the window. "George reckons he knows this motor. It's been really well looked after and never had any problems until it developed that fault. The owners just got fed up with their dopey mechanic not being able to fix it and bought another car. They were so pissed off with it they drove it into George's yard to scrap it and he bought it off them for nuppence. It looks alright and it drives really well when it goes. If you like that sort of thing. It's a super dooper TS with twin carbs, a log book, six months tax and MOT and it's all yours and ready to go. It's even got pump-up tyres!"

"Pump-up tyres? Now that is posh. Well you seem to have sorted out a runabout for me and got rid of that Mini. The Boy's done good. I'll change the log book over and register it here to the garage. I don't think George would be too happy getting my parking tickets and if you could give it the once over I'll take it away after the weekend. You can drive it around 'til then as you seem to like French motors so much."

"I will, but it won't change my opinion about them. You can't beat an old Jag. Speaking of which, how is the old Porsche going? It sounds like the carbs are still in tune."

"It's such a pleasure to drive. Everyone just loves it. Michael's girlfriend nearly had a heart attack when she saw it and offered to buy it when I was fed up with it," Peter said and laughed at the idea.

"Yeah I bet she'd give you 50 quid for it now."

"No, she is absolutely loaded. Her grandad gave her a fortune and will leave her more when he pegs it. You won't believe it when you meet her. She is an absolute stunner."

"Where did Michael manage to get her from then?"

"I believe she was living with a dope smuggler for a while and she got fed up with him and met Michael," Peter explained.

"Well that's what I call moving on. Though he is a nice feller, I'll give you that."

"Good, I'm glad you like him because he wants to use the lock up over the weekend. His Land Rover has got back from Afghanistan and he needs somewhere quiet to get the dope out. It's all concealed inside the wooden roof rack so there is no metal cutting to do. If we let him use the garage you can help him split the wood open and he will give you a nice 'drink' if you like."

"Too right 'I do like'. I haven't done anything hooky for weeks now and I am getting a bit bored with all this honest mechanic-ing. So I will look forward to that."

"Right then I'll tell him it's on. He'll ring you and arrange to meet you here. I've got to go now, I promised I would go and see Lady Bradley so I'll see you later at the pub."

"And I'll make sure this piece of Frog rubbish is safe enough to drive if I have got to be the guinea pig who tries it out first."

Peter was really enjoying nipping around town in the Porsche. Although it wasn't really fast it was still a beautiful car to drive. Also it hardly stood him in any money so it didn't really matter if it got damaged in traffic. However it would be a relief to have a nondescript motor to drive around when he was moving dope or carrying money around and he liked the look of his Renault. He parked outside Christine's house and rang her bell. When she came out she smiled and said, "Oh my God! That is so lovely. Is it a Porsche? It's perfect. Hang on here a moment, I'm going to take some photos, while it still looks new, if you don't mind," and she went inside to get her camera. Peter had never owned a car that had such an effect on women as this one. He had no idea when he bought the unassuming, shabby little motor that it was already a style icon. Christine took some photos with her Nikon, from all sides of the car admiring all the different curves and angles. When they had been developed, she gave some prints to Peter who thought they were a perfect memento of the car and he never got rid of them.

They went inside and smoked some of the Thai grass and drank tea and lay around listening to *Astral Weeks* as the music was so trippy. There had been no word from Ian since he left in such a hurry and Christine said she was a little concerned about him as he was so crazy.

"We had a brilliant time on Monday," Peter said. "Michael is strange. We went to a really weird wine bar for lunch and ended up at Sotheby's for a Pop Art sale in the afternoon."

"Did you manage to buy anything interesting?" Christine asked.

"Yes I did! Apart from two cases of Chateau Margaux, I bought about seven prints by some different American artists for only £170 and even if they don't go up much in value I really like them as kooky pictures. Michael has a wealthy girlfriend who knows all about that stuff and she helped me make the choices. I think it is such a good idea to put some money away like that because it is so easy to get single-minded in the dope game. Look at the Boy Wonder putting all his eggs into one basket, so to speak. I don't want to be like that. If he gets captured on this Kamikaze run, he will have lost everything he has made up to now."

"You're right Peter, everyone is chasing the next big scam and they keep investing everything they have for bigger and better things. I heard that last week Howard Marks brought in 650 kilos. Can you imagine that? He is the one who says he isn't in it for the money! What a tosser."

"He sure is a tosser and he'll carry on getting bigger and bigger until he cannot be ignored any more by the authorities, and they'll hunt him down and everyone else will be dragged down with him. Everyone knows all about him and he is just too greedy for his own good."

The pub opened at half past five and Peter left Christine's house for the evening session. He had a few things he wanted to talk about with George and when he got there his Renault was parked up outside. The paintwork was sparkling like new with a deep shine. Steve was propping up the bar with a pint in his hand and a 'toof' in his mouth and said, "Did you see how we buffed up the old Renault? They just ran the polisher over it next door and it came up lovely."

"It certainly did come up lovely and it just shows what good cars they are," Peter joked.

"Well I must admit it goes like a rocket. If it don't break down on me I might agree with you."

George came into the pub and laughed at Steve. "You'll take all the paint off that old nail if you polish it too hard. I'll have a pint. Thank you. I can get you as many of those poxy French motors as you want. Nobody wants to buy them cos they look so funny."

"We can take a couple more but not Renault 16s as we will look like a French minicab firm all driving the same motors. Mix it up a bit with some Peugeots. They are perfect as no one would guess you are up to mischief in such a boring car. And can you find something for Steve? He seems to have fallen in love with my car."

Everyone laughed at the thought of Wilkins driving a foreign motor and he said he would settle for a proper English motor. Thank You Very Much.

George said that the Mini was perfect for his boy to start with. He was only 12 but already car mad and loved the lowered look of the car. It wasn't too fast for him to tear around the yard and it was simple enough to work on as he was already a useful mechanic. It wouldn't be long before he wanted to soup it up but it would do for starters. He said he would sort out a couple of cars that Peter could buy for Steve to work on and he would supply any bits that needed replacing. He now had a good idea of what was wanted and it would be easy to sort them out. He said that he loved the idea of Peter using boring, ordinary looking cars to deliver dope around London instead of flashy expensive ones as everyone would expect.

"Well not everyone agrees with that idea and they

continue to drive around in huge Camaros and Jags, but maybe I can persuade them to tone it down a bit and sell them something a little less noticeable just for working in. Just let me know what comes in and I will sort you out with the money," Peter said.

Later on Peter said he had to go now and he would be away for the weekend to attend the festival. This caused a huge laugh from the group at the bar.

"What? What? I'm just doing my real job. I'm not a grease monkey like all of you wankers. I'm the festival director, if you didn't know, and I have to go and pick up all the money I'm owed for setting up this festival."

This caused a riot of laughter and abuse and Peter slipped out of the door to catcalls and waving fingers.

"Only joking!" he mouthed as he went through the door.

CHAPTER 28

I could drink a case of you

Thursday morning started ominously with gale force winds and heavy rain falling, and Peter cursed the foul weather as he had to do some running around before he left for the festival the next day. He rang Susan and told her he would be bringing over the wine around lunch time if that was ok, and he threw some clean clothes and six of the half-bottles of wine into his hand stitched leather holdall to take away with him. The stash of grass and hash was slipped into a disguised pocket inside the bag and he checked that his stash of money was well hidden in his secret hole in the wall. Please God don't burn the place down while I'm away. He picked up two cases of Margaux and walked down the stairs and put them on the front seat of the car. Traffic was slow because of the heavy rain and Peter was reminded of the horrendous storm he had to drive through when he left Somerset. Was it really only six months ago? He really should go back and visit them all soon. Eventually he arrived at Cadogan Gardens and pulled into a space that a car had just vacated opposite the entrance to Susan's flat. He wasn't going to get soaked after all. Scooping up the boxes he ran to the sheltered doorway, rang the bell and was buzzed into the building. Carrying the two boxes up four flights he arrived at the flat with them under his arms.

Susan was waiting for him at the door, still looking as lovely as ever, and greeted him warmly.

"Peter Bear. How kind of you to come all this way to drop off the wine. Come in I am just grinding some fresh coffee. You are just in time. Excuse the building site but I'm having some renovations done."

They went into a simple rustic kitchen that had obviously just been refurbished immaculately with natural reclaimed wood and stainless steel and Susan poured three cups of coffee.

"Michael has gone out to do something with his Land Rover or something so you will have to make do with me, I'm afraid. Let's go to the front room. Tony Reggie is redoing the walls so it's a tip, I'm afraid."

When they entered the front room the fourth-floor views were spectacular through the trees into the gardens opposite. Tony Reggie was occupied plastering a perfectly straight edge where two walls abutted at the window alcove.

"That's better, Tony, But it's still not straight. Can you do it again, Darling?"

Tony appeared to be used to this degree of perfection and nodded and they drank their coffee from some earthenware Portuguese cups. There was little evidence of any dust or mess and Tony Reggie appeared to be the tidiest builder in the world as well as being the most long-suffering one. It turned out that he was an excellent builder, who was also an old friend from Southend, and was staying there on the sofa until the refurb was finished. Michael had got fed up with it all and that was why he was living in Bethnal Green. His house had been stripped and finished in the time it took Susan to choose the right mixer tap for the kitchen.

"Are you going to let me drive your car today, Peter Bear? Because if you are, we could go down the King's Road and have a little lunch somewhere lovely that I know."

"That would be great and maybe we could drop into the Deli to see what I can get for tomorrow?" Peter replied looking forward to having lunch with The Babe.

Susan casually slipped on a jacket and they went downstairs to the car.

"I am really excited about driving this car," she said as she sat behind the wheel. "I am serious about buying it from you as well and I want you to know that I will wait for you. You know, until you want to get rid of it. I will wait for as long as it takes."

She drove the car as if she had owned it for ever, keeping the revs up but not hunting it, and treating it with care and consideration. They went for a spin down by the river and drove along the Chelsea Embankment with the Thames on their left. Considerably more people noticed the car when she was driving it and when she parked outside the restaurant on the King's Road, a small group of admirers stopped to ask her about the car. She just laughed and said it wasn't hers yet but it would be one day. Lunch was strictly vegetarian and Peter really enjoyed it and they had a bottle of wine that was nowhere near as good as the wine at Jimmie's. She was easy to be with and they mainly talked about Peter. Where he came from. What he did. Was he going to carry on working in The Music Business? As before Susan attracted lots of attention from the other men in the room but she didn't seem to notice and all her attention was centred on her lunch partner. He knew it was stupid but she really made him feel special for the time he was with her.

When the meal was finished she drove back to the deli in Sloane Street and had the assistant write a list so Peter could just nip in the next day and collect the freshly made up order.

"We need two sirloin steaks to keep your strength up, French mustard, potato salad, stinky cheese, smoked salmon, two crusty loaves, ground coffee, fresh eggs, bacon, olives, olive oil, some lettuce and salad bits, some asparagus quiche, coleslaw, pickled beetroot and some butter. Ooh and two of those lovely creamy chocolaty desserts. Would you please make this up in a box for Peter to collect first thing tomorrow?"

"Certainly Susan. It will be made up to be ready for nine tomorrow morning."

"I hope it won't be too heavy for you to carry." She said to Peter.

"Oh no I'll be ok. I'm meeting my driver just over there by the Tube station in the morning."

"Your driver, eh? That is grand but I am still worried about this weather. It doesn't seem to be easing off yet and a bit of rain can easily wash out a festival especially if it's as early in the year as this." She seemed concerned. "Still you will be alright locked away in your caravan enjoying your new 'festival friend' and eating all those lovely goodies I've chosen for you."

"Well I will be thinking of you as I enjoy them both," he joked and she pulled a sour face at him. He dropped her back at her flat and thanked her for choosing the lovely food and asked her to remind Michael to ring Steve who was expecting him on Saturday at the lock up as arranged.

"Of course I will. Bye babe. Do try to have a lovely time." She waved as he drove back down the King's Road to Shepherd's Bush without attracting half as much attention in the car as when she had driven it. His mind was fixed on the 50 keys of Afghani dope Michael had smuggled back into the country. He had been told that he could move half of it and he was working out the best people to sell it to for the most amount of money. He could think of at least ten people who would take a kilo at a high price and if it was as good as Michael said it was, they would be back for more the next day. He would offer it to Gill's music business dealer as he would be able to sell loads of it to musicians and all the other dope connoisseurs associated with The Business. Apart from all the musicians there were the A&R men, the record producers, engineers, studio managers, the sound guys, the lighting guys, the roadies, bookers, the record pluggers, the record company workers and the many other smokers in The Business. They were always looking to buy really good dope and there were so many of them. Everyone wanted a piece of it and were prepared to pay well for the best.

CHAPTER 29

Looks like we're in for nasty weather

As he was climbing the stairs to the flat Peter could hear his phone ringing. He unlocked the door and picked up the receiver and heard:

"Where the fuck have you been? I've been ringing all morning."

"Hello Malcolm. And what can I do for you on this very rainy Thursday?"

"What can you do? I'll tell you what you can do. You can get yourself up here right now. That's what you can do."

"You appear to be mistaking me for someone who actually works for you, Malcolm."

"Oh for Heavens sake just get up here. It's a total disaster. A huge storm blew in last night and the whole site has been flattened. The stage went first, then the Big Top closely followed by all the smaller tents, most of the concession stalls and then all the loos blew over. Anyone camping lost their tents, which are now floating somewhere in the North Sea, and the only thing that is still in pristine condition is the security fence. The whole site has turned into a sea of mud and as the punters arrive they churn it up even more. Will you stop laughing? I'm not joking, the whole site has been devastated."

Peter was laughing so much he had tears in his eyes and could hardly speak.

"You make it sound so inviting, Malcolm. I was going to come up tomorrow morning with Chris but now I think I'll give it a miss. I really do have an important job I should be doing on Saturday."

"No hang on. Just come up tomorrow and back me up. I'm getting a lot of flak here and I need some help."

"Why would you be the one getting stick for the site being devastated? It was them that put the whole shonky show together."

"Just get up here, please."

"Alright I'll come up but I want you to remember that I am not working for the company any more. No one is going to be telling me to go and fetch anything for them. I don't work for you anymore and I don't owe anyone any favours. Understood?"

"I understand and appreciate you coming up. Come to the headquarters and find me tomorrow."

"I will do that. Oh, by the way. Did all the caravans I ordered survive the storm?"

"Yes they are all alright I believe. Why are you asking?"

"No reason. Just that it was my last contribution to the festival and I hoped they weren't damaged. Has it stopped raining yet?"

"No but it isn't raining as hard and the wind is dying down. The Production Managers are having hysterics trying to think of ways to put a sticking plaster on the damage. I'll see you tomorrow then."

"Ok see you tomorrow."

He hung up the phone and could not believe what he had just heard. The stage and the whole site flattened. Even allowing for Malcolm's ability to exaggerate it still sounded like it was a disaster. But every cloud has a silver lining. The caravans were undamaged so he had somewhere to stay. Now he really wanted to stay in London and help unload

Michael's Land Rover. His current interest in the festival was only a vague wish to see it fail and he now didn't need to see it first hand. Why had he listened to Malcolm and agreed to go up there? He would have to keep his head down and not get involved.

The alarm clock went off early the next day as he had to get to Sloane Square to pick up the food from the deli and then meet Chris at ten o'clock. Chris was a professional driver and was always on time so Peter put on his ratty old Barbour jacket and strapped a pair of wellies to his bag and headed off to the Tube station.

The box of food was waiting for him at the deli and he settled up and carried everything back to the Sloane Square Tube station. Chris was waiting in his car at the kerb and they put the box in the massive boot.

"You do look quite the country squire in that tatty old jacket. I must say," Chris said as he slammed the boot shut.

"Yes. Well, I got a phone call from Malcolm yesterday and apparently the site has been flattened and it's still pissing down."

"That's what I heard as well. It was fine when I left there on Wednesday afternoon. I heard that a mini-hurricane blew through and not much apart from the fence survived. Let's go and see what is happening up there."

They set off on the long arduous journey to Lincolnshire that got wetter and wetter the nearer they got to their destination.

By the time they were about five miles away all they started to see was wet and bedraggled festival goers walking beside the road carrying all their stuff on their backs. Most of them looked like they were drenched and miserable. All kinds of plastic protection had been improvised from black binbags to clear polythene sheets wrapped around them to try to avoid the driving rain. Some had wrapped supermarket bags around their feet and some of the crazier ones just embraced the rain. The closer the car got to the site the more people were walking by the road. A large number of people were actually walking away from the festival having been beaten by the atrocity of the cold English springtime weather and were waving their passouts for sale. Everyone looked like a refugee whose home had been flattened by a typhoon and they were making their way to safety with what belongings they could save on their backs. It soon became obvious that where they were heading didn't really offer any protection. Chris pulled up to the Artists' Gate and waved to the two men who were huddling under a large piece of polythene. He wound down the window and greeted them.

"Alright Danny? Danny Junior? Wet enough for you?"

"Fuck off Chris. This isn't even funny. We are only doing this as a favour for Stanley."

Peter waved his pass at the two Dannys and they were let into what essentially looked like a Haitian Hurricane Refugee Camp without the sun.

"What the hell is going on here?" Peter said.

"This is not going to dry up for days, even if it stops raining now. I'll try to get us close to the caravans if I can get through the mud"

"How do you know where the caravans are and who are those two heavies on the gate?" Peter asked.

"I've been up and down to the site all week, ferrying people up and down. My firm got roped into hauling a lot of the caravans up here and I brought some up and luckily managed to sort out a nice one for me to use. The whole site is filled up with old East End villains who are staying in the caravans. They are all friends of Stanley and are supposedly doing the security but are just getting drunk, partying and trashing the caravans. There's also 700 policemen and other people recruited by Barry and Michael. I'm assuming you've got a van sorted as there was a big one with a 'Danger Gas' sign on it. It does look like a beauty."

"Is there anything that gets past you, Chris?"

"Not much. That's my van over there so if you want to go back on Sunday call in or leave a note. I am leaving just after 12. There you go… I assume this beauty is yours."

"Wow! Look at that. They've done me proud." He climbed out of the car and retrieved the keys from the gas bottle container. Pulling his things out of the boot he opened his holdall and grabbed a bottle which he gave to Chris, saying, "Thanks Mate, I'll see you on Sunday. I've nearly had enough of this already. If you want a bit of Thai grass come and ask me. Thanks again."

"Wow this isn't just a bottle of wine, is it? Thanks a lot, I do like a nice bottle of wine. I will enjoy this. See you around." Off he went slipping and sliding the large car through the liquid mud.

Peter then saw a Land Rover parked just down from his van. The sign on the window said 'Broken Down. To Be Collected'. Peter ripped off the sign and found the keys under the driver's seat and they went into his pocket. Sorted, he thought and went back through the rain to his caravan. His belongings were on the step and he opened the door with the key. Removing his muddy boots and tucking them away he entered the caravan. They really had done him proud. The van was a deluxe model with a large separate bedroom and on inspection had been left with more than the essentials for a weekend stay. They had gone the extra mile and the sheets were crisp and the towels were plentiful and newly laundered. Pots and pans, crockery, glasses, corkscrew, candles and even milk, butter, bread and a bottle of wine all neatly stored in the cupboards. All he had to do was light the fridge and put his food away.

A note on the table said 'Check Freezer Before Use' so Peter opened up the little door inside the fridge. Lying inside was an envelope and when he opened it he saw it was full of money. What a result. They were as good as their word and had given him a finder's fee. He quickly counted it and discovered it was £750. Result!! That was a lot of caravans. At least someone appreciated his value.

He wasn't yet ready to go off and see what was happening in the festival so he unpacked his box of food into the fridge and his clothes into the drawers in the bedroom after lighting the gas fire. He replaced the stash of dope with the bundle of cash in the inside pocket in his bag and rolled a one skin neat grass joint and sat at the table considering his options. 'Jeez this grass is good'. He thought that every time he smoked it. The next shipment must be on its way now and he could make at least £5000 even if he just knocked it straight out in one hit. If he and Michael bought it together they could make so much more, maybe nearly double that, also it was worth looking into the much more profitable possibilities of selling to the music business. It would be perfect for them. Anyway it was now time to go and look at what was going on around the site. Dressed for the weather, he climbed into the Land Rover and fired up the engine. The usual cloud of black smoke belched out of the exhaust then faded away. It sounded good and putting it into four wheel drive he set off over the ground that was so soft and muddy even the little Land Rover was having trouble getting through, so Peter picked his route carefully. He found himself approaching the rear of the stage and could not believe what he saw. The original stage had been blown over and the roof had been scattered around like giant pieces of confetti. The structure had been hastily rebuilt out of scaffold poles and covered in heavy duty polythene sheets. The roof was being held suspended by, of all things, a crane.

"For the love of Jesus," as Bruce would have said. "Couldn't you think of a more shonky way to fix it?" It was unbelievable. Whoever thought that was acceptable for a festival stage in this kind of weather? Hanging the roof from a crane. How on earth did that get past the safety regulations. It didn't appear to offer any protection from the wind and rain but some hardy musicians appeared to be playing on it.

Peter immediately thought of the band called Stone the Crows who had been booked to play. Their lead guitarist was called Les Harvey and was the brother of The Sensational Alex Harvey. Unfortunately two weeks previously Les had been electrocuted while playing on stage, and had died. Several famous guitarists offered to stand in for him for this gig but when they saw how dangerous the conditions were, they dropped out. When Steve Howe, the guitarist from Yes, offered to play the odds of him completing the set alive in these conditions must have been pretty short in the back-stage sweepstake. However, more by luck than judgement nobody died at the festival.

Driving on, Peter was aware of the total destruction to be seen around the site. Malcolm wasn't exaggerating, the whole site had been totally flattened and a half-hearted effort had been made to rebuild some of it. Many of the demolished structures were left just lying around as they were too far gone to repair. Also there didn't appear to be too many people to be seen around. They must be sheltering from the weather or maybe no one had bothered to turn up. The rain was still falling and the Desolation Row look continued everywhere.

At the start of the festival the farmer had a large hay-stack made from bales stacked carefully on top of each other. Some clever soul realised the wonderful insulating properties of hay and started removing a few bales to build a little shelter to escape the elements. Obviously this was spotted by others who thought it was a great idea and in half a day the whole haystack had completely disappeared and a shantytown, with all kinds of weird and wonderful designs of hay huts, appeared in the shadow of the ex-hay-stack. Some looked like the Maasai huts seen in Africa but had the advantage of being waterproof. Some had polythene sheets flapping wildly in the wind and Peter was amazed at the ingenuity and skill of these hay builders and hoped they managed to at least get a comfortable and dry shelter. These improvised buildings also added to the disaster zone look of the site, he thought as he slowly drove through them. It was proving too difficult to get round the site without bogging the Land Rover down in the gloopy mud and he decided to drive down the metal emergency road and go and see Malcolm.

The festival headquarters, which appeared to be totally untroubled by the storm, was housed in the farmhouse and Peter showed his pass to the security guys who were guarding the gate. They waved him through and he let himself into the house. Someone pointed him in the direction of a downstairs room, when he asked where Malcolm was, and he walked in to find him sitting by a coal fire in a comfortable armchair with a glass of whiskey in his hand.

"Looks like I got here just in time," Peter said, helping himself to a large shot of Laphroaig from the bottle on the table.

"No, you are two days late. There is nothing left for you to do now. The whole site has been flattened and it isn't possible to put it all back up in time. Those winds were in excess of 100 miles an hour and just took everything away."

"I can see that. I was particularly impressed with the repairs done to the stage. That crane holding up the roof really looks the part."

"Don't talk about the stage. That idea was thought up by Barry and Michael and they think it is a brilliant off-the-cuff repair," Malcolm said.

"Well it doesn't look too brilliant to me. The rain is blowing onto the stage which is full of electrical equipment and that cannot be a good idea. This may turn out to be the Les Harvey Memorial Festival if anyone else gets electrocuted. The only thing that could make this worse is Jeremy Beadle's high dive tank, full of water, exploding in front of the stage. Remember how we laughed at his misfortune?"

"I do, I do. But mud is mud whether it's black or brown," Malcolm mused.

"Right then. I'll have that wise saying carved on your gravestone, shall I? Anyway I've got more bad news for you. There are hundreds of waterlogged kids, who have had enough and given up, walking back to the train station," Peter told him.

"I know that and as long as they have already bought their tickets I don't really care."

"Well there might be a problem because they are either selling their tickets, or giving them away, to the people who are on their way coming to the festival. There also appear to be a lot of passouts changing hands for money. Whatever happens their money is not going to be paid into the festival coffers."

"Sweet Jesus, how many more things are going to happen before we can start to make a little money?" Malcolm said, pouring another large shot of whiskey for himself. "If it goes on like this there won't even be 50,000 people here. With the publicity Deeley and Spikings have been giving to the television people about this festival everyone is now so interested in seeing it fail."

"That is not the problem though. Barry and Michael are already looking for a way to avoid being blamed in any way for anything that has gone wrong with this festival. The list is long and everyone but them is responsible for the failure. You are partially at fault as am I and they are entirely blameless."

"That is exactly what I predicted in that club in Soho. I couldn't care less what those tossers say as there is nothing with my name on it. Maybe it would have been better for them if they hadn't made so sure of that while they were going for glory. Anyway I can only imagine 'The Teflon Twins' will have already worked out their escape plan. Are you sure they can't put it all on you?"

"No chance. I have made sure I am in no way implicated in the failings of this festival and have had several discussions with the Money Men. Don't worry about us getting any of the flak. Anyway I want you to do me a small favour, if you wouldn't mind?" And without waiting to see if he did mind, Malcolm continued:

"Would you take this crate of beer to the guys who are looking after the Artists' Gate? They are both called Danny Holland and are father and son. They are stuck on that gate all weekend and won't take a break, as they promised Stanley they would make sure nobody got through without a pass, and they are taking the job really seriously. You don't have to do it right now but just pop down to see that they are alright, some time, would you? I would go but I can't get through all that mud. Danny senior is an old school East End 'Hard Man' and is a great character and 100% reliable and honest. He wouldn't steal a penny from Stanley, and his son Danny Junior is just the same. The whole site is filled with old villains who are just here to party and get drunk at Stanley's expense. They all love him! It's so weird that Stanley's Hard Man character in a few films has turned him into the big friend of the real villains from the East End. They are really taking advantage of his hospitality and are the only people here who are really getting the full enjoyment from the festival. It's all one huge drunken party for them!"

Peter took the crate of beer and promised he would give it to the Dannys but said it might not be tonight. He left before Malcolm could come up with any more little jobs for him and before he found out about the Land Rover. If he knew about that, Peter would have to drive him around the site all day and night. So it would have to be his little secret.

CHAPTER 30

Wouldn't it be nice if they were all California girls?

Peter left the festival headquarters carrying the crate of beer hoping he didn't bump into Deeley and Spikings as they would be sure to try to find something for him to do. The Land Rover's wheels looked as though they had already sunk deep into the soft ground and Peter opened up the rear window flap in the khaki canvas cover at the back and shoved the crate onto the floor and worked out the best way to get back to his caravan without getting bogged down. He would see the Danny boys later.

Even the Land Rover was having difficulty with the conditions on site and he certainly didn't want to be asking for a tow out of the mud. The rain was still falling, but thankfully not as hard as before, as he drove off with the four wheel drive still engaged. He decided to go back down the safety road. He had an 'All Areas' pass after all, and it was the only road on the site that was not under a foot of mud. When the road finished he was back in the mud and started to head for the area behind the stage and he found himself driving back through the collection of straw shelters. Taking great care not to slide into the huts he reduced his speed to walking pace. Just then he could see in front of him a neatly made shelter and coming out of the straw was a striking looking girl who looked amazingly free of mud and hay considering her accommodation. She spotted Peter in the Land Rover and caught his eye. She looked tall. Almost as tall as he was, maybe. She also looked pretty. As Peter drove slowly towards her shack she walked out in front of him forcing him to stop. He slid to a halt and she went round to the passenger door, opened it and got in.

Her fair hair was curly and wild. Her eyes were light blue, she was tall and tanned and her accent was American. She was really pretty.

"Hi there. I'm so freaking cold I think I am going to freeze to death. Can I sit in here for a minute, enjoying your heater, and warming up a little? I can't believe the weather in this country. I was told it was bad but I didn't think it was going to be this bad. My name is Sky and I have come all the way from California to sit in this shitpit, and I am pleased to meet you."

"I am pleased to meet you too, Sky. I'm Peter and I'm afraid the heater on this motor doesn't really give out a lot of heat. I think it's just for show."

"I don't really care just as long as I can get out of the rain and cold for a while. So what do you do that gives you the right to drive around the site in a Willy's Jeep wearing a laminated pass?"

"I'm not really doing anything at the moment." He said truthfully. "I kind of helped to get the festival started a few months ago but I don't really work on it anymore."

"What did you do to get the festival started then?"

"Well I helped to stop the Government from legislating to put an end to all festivals, for one thing."

"So you are a lawyer then."

"No I'm not a lawyer."

"What did you do before you worked on the festival?"

"That's an easy one. I was a shower salesman."

"How many showers did you sell?"

"I nearly sold one but they cancelled and bought a Dolphin 'Shitey' Shower."

"You Brits are so funny. You make me laugh but I really don't understand what you are saying. But the way you speak is so sexy. I could listen to you all day."

"Are you here with anyone?" Peter asked her.

"Yes. My friend Patti is inside there snuggled in her sleeping bag trying to get warm. Why do you ask?"

"Well, it's just that I have got a caravan over there with gas fires and a shower if you wanted to take a hot shower."

" Oh my God. I think you have just saved my life. Have you got any food there?"

"Yes I've got some food there."

"Ok show me some ID." He showed her his 'All Areas' pass and she said, "Alright Mister Peter Whitehead I am going to tell Patti that I am going to visit your caravan and if I don't come back, to call the Feds."

"That is a good idea but we don't have any Feds here. We only have Bobbies."

"Then I will get her to call the Bobbies, but it doesn't sound quite so threatening as calling the Feds."

"That doesn't matter as nobody is going to be 'Picked up by the Fuzz'."

She gave him a quizzical look and got out of the motor and ducked back into the straw hut. After a few minutes she reappeared clutching a small leather holdall with another girl in tow.

She introduced Patti and told her she was going off with Peter for a while and would catch up with her back here at lunchtime tomorrow.

Peter realised the implications of that and felt very lucky to have been chosen by Sky the way he had.

She threw her bag on the seat between them and said, "That bag is very important, we really don't want to lose it."

"Then we must make sure we don't. It'll be safe in my van."

"Does having a caravan make you Trailer Trash?"

"It can do. Is that what you would like me to be?"

"I don't know. It might be fun for a while."

Soon they arrived back at the caravan and he parked right next to the door so they didn't have to walk far and get too muddy.

"This sure is a rinky-dink little trailer you have here."

"Is that a good thing? I don't really understand American properly," he joked.

"Hell yes it's a good thang," she said in a Southern drawl and they were laughing as they went into the relatively warm caravan. He lit the gas fires as she stashed their muddy boots away and soon it was warm and cosy.

They sat on the naff pink nylon velvet covered banquettes at the table and Peter asked if she liked wine and she answered, "Do I like wine? I've lived most of my life on a Winery in the Napa Valley. That is the home of the very best wine in America. My dad taught me all about wine from a very young age. I've visited most of the vineyards in Napa. Of course I like wine."

"That's good. I'll open up this, then." Gently easing the corkscrew into the cork he carefully pulled it out so he didn't break off any into the wine.

"Let me see what you are opening there in that dinky little bottle. Oh Jesus! Is that for real? Is that really a Margaux '62? Of course I've heard of Margaux, who hasn't, but I have never tried it and have always wanted to. You freaking British are so understated. An American would have been waving the bottle around shouting out 'It's a Margaux. Look at my Margaux!' and you just ask me if I like wine. I love that about you so much."

"Well I am going to open another one as well, cos they're

only half bottles, and they can both breathe and we won't have to wait for the second one."

"You sure are full of surprises, Peter Whitehead. Especially for a Brit."

"That's good then, isn't it? Now, I guess that as you come from California you like to smoke grass?"

"Yes I do like to smoke grass. Don't tell me you have got the English Home Grown equivalent of Margaux in grass form. Like some Maui Wowee."

"Sorry I don't know what that is but it sounds good. No, I've got some grass from Thailand that comes tied to a bamboo skewer that we call Thai Sticks. Look, it's not bad."

"If you say it's not bad I suppose that means it must be terrific. What with the way you describe things."

She sniffed the grass and said,

"It smells good. I can't wait to try it."

Peter was wrapping some neat grass in a single paper and when Sky saw that she exclaimed: "This is the first time since I got to England that anyone has not mixed tobacco into their joints. I hate tobacco and can't bear to smoke it. All I have smoked here is brownish dusty stuff mixed with tobacco that tastes like shit and doesn't do anything for you. Did you learn that in America?"

"No, I've never been to America. I really want to go as it all sounds so exciting and different." He lit the neat grass spliff and took a toke and passed it over. She inhaled deeply, didn't cough, smiled and waited to see what happened. She had smoked a lot of grass and immediately knew this was good.

"Another surprise. This is really good. Did you say it came from Thailand? I don't even know where Thailand is, and I didn't know they grew Ace grass there. Do you get much of it here?"

"No not much but I have got access to a little bit."

"I knew it! I freaking knew it! You're a dealer, aren't you?

You look like a dealer and you act like one too. I bet you do a bit of smuggling too."

"Well I do deal a bit and I know some smugglers as well but I don't do a lot."

"Yeah, yeah, Mr Understatement. Wow this shit is really good, are you sure it doesn't come from California?"

"Ha Ha. I didn't know you grew grass in California."

"Yeah right. If you ever come over I'll take you to where they grow some of the finest sensimilla you will ever smoke."

"I'll take you up on that. Now do you want to try the wine?"

He found a couple of glasses and poured out two small tumblers of wine and they warmed it slightly in their hands. They sniffed the bouquet and anticipated the taste. They took a sip and it was as wonderful as they were expecting. Full bodied, rich, fruity, aged, long on the tongue and just gorgeous. She laughed with pleasure and said that it was the finest wine she had ever tasted and thanked him for sharing it with her.

They were sitting on opposite sides of the table listening to the rain hammering on the tin roof making it feel particularly snug inside. Peter couldn't read what it said on her tee shirt as she was wearing a fringed suede jacket that covered some of the writing.

"What does it say on your tee shirt?" he asked.

She laughed and said, "Let me show you."

She pulled the jacket off and revealed the writing. What she also revealed was a spectacular pair of breasts that looked like they were straining to escape from the flimsy fabric. Peter read the words written across her chest.

'Dear Lord Please Buy Me a Mercedes Benz.' He could hardly read the words as he was so distracted and Sky was fully aware of the effect her large breasts were having on him.

"Do you like my tee shirt?" she asked playfully.

"I don't think I have ever seen anything like it before."

"It's a bit of a joke really. It's from a Janis Joplin song. She's begging for a Mercedes but I have really got one. My daddy is an orthodontist with a big practice in Napa so he's loaded. He asked me and my sister what cars we wanted and I asked for a Mercedes 190 SL and he bought me a bright red one. Look here's a photo of me in it."

She dug inside her bag and produced a picture of her smiling at the camera from the driving seat of a vintage bright red Mercedes 190 SL soft top with a sunny backdrop of vineyards disappearing into the hills.

"I love driving through the Valley with the top down and the sun shining through the vineyards. You would love it there. I also really like the tee shirt because the material is thin and it makes my breasts look bigger. It is also perfect for doing a 'Titty Drop'. Do you want to see one?"

"I don't know what a 'Titty Drop' is, but I think I would love to see one."

She stood up in front of the table and smiled at him. She gripped the hem of her tee shirt and with one slow movement she pulled it taut with both hands and inched it up over her tanned, slim stomach. When it reached just under her breasts she snagged the material so it lifted them up, then she set them free from the material, allowing them to drop back down. It was mesmerising for Peter as he got his first sight of those large, firm breasts tumbling out of the fabric and settling back in place with just one small bounce. She stood there, tee shirt raised, proudly displaying those incredible breasts, smiled a thousand watt smile and asked, "You like?"

He moaned theatrically and then said, "Oh my God, I love. That is the sexiest thing I've ever seen. Most girls over here would not have the bottle to do that, even if they could. Are all the girls like you in California?"

"Baby. You ain't seen nothing yet." And with a little shimmy she pulled the shirt back down. "I'd like to take a shower now, if that's alright. I have really missed taking a shower. Have you got plenty of hot water and towels here?"

"Yes, there's as much hot water as you want, fresh towels on the bed and everything you need in the tiny bathroom. I think there is a clean tee shirt on my bed if you want it. I will make us a bit of lunch so you can take as long as you want. The wine should have properly breathed by the time you have finished your shower and hopefully it will taste even better."

"You keep thinking about my 'Titty Drop' while I take a shower and I have got a couple of surprises for you later on."

"I can't wait."

She put her hands behind his neck and kissed him languidly and then disappeared into the bathroom and Peter started getting some lunch out of the fridge while unsuccessfully trying to calm down a raging stiffy. He chose the asparagus quiche and some stinky cheese, as Susan had called it, with a bit of salad and coleslaw. The crusty French loaf was sliced into chunks and he decided they could eat the steak later if she was going to stay, and it certainly looked like that was going to happen. With the food on the table and happy showering sounds coming from the bathroom he took a little sip of the wine and rolled another little neat grass joint. He heard her come out of the bathroom and call from the bedroom,

"Can I borrow this white tee shirt?"

"Yes of course you can. It should fit you fine."

Then she was back wearing his white tee shirt that was slightly damp and that did very little to disguise her magnificent breasts, she was also wearing her jeans and no socks. A white towel was swirled around her wet hair in the sexy, casual way that women do and men find impossible. As she was almost as tall as him the tee shirt fitted her perfectly and she looked so incredibly sexy.

"I must say that the tee shirt looks much better on you. Here I've rolled a joint and got us some lunch. Are you hungry?"

"I am absolutely starving. I haven't had a decent meal since I left London, and that wasn't anything special. Do you have something nice?"

"I think so. I went with a friend to a really fancy deli in Chelsea and she helped me choose some bits and pieces to bring here to go with the wine. I hope you like it."

"Well I must say it looks delicious. Is she your girlfriend?"

"No she is not. She is way out of my class but she is a good friend."

"You shouldn't put yourself down, you know, as I think you are pretty special, and I've only just met you."

They sat and smoked the joint which made them both really hungry. Sipping the wine and eating the lovely food made them feel miles away from the devastation going on outside the caravan. It was so warm, dry and comfortable in there.

"So do you have to do any work now you are here?" she asked, between chewing hungrily on a piece of quiche.

"Not really. I do have to deliver a case of beer to some gangsters who are running the Artists' Gate, but apart from that I don't have anything to do."

"That's good. So you have plenty of free time then?"

"Yes I do but I wasn't really very keen to come up here. I am not interested in any of the Bands. The only one I am remotely interested in is The Beach Boys. I used to really love them in the sixties but I am not as keen on them now as I was a few years ago. I don't think I can be bothered to listen to their music in the mud and rain. That doesn't really work for me."

"Yes I do know what you mean. I imagined this was going to be like Monterey, not like mud wrestling. Everyone tried to warn me but I had no idea. I also never imagined I would be experiencing the delights you are offering me here. This food is awesome. It's the best I've eaten since I left San Francisco and it really reminds me of eating at Doidge's cafe. Your grass is amazing and the wine is the Best Ever. I'm so glad I flagged you down when I did. I have to admit that I noticed you driving past on your way out and was hoping I could catch you coming back." She looked at him, laughed and said, "We are going to have such a ball!!"

"I'm muddy and wet as well so I am going to take a shower and change into something dry," Peter said heading for the bathroom. "Make yourself at home."

He had a quick shower and put on a clean tee shirt and jeans and went back to see what Sky was doing. She was reaching into her 'important bag' and unpicking some stitching in the lining.

"I've got something really amazing for you, in here. I've been saving it for a special occasion and this is as special as it gets. Come over here and take a look at this." She poked her fingers inside the lining and came out with a small envelope made from folded white paper and a crisp brand new $100 bill.

"This is my emergency pack," she quipped.

She reached over and started kissing him softly at first and then more passionately.

"Jesus you make me so horny," she whispered in his ear. "You won't believe what I've got in store for you."

"Well don't keep me in suspense for too long," he said.

She opened the paper packet and inside was a pile of tiny white powdery rocks. "Have you ever snorted cocaine before?" she asked him.

"No. But I have heard a lot about it and have wanted to try it for ages but I haven't seen any over here yet."

"Then this will be my special treat for you. My friend went to Bolivia to buy some grass and brought back an ounce of pure cocaine and let me have a few grams. I smuggled a couple of grams through with me just in case, and I'm so glad I did. This will blow your mind. It's so pure. It is not usually possible to get pure coke before it has been stepped on, and then it's just not the same."

Sky got up and removed a mirror from the wall and wiped it clean with a tissue. She then put the corner of a gold American Express card into the packet, scooped a few rocks out and tapped it onto the mirror. She removed the silver signet ring from his finger and used it like a pestle to crush the tiny rocks into powder, finishing off the process with the edge of the card. When the rocks had been fully turned into a fine powder, she used the card to make four large lines on the mirror. Taking the crisp $100 bill she rolled a tight neat tube and sniffed up a line into each nostril.

"That's how you do it." And she passed him the note.

It was at this point that Pandora's Box was well and truly opened for good or bad. Mostly good, then really bad. It would be another nine years before the lid was firmly slammed shut again.

He snorted the powder and immediately felt a rush in his brain. It seemed to envelop him in a white light and everything looked clear and bright. It was the best feeling ever and also he started to feel hornier than he had ever felt before. It was outrageous how he was feeling and he looked at Sky who was smiling at him.

"Do you feel it as well?" she asked.

"Oh… My… God. What is happening?" It felt so good.

"I'll show you what is happening and you will not believe it."

She undid her jeans and slipped them off and stood there

wearing only his tee shirt. Smiling at him she pulled the shirt over her head and stood before him totally naked. The coke was affecting his whole body, concentrating his mind, and his dick felt like a rock. Her breasts were still as incredible as before. Large and firm and luscious but she had another surprise for him.

She was standing there proudly displaying her freshly shaved pussy. Apart from a narrow strip of trimmed hair it was completely bare. Peter thought it was amazing. It seemed like she had undressed for him, and then undressed some more.

"So what do you think? Is it too much for you? It's the latest buzz in California and I have only just had it done. Do you like it?"

"I can't believe it. It is fantastic and looks like a beautiful ripe fig and I just can't wait to eat it," he said, hardly believing the words that were tumbling out of his mouth. He seemed to have lost all of his inhibitions and was totally fired up on the coke.

"That is why I did it. Apparently it is just perfect for that. But first I want to have a look at you."

Peter stood up and took off his tee shirt. Not as impressive as Sky. He undid the buttons on his jeans and slid them down releasing his erection which sprang up eagerly. Now he felt on equal terms. All the blood in his body seemed to have rushed to his dick and it felt harder, and bigger than it had ever been before.

"Holy Mother of God," Sky said, "are all you Brits hung like that?"

"I think the coke has made it bigger," he answered.

"Well you don't need to take another line for a moment or two. That thing is plenty big enough for me," she said laughing with pleasure.

They stood there naked, kissing and exploring each

other's bodies, whispering into each other's ears, building the sexual tension to boiling point. Running his fingers softly down the line of curly short hair he tickled her gently and then stroked all around the soft shaved pussy thinking that this was the sexiest thing ever.

"Me first," she said and dropped to her knees and started to suck him like he had never been sucked before.

"How's that feel then?" she said.

"Like nothing I've ever felt before. Don't stop."

"Ok now watch this and see how you like it." Then she slowly took him in her mouth and then down her throat with the dangerous ease of a sword swallower as she swallowed him completely. With a slight gagging sound she pulled back and released him from her mouth and he was overwhelmed.

"That's what we call a 'Cheerleader's Special'!" she said beaming with pride.

"I love cheerleaders," he said as she resumed working on him. Had he not snorted some coke he would not have had so much self-control but he seemed to be able to contain himself to a much greater degree.

Not for much longer though and when he came it was unbelievably intense.

"I don't believe I have ever felt anything like that in my life," he confessed.

"Well thank you for coming," she said politely.

"Now let's go into the bedroom as I have something for you now."

While she was lying on the bed, he lay on top of her, kissed her, and then slid down and kissed her breasts and then very slowly slid his tongue down over her flat stomach until he felt the soft, narrow line of hair under his tongue. He gently nipped her with his teeth and continued down to her pussy. He had learnt about pleasing girls from his

Korean girlfriend Yasuko and was delighted to show Sky his newly acquired skills. Essentially the best way, he had been advised, was to get onto the clit with your tongue and stay on it until you hear cries of surrender. With cocaine fuelled determination Peter used his skills and soon enough he could feel her pleasure levels rising. His tongue was turbo charged by the coke and relentless. He pinned her down and continued teasing her. Now she was wild and she was becoming very vocal. It had never felt this good for him before and he was seriously fired up. Sky was totally helpless and just about to have a climactic orgasm and was shouting obscenities and 'Yes, Yes, Yes', and then she seemed to erupt from deep within her body. Finally she begged him to stop and when he looked up he saw her skin was covered with a rosy glow and there was a fine sheen of sweat, all over her body.

"Where on earth did you learn to do that?" she asked him.

"Oh, I studied at The University of South Korea. I got a first-class degree in Oragasmi. My teacher said I passed with flying colours but the coke certainly puts a different perspective on things."

"I don't know when to believe you but from now on I will call you 'Beaujolais'."

"Why is that, then?" he asked, already knowing the joke.

"Because," she answered with a New Orleans drawl, "ain't Beaujolais some kind of fancy 'likker'?"

They lay exhausted on the bed for a while drinking some wine and smoking another joint still feeling the buzz from the coke. She noticed he had recovered enough to get a hard on so she rolled him onto his back then climbed on top of him and he slid inside her. He couldn't believe how joyful making love was with her. She was completely unembar-rassed and uninhibited unlike most of the English girls he had slept with and he found himself constantly forcing himself to abandon all the hang ups he had been saddled with while he was growing up in the repressed 1960s in England and remember what Yasuko had shown him. He lay back and enjoyed watching the sight of her breasts bouncing as she rode up and down on him. They rolled all over the bed and made love in all kinds of ways and finally when she came, she came hard and he followed just after. They both laughed with pleasure and said that it had never felt that good before and they lay together just feeling easy with each other. They were stoned, slightly drunk and coked up all at the same time and they both agreed that cocaine really was something else!

"Mr Freaking Understated! If you ever get to California you be sure to look me up. I know that the girls there would love you and your subtle charms."

"It is high on my list of things to do but I don't think I will be able to go to the States for a few years yet. As soon as I can, I want to visit San Francisco. I've heard so much about it and I'd love to visit for a while."

"Here is my dad's Number, he will always know where I am." She said writing it down on a scrap of paper and passing it to him. "Even if you don't want to get it on with me when you arrive there, promise me you will give me a ring and I'll show you around. I know some great places and some of my really cool friends are dealers. They would love you."

"Well if I ever get over there I promise I will find you and if you are married with kids, just let me know and we can all have brunch or something."

"Yeah right. Like that will happen. But I do mean it. Look me up."

"I promise I will. Scout's honour."

Sky got out of bed and went to take a shower leaving

Peter lying in the bed wondering what had just happened to him. He thought about getting something to eat but found he didn't appear to have any appetite for food so he got up and opened a bottle of beer he had nicked from the crate he was giving to Danny. Sky came back dressed in his tee shirt and her jeans and he gave her the bottle and also went off to take a shower. When he came back he opened another bottle for himself and they sat at the table and she asked him where he lived.

"I share a cheesy flat in London above a really busy Kentucky Fried Chicken takeaway, with one other bloke. It's in a place called Shepherd's Bush. I really like living there but it's not at all fancy, it just suits me at the moment. When the wind blows in the right direction you can smell the delicious aroma of fried chicken fat, so it's not all bad."

"I just don't know when to believe you or when you are winding me up. It seems so easy for you to make fun of me."

"I'm not making fun of you, I am making fun of me, actually. So tell me about you. Where do you live?"

"Oh it's a bit boring, you know. I have just moved back in with my folks in Napa, after a miserable, failed relationship in San Francisco. My dad is loaded and lives in a huge house on a huge Winery in Napa Valley. He's ok and he gives me and my sister loads of money and stuff. He just bought us both a car. I got a Mercedes, as I told you, and my sister asked for a Porsche. She is so straight and when he gave it to her, he had put a personalised number plate on it. It read 'JUGS' and she went completely mental. My dad thought it was hilarious because she has got huge tits. You know, really big. Much bigger than mine which aren't small, as you may have noticed, but she is so embarrassed by them and won't even let anyone touch them or have any fun with them.

"Anyway she made him take the plates off the car and re

register it but he kept them and stuck them on the garage wall at the back, to remind everyone of the joke as they drove in. I finished college a couple of years ago and never really learned much there, except for how to give a good blowjob. That is the most important subject at high school in California because it is the number one way for a girl to get ahead in America. Everyone learns how to do it well, when school is over, after cheerleaders' class."

"Well it sounds like the place to be if you are a young boy in California. Hanging around the cheerleaders offering them something to practice on."

"Do the girls in England give good blowjobs?" she asked him.

"Now that is a tricky question. It's not a subject that is discussed much over here. We are a little embarrassed to talk about sex at the moment and have only just started out on a bit of a sexual revolution. Girls feel a little more emancipated about themselves now, but the idea of sucking a dick is sometimes a little more than some of them can handle. Of course there are some girls who love it but a lot of them think it is a demeaning thing to do."

"How weird is that? I love doing it and I love what you did to me and can't wait to do it again," she said with a sparkle in her eye.

"Do you want us to take the motor and have a look at the festival and then we can come back and eat some steak? Unless you are a vegetarian of course."

"That sounds like a good idea. After all, I did make a huge effort to come to this godawful place to see some dreadful bands while sitting around in the freezing mud. And no I'm not a vegetarian. I like eating meat too much."

They put on their wet weather clothes and boots and jumped into the Land Rover and headed off towards the festival. Although Peter's pass got him access to anywhere on site he didn't want to use it to get backstage. He could have blagged Sky through with him but there was no one playing that night that he had any interest in seeing and he wasn't prepared to take the chance of being electrocuted. They drove alongside the stage, giving it a wide berth in case the crane fell over, and when they could see who was playing, he stopped and turned off the engine.

"That's Alexis Korner. He plays American Blues and has had a big influence on a lot of bands who are around at the moment. He particularly influenced Mick Jagger and Keith Richard who also like the Blues."

"Is he any good?" Sky asked.

"He's pretty good but I prefer to listen to the songs played by the original Blues men. Lightning Hopkins, Howling Wolf, Robert Johnson, Sonny Terry and Brownie McGhee and people like that are the ones I really like. I don't think cover versions have any authenticity."

They sat in the motor, sheltered from the rain, and listened to a couple of numbers from Alexis. His guitarist was good but the weather was pretty much destroying any atmosphere the band was creating.

"I want to try and find someone, who should be on site, if you don't mind," he said and she didn't mind so they set off towards the food stalls.

"I asked someone if they wanted to bring a food stall up here and I would like to know if they are alright."

The food area was in another part of the site and looked as if it had been pretty much flattened and had been rebuilt as well as possible because the owners were here to make money and had to get on with it. It did have the tattered, ramshackle air of the street food stalls in the markets in Marrakesh, which really was not such a bad look even if it was unintentional. Peter was looking for the Asterix stall and spotted it easily as it was a striped red and white affair that appeared to be in pristine condition. There were a few customers around it but it was quite early and Peter pulled up near the stall. They got out and walked over to where the owner Jean-Pierre was mixing up a huge bowl of batter. Peter felt a little nervous about being responsible for getting them involved in what had turned out to be such a disaster. Jean-Pierre looked up and recognised Peter.

"Hi there," he said, "it's good to see you again. What a storm we had. Most people got completely blown away."

"How come you have survived so well?" Peter asked.

"It was pure luck really. We were going to come up on Thursday in my old Citroen H van. You know, the large one with the corrugated sides, but we were so late getting loaded up and only just driven out of Chelsea before it broke down. By the time we had borrowed a Transit from my brother-in-law it was late so we started early this morning hoping we weren't going to be too late to get in. We arrived to find all the stallholders who had come early trying to rebuild their shredded stalls. We missed the worst of it and we set up our brand-new shiny stall. Lots of traders gave up and went home but we are doing really well considering the weather and a lack of people here yet."

"I'm so glad because I thought you would be pissed off with me for dragging you into this disaster."

"Au contraire," John Pierre said. "We have a distinct advantage here as a lot of the competition has left already and we paid nothing to get in here. Thanks to you.

"We look smarter than the other stalls and our food is quick and people like it. We are doing well as the thousands of people have to eat and I think this festival will be very good for us and I can only hope the weather will improve tomorrow. Would you like something to eat?"

Sky thanked him and said she wasn't at all hungry but said the pancakes looked delicious and Peter said he couldn't manage anything either so they had a glass of wine and then went off in the Land Rover.

"I am so pleased he isn't having a disaster," Peter said, "because it was me who persuaded him to come up here. Who could have known this was going to happen?"

"Well I'm sure he'll do well as he's got the smartest place on the block and that means a lot to some people. Those pancakes looked good too but the coke has completely ruined my appetite for now. I'm sure I'll get it back soon and I'm looking forward to eating steak later with some more of that lovely wine to wash it down. If you don't have anything more to do why don't we go back to your trailer. We can clearly hear the bands from there and it is so much warmer and more comfortable."

"That sounds like a plan!" he said and spun the Land Rover round and headed back to the caravan.

They drove past the stage where the crane was still valiantly holding up the roof of the stage for Rory Gallagher to try and play an acoustic set to a few thousand sodden people who were mostly hiding under sheets of polythene trying to ignore the weather. It certainly didn't make it easy to enjoy the music but Rory was giving it all he had and the crowd respected him for that. Normally he would be belting out a rocking electric guitar driven Bluesy set that would have had a greater impact on the crowd but to strap on a wet electric guitar while using a wet electric microphone standing on a wet stage in the driving rain was easily spotted as an elementary mistake by an old campaigner like Rory and he had to abandon his set.

The mud seemed to be getting deeper as the Land Rover was slip sliding its way back to the caravan and they did get stuck once in a large puddle but managed to reverse out throwing rooster tails of liquid mud everywhere. When they got back to the caravan they saw the Land Rover was completely covered in mud except for where the wipers had almost cleared two arcs on the windscreen.

"This is a nightmare." Sky said as they carefully entered the caravan, trying not to bring in any mud onto the carpets.

"I know," Peter replied. "I don't understand how anyone could stay here to listen to such a piss poor line up of bands in these appalling conditions. I do know for a fact that they have no chance of getting a refund, but why would they stay for four days in these conditions? I feel really guilty about having been involved in helping to perpetrate this fraud."

"Don't worry yourself. It's not your fault the weather turned so bad and you told me you kept saying the acts that had been booked weren't strong enough. You did your charitable duty by rescuing me from the mud and mire and I am entirely in your debt!"

"Well that's ok then, let's smoke some grass and eat a fine piece of steak," he said ironically, but it was lost on Sky as she was American. He opened another bottle of wine and let it breathe as he poured a glass from the one he had opened earlier. They sat at the table and she rolled a neat grass joint and said, "I am beginning to feel hungry again. The coke has worn off now so maybe we should eat something before we do another line. What do you think?"

"That is a great idea. I've got potato salad, green salad, coleslaw, mustard and French bread to go with the steak. We just need to fry the steak in a really hot pan for a couple of minutes and dinner is ready."

"That sounds great, let's smoke this dooby and then eat."

Sitting in the warm comfortable caravan made the festival not seem too bad, but Peter did wonder what he was doing there. He thought he should be back in London working and it would be more exciting helping to unload the 50 keys of dope with Michael but he managed to put that out of his mind. It would still be there when he got back and he was having the time of his life with this American chick.

"You know I think this grass gets better the more you smoke it. I never thought I would find anything this good over here. I think it makes me feel even more horny than usual. I know that all I can feel at the moment is the inside seams of my jeans rubbing on my shaved pussy. It feels so incredibly sexy. Every time I move it reminds me I am not wearing panties and my bare pussy is in a constant state of arousal. It feels amazing. Like I've got a constant itch that needs scratching, if you know what I mean?"

"Yes I do know what you mean. I can't stop thinking about it either. I have got a permanent hard on and I'm always thinking about you."

She leaned over the table, kissed him and slid her hand up his thigh and gripped the bulge in his jeans.

"Ain't dat da troof," she said and stood up to start frying the steaks. The pan was getting hot as he put out the salads, bread and mustard. He poured two large tumblers of wine as she seared both sides of the steak asking if he liked it rare.

"I like it as rare as possible and slightly charred on the outside, but anyway you can do it is fine with me."

"Well I think this is done now, so… whatever."

The steak was perfect and so were the salads which went well with the crusty French bread. The wine of course was sublime but there was only one thing on both of their minds as they ate the food. They both took their time enjoying the delicious anticipation and when they had finished eating Sky scooped the dishes away into the sink and picked up her bag and put it on the table.

"Do you want to do another line?" she asked.

"Well, it would be rude not to, wouldn't it?"

"I think you can be rude any time you like, Mr Beaujolais," as she scooped out some more of the magic dust onto the mirror. Before she put the packet away she tore a square of paper from her notebook and folded it in half diagonally. She then chose some of the larger rocks from her packet and put them inside the folded paper. Tucking the two opposite ends into each other she then folded the pointy bit at the top inside the gap at the bottom making a neat little envelope just like her original one.

"This is a present for you. I hope you enjoy it. Maybe you could snort it with your classy friend and then lick her into submission. I can assure you that she would never have felt anything like it before. You are a freaking 'one off' and it doesn't matter how classy or rich you are there is nothing better for a girl than a screaming orgasm. Well that is my humble opinion, anyway."

"Thank you for that present. It's very generous of you. You know I'm not sure how her boyfriend, my business partner, would feel about that idea. Not that I don't think it's a great one but there is too much for me to lose right now. I do know who I can share this with and I know she will love it."

"Good for you! But I do have to warn you this stuff is very moreish. I'm not bothered about giving you this small bit, but once you do it you want to keep on doing it and then it can become a big problem. It's not as addictive as heroin but it can be hard to stop doing. So be careful."

"I don't think that will be a problem, as I have said, I have never seen any coke in London yet. It won't be a problem. Thank you for your kind gift. I really appreciate it," Peter said, blissfully unaware and having no idea what highs and lows the future held in store for him and cocaine. "But it certainly is an amazing drug. You feel like you can do anything you want to, when you take it."

"Yeah. Bolivian Marching Powder. Right then. Here we go." And they both snorted the lines and felt the white light again.

Picking up his holdall he pulled out his stash and gave her five Thai Sticks that were in a polythene bag which she put in her bag.

"Oh they look so cute. I will really enjoy smoking that. Thanks."

They tumbled into bed and began the slow path to ecstasy, fearlessly riding the white-capped cocaine wave, until they had thoroughly exhausted themselves and they lay there entwined talking about anything and everything until the coke finally wore off and they fell asleep.

Peter couldn't believe it when he found himself back in Susan's living room and she was undressing for him until all she wore, bizarrely, was an antique Indian silver snake chain around her waist. He wondered how this had happened. He was scared Michael was going to come bursting in and catch them. He didn't care, it felt so good. Slowly the dream faded and he opened his eyes to see that it was Sky who he had woken up with. She saw he was awake and smiled and said, "You were fast asleep with a huge hard on and seemed to be dreaming about something nice. I couldn't resist. Did you have a good dream?"

"Not as good as how I woke up," he answered diplomatically.

"You are a liar because your dreams are usually so much wilder, but I don't care because you are with me now and that is all I want. It was so sweet when you called me 'Babe' in your sleep. I like that, it's so English."

She then asked if he had been to a festival before. He told her all about Green Lanes and how he took one to the Pilton Free Festival and how Gill had given him an unexpected farewell present driving back down the lanes.

"The weird thing about Gill's blowjob was that she never actually sucked when she did it."

"What do you mean 'didn't suck' isn't that the point of it? Didn't you say anything?"

"Well, no I didn't say anything because I thought it was cute and it felt good because she did everything else. If she wasn't actually sucking it lasted a lot longer and gave me a lot of pleasure. If that is how she chose to do it, I don't mind."

"Do you think she knew what she was doing?"

"I don't think she realised there was any more to it and I never told her. I guess someone will tell her one day but it did feel good at the time."

"Wow, you English are so weird!"

"Well we don't have the advantage of having cheerleaders over here so there are no lessons."

"No you don't but we don't have Green Lanes and they sound cool. Did you take a Green Lane to get here?" She asked.

"I don't know. Maybe I haven't got off the first Green Lane yet and this is still part of the same journey."

"Now that is really weird," she said as she wondered what Peter had meant.

"I am going to make us some eggs for breakfast. I am always hungry when I'm around you." With that, wearing his tee shirt which didn't quite cover her ass, he watched it as she sashayed out and she winked at him over her shoulder as she went through the door.

"There's some Scottish smoked salmon in the fridge if you want, to go with the eggs," he called out to her when he heard the rattle of pots and pans.

"Of course there is. I expect you caught it and smoked it yourself."

"Don't be silly, I've got a little man in Chelsea who does that for me."

It was getting on for eleven before they started to enjoy breakfast in bed. The salmon was lovely with the scrambled eggs and while they were drinking their coffee, Sky said,

"Much as I am enjoying getting fucked senseless, I do have to get back to see Patti. I need to let her know I haven't been kidnapped, so she doesn't call the Bobbies. I need to spend a little time with her. Not that I really want to, but we met up here and I can't leave her totally alone. Would you take me back to her for a little while? If you have something to do now, maybe you could come and get me later and we can pick up where we left off."

"That sounds like a great idea as I have got to go and see a couple of villains and give them a crate of beer for some reason. It's the only thing I have to do but we can go now and I will come and get you when I've finished."

Sky took her freshly washed clothes from over the gas fire and stuffed them into her bag laughing and saying, "I'm still not wearing any panties so by the time you get back to pick me up I should have a very big itch that needs scratching."

They were laughing about that as they drove the Land Rover through the gate and into the site. He didn't slow down in case he couldn't get out of the mud again and soon found the little cluster of hay huts.

"That's mine over there." Sky yelled over the noisy diesel engine so he pulled up to let her out. She leaned over and kissed him and said, "Make sure you come back and get me as we have hardly started yet and I will be so hot for you."

"I wouldn't want to miss that. I'll come back after I've seen the Dannys. If I miss you, just make your way over to the van. I'll leave the door unlocked for you and I won't be away for very long." He drove off watching her in the mirror as she ducked into the hay shack. What an amazing girl! He had never met anyone like her before. He couldn't wait to get back and see how hot she actually was.

CHAPTER 31

Altamont it ain't

Peter drove past the farmhouse headquarters towards the Artists' Gate and caught a glimpse of Michael and Barry frantically waving their arms in the air about something. He drove quickly on and arrived at the huge reinforced sheet metal Artists' Gate to find a little garden shed had been erected for the Gate Guardians who were both still sitting there fiercely controlling the access. He parked behind them and got out and retrieved the crate from the floor in the back. They spotted him as he walked over and both got up to see what was going on.

Little Danny Holland was about 60 years old and although he was quite short to say he looked hard was an understatement. He actually looked as though he had been carved out of a solid lump of oak. He was dressed immaculately for the country in a tweed check jacket and cap, shirt and tie, cavalry twill trousers and wellingtons which somehow made him appear even more menacing. Big Danny Holland, his son, was bizarrely dressed in the same outfit, however he was about six feet six inches tall and was built like the proverbial brick shithouse. Nobody in their right mind would want to cross either of them and they were both friendly as Peter handed over the crate of beer.

"I come bearing gifts from Malcolm," he said.

"Is that the little Scottish iron?" Big Danny asked.

"Yeah, that's right. My name is Peter and I used to work for him. He asked me to drop this off for you last night but I got a bit involved with something and couldn't get over here. Sorry about that."

"Don't you worry about that, son. This involvement didn't have anything to do with a young lady, did it?" Little Danny asked.

"Well I have to say yes it did. And I have to confess that I did give her one of your bottles of beer, I mean. I hope you don't mind?"

"Ha Ha, not at all. I hope that's not all you gave her. We did happen to run out of beer last night so this will do us nicely. So what do you do here, Peter?"

"Well apart from delivering beer around the site, not a lot really."

"Good boy," Little Danny said. "We didn't think it was going to be like this when Stanley asked us up here to look after this stupid gate. It's turned into a nightmare."

"You've turned it into a nightmare," Big Danny, his son interjected.

"Well you've got to do something to stop yourself from going mad. Haven't you?" Little Danny said, grinning.

"Well that is true but you do take it to the limit, Dad. Tell him what you did."

They knocked the tops off three bottles and sat on empty crates in the shed drinking as Little Danny started his story.

"Well, we was on this gate Thursday in the pissing rain and we was promised a shed to shelter us but it never came so we sat under a pissy piece of plastic all day, as you might remember. The weather got worse and we got frozen and wet and finally we were relieved about ten at night. All day kids had been trying to get in by offering me a quid to let them through. I told them I wasn't doing this for the money I was doing this as a favour for Stanley so fuck off and buy a ticket. We got back to our caravan and had a bit of dinner and a beer and passed out from the cold and wet. We started again in the morning and these musician blokes started to arrive by the afternoon. We had been told to make sure we only let in people who had passes. Weren't we Dan?"

"Oh yuss we was, dad."

"Some of them were O.K. and a few of them got a bit shitty with us and in the end we thought if they wanted to give us some stick we would have a bit of fun with them. Late in the afternoon this young Irish kiddy drives up and says he was Rolly Gallagher"

"No he said he was Rory Gallagher, Dad."

"I know but I liked to call him Rolly and he didn't mind. So he said he was late and was due to play on stage soon and could he come through. I said of course he could, just show me the paperwork. He said that he had it with him somewhere, but his car was an absolute tip and he didn't know where it was exactly. It was full of rubbish and guitars and he started rummaging around to try and find it and said that he was sorry but he couldn't exactly locate it."

Big Danny joined in: "He was such a nice feller, really polite and I felt a bit sorry for him."

"Yes he was a nice feller but he was blocking the gate for people to come through so we sent him back out again in his car to find his tickets."

"Isn't all this a one way system?" Peter asked.

"Yes it is. It's a six-mile circuit to get back and it took him about an hour and when he got back he had all the tickets and paperwork neatly folded in an envelope. We didn't even look at it. We just waved him through. He couldn't believe it and he stopped and asked us to look at it but we said that we knew he was Rolly Gallagher and to just go on in or he'd be late on stage. He was a good kid and didn't even swear at us. Well not much anyway."

"That was just the start," Big Danny said. "He's a lunatic when he gets like this. So tell him what happened next, Dad. "

"Yuss, well this bleedin' great Charabanc drives up to the gate full of what looks like 1950s teddy boys. I couldn't believe it, so when they open the door I climb in. They had a geezer in charge who had a clipboard of paperwork about a foot thick with everything immaculate and all in order and complete. I says 'Fuck me. What's this? A Sunday school outing?' and he says, as polite as you like, 'No we are Sha Na Na'. I told him that meant nothing to me and he told me they were a Doo Wop Band.

"'A do what? Band' I says."

"'No a Doo Wop Band', so I told him that was alright but I had to count the tickets. I started counting through them and it took me about four tries to get to the total he had written at the top, 43."

Big Danny was laughing at the memory and his Dad continued.

"Yes I know I could hardly keep a straight face but having counted the tickets I said I had to count the people to make sure there wasn't an extra body on the coach. I started counting them from the back and when I got to ten I said I was sorry but I had lost my place and I started again. This time I got to 15 and started again. I said it would help if they stood up when I counted them and off we went again with them bobbing up as I counted. This time I got to 19 before I lost count. Then I got them all to stand up and only sit down when I had counted them. This didn't work either but they happily did everything I said without complaint."

"It was so funny." Big Danny said, "They was bobbing up and down like 'Simon Says' and they didn't really get the hump at being treated like that."

"No but the joke was wearing a bit thin by then so I says that I wasn't going to make them get off the bus and count them back on as I had an idea of how many there were. He asks me how many is there and I say, 43. 'How do you know that,' he asks and I tell him that it's a 50-seater coach, as the sign over the driver says, with seven empty seats. He finally twigs and starts to laugh and the whole coach begins to get it and they all laugh as well so I jump off and we wave them through as they pulled faces at me through the windows."

Big Danny was laughing at the memory of it and had another swig from his bottle.

Little Danny said: "I swear I wouldn't be sitting in this bastard field if it was anybody else apart from Stanley who asked me. He is a diamond geezer but I don't give a toss for those other two. I just don't trust them."

Big Danny piped up: "Finish your story then Dad." So he continued.

"It went a bit quiet then and we was getting a bit bored until a whole load of kids drove up on some clapped out old motorbikes. They parked them right up next to the gates and a little feller, with what looked like a furry tea cosy on his head, got off his Triumph and marched up to me.

"'Hello Grandad,' he says to me. 'My name is Buttons'.

"Do you know you've got a tea cosy on your head, son?" I replied, nice and polite, like.

"'Don't call me son, grandad. Anyway we are The Hells Angels' he said proudly.

"'I can see that, son. You've got it written on your back so you don't forget.'"

"'No. I've got it written on my back so YOU don't forget. Anyway my name is Buttons and I'm in charge of The Hells Angels, as you can see, and we have come here to do the security,' Buttons proudly explained.

"'Well that is kind of you to offer but we have got the

security sorted between me and my China's, but thanks for offering to help,' I told him.

"'You don't seem to get it, Grandad. We are the Hells Angels and we are going to do the security here.'

"'No you don't get it. We are doing the security here, son.'

"'Listen to me you stupid old man.' That's what he called me. Fucking liberty! 'When The Stones played the Altamont Festival they invited The Hells Angels to do the Security so we are entitled to come and do it here.'

"'Well The Stones aren't here and as I've tried to explain, the East End is doing the Security, thank you.' As you can imagine by now I was beginning to get the Bollock Ache with this little feller. He was strutting around and puffing his chest out and thinking he was quite the hard man. I let him carry on for a bit and then he played his trump card.

"He got right into my face and said as menacing as he could, 'Alright Grandad. If you don't let us in to do the security I'll go down to the village, get on the phone and within an hour I'll have all the Hell's Angels from Great Yarmouth, Ipswich, Norwich, Lincoln and the surrounding area here. We will march straight through this gate and we will take over the security and there's nothing you can do to stop us.' All his mates were cheering and hooting and shouting out suggestions to Buttons. I'd listened to him for long enough. Before he could move away I had him in a headlock with my arm round his throat and was squeezing harder than he thought was possible. He couldn't breathe and just as his mates were thinking about getting off their bikes and helping him. I reached behind me under my jacket and pulled my gun from the waistband of my trousers and jammed it into the side of his head. Very calmly I said, 'If you and your friends don't get on your stupid little motorbikes right now and get out of my sight, son, I will blow your fucking head off!'"

"That's right. And then the little feller's legs went and I shouted out 'Don't shoot the Angels, Dad, they're not worth it,'" Big Danny added wiping away a tear of laughter as he recalled the scene.

"That Buttons stumbled back to his bike holding his throat. I don't know if he actually pissed himself but it was close and they all started their bikes and rode back down the road waving their fists at us while I just calmly pointed my gun at each one of them."

They were all laughing so hard at the memory they had forgotten about looking after the gate and had to go and wave a few artists into the site and when they got back Peter asked, "Did they come back?"

"No they didn't cos he knew that if he had come back I would have shot that little feller. I wasn't joking and he knew it. They are just pussies." To prove the point he pulled the gun out from his trousers and showed it to Peter. It was enormous and looked scary and malevolent with its taped-up grip, certainly not for decoration or show. No wonder Buttons had run away.

"Stanley did tell me not to bring my shooter but It's a good job I did or we may have been in the care of The Angels," Little Danny said, taking the last swig of beer from the bottle. "You tell that little Scottish bloke thanks for the beer. No one else thought about us and we appreciate it, and we owe him one."

"I will do, when I see him, but right now I have got to go and meet someone over there in all that mud." With that Peter walked back to the Land Rover thinking about what they had just told him. What would have happened if The Angels had come on a little stronger? It didn't bear thinking about, but they were certainly no match for Little Danny.

CHAPTER 32

If this is goodbye

Peter climbed back into the Land Rover and carefully eased it out of the mud and headed back to the site and had only got a short distance when he saw Chris standing beside his car which was completely plastered in mud and appeared to be well and truly stuck. Pulling up next to him he climbed out and asked,

"What's up, mate?"

"This must be the 50th time I've been bogged down on this stupid, poxy site. I've had quite enough now and my boss has called me back. He doesn't want his car to be trashed by using it as a taxi cab round this swamp. Look at the state of the carpets. I'm on my way back to London as soon as I get out of this quagmire. You can come back with me now, if you want, or you can make your own way back later."

"I've had enough of this festival now and I'll come back with you, thanks. I'll tow you out of there if you like but I have to tell someone I'm leaving and also get my stuff from the van."

"O.K. I'll come to your van in half an hour and we can leave." Chris pulled a muddy, well-used tow rope out of his car and was towed backwards, by the tow hitch, out of the mud for the 51st and final time and Peter continued on his way. He would have to tell Sky he had been called away. There was a huge twinge of regret but Peter was by now completely bored with the whole festival and wanted to get himself back to London. In one way he was relieved he hadn't been involved in any of the major decisions as they had all turned out to be wrong. The line up of bands had been so weak that it had hardly drawn much of an audience, which turned out to be lucky for them. The facilities were so woefully inadequate, even before the storm demolished them, so if 400,000 had turned up it would probably have turned into a full-blown disaster ending with people dying in the mud. What a let off for the 40,000 or so punters. Also he thought that if he hadn't met Sky he would have left earlier but he did regret he was leaving her there. Maybe she would like to come back to London with him.

When he arrived back at her shack there was no sign of either her or Patti. They must have been out seeing some of the festival, but after waiting around for 15 minutes or so Peter left on his own and went back to his caravan. There was not much for him to pack into his holdall and he cleaned up the van a little before checking that he had his money and stash of dope. He remembered he had told Sky to come back here if they missed each other so he rummaged through his bag and found a pen and some paper and wrote a brief note explaining that he had been called back to London. He said that he was sorry and he had loved meeting her and she was welcome to stay in the caravan as long as she liked. Also if he ever came to the States he would look her up. He said that he had waited at her shack but she wasn't there and he was sorry but he had to leave right now but he did have a ball! He signed it, "With love, Beaujolais!"

Chris drove over from his van to Peter's and they put his bag in the boot. Leaving the Land Rover where he found it, with the key under the driver's seat, he got into the car with

Chris. They managed to slide the car around to the Artists' Gate without getting stuck and they stopped and said good-bye to the two Dannys. As they were let out of the gate Peter leaned out of the window and called out to Little Danny,

"Don't forget Danny, Don't shoot The Angels. They're not worth it."

Little Danny laughed at them and slammed the heavy metal gate shut behind the muddy car. Coincidently it also slammed shut on any involvement Peter was ever to have with organising pop festivals again. Realising it was time to make a decision about which path to take he considered his options for all of two seconds and chose the integrity, honesty and trust of all the people he knew in the illegal world of drugs. It was so easy to walk away from the whole shambles that was called Great Western Festivals and he hardly gave them another thought again. It was just a crazy episode in the story of his life. Now he was just looking forward to continuing with all the business he had waiting for him back in London. That side of the music business was of no interest at all and he would leave it alone now and concentrate on supplying drugs.

However he failed to realise that taking cocaine had opened Pandora's Box which he was carrying with him. It would not be long before it would start to shower its malev-olent contents onto the head of the unsuspecting Peter.

Three months later

Peter had not really thought much about the festival fiasco as he had been far too busy dealing with the constant flow of campervans from Morocco and their well-hidden contents. He was surprised to get a phone call from Malcolm who tried to get Peter to come and work for him as tour manager for some idea he had involving a country wide tour of Thai boxing exhibitions. With his usual bulldozing manner Malcolm got Peter to agree to meet him for lunch the next day. They decided, at Peter's suggestion, on Jimmie's Wine Bar in Kensington which had become a regular haunt of his.

Driving down there the next day he decided he would not be coerced into Malcolm's hair brained scheme, however much fun it may sound, whatever he said. Entering the gloomy bar, he sat at his favourite table in the corner and ordered a good bottle of wine and started to drink it as he waited the customary thirty minutes for Malcolm to arrive. A couple of glasses and a brief chat with Jimmie were enjoyed before Malcolm stuck his head round the door. He peered through the gloom and saw Peter in the corner and made his way over.

"Is that you?" He said in his strongest Glaswegian accent as he sat down and took a sip from the glass that had been poured for him. "Are you hiding from The Law in this dive or what? Though I must say those steaks smell awfully good and this wine is superb so it's not too bad a choice after all."

They ordered steaks from the grill and another bottle of wine was left to breathe as Malcolm tried his hardest to get Peter to work for him. There was no way Peter could find any time to go on tour and he was making so much more money than Malcolm could offer.

"So you've wasted my time and money coming here?" Malcolm said with a mock hurt look on his face.

"Not exactly." Peter replied. "Think of it as a very small part payment of the bonus I was supposed to be getting from you for working on that stupid festival. However, there is something that I wanted to ask you about if you don't have to kill me after you tell me. It's the idea you had for a film about laundering money. Are you prepared to enlighten me?"

"Och. That old thing. I've moved on from that now. I'll even let you have the idea if you want it. Let me give you the outline." Then he started with his tale.

"A gang of safe breakers tunnel into a bank vault full of safety deposit boxes and get away with few million pounds worth of bullion, jewellery and cash."

"Oh yeah and how did they do that then?" Peter asked.

"That's not important. This is a film. We can work out the details. On the other hand, we could use a drug smuggler who brought in a huge consignment of drugs and has a large amount of money he can't account for, but people don't like drug smugglers as much as they like bank robbers. I can't imagine many films being made about heroic drug smugglers."

"You've got a point there." said Peter.

"Anyway, we just need someone with a shit load of illegal cash. So, the heist goes off smoothly, however they do it, and they fence all the jewellery and bullion and end up with a couple of million pounds of illegal money which isn't as wonderful as it seems as you can only buy so much with cash without alerting the authorities. They need to launder their cash and try the casinos but there is no way they can use them to clean so much money anymore after the London clean up, as I explained before, so they look for another way." Malcolm was relishing the story he was telling.

"Don't keep me in suspense any longer." Peter said.

"Well, my naive young friend he organises a Pop Festival. That's how he does it."

"Oh yes that's a great idea. He puts in a hundred grand on the slim chance of making three hundred grand profit." Peter said dismissively.

"No he doesn't. My dear stupid boy. He puts up £100,000 in order to launder one million pounds. This is how it's done. First and foremost, it is important that the festival in my film has to be absolutely legal. It must be paid for with legitimate money and made sure it's one hundred percent perfectly legal and squeaky clean. When the festival is over, and the gate receipts have been counted, they can only proceed with the scam if they have attracted an audience of at least 300,000. This figure is absolutely necessary because it is almost impossible to accurately estimate large numbers of festival goers. Most festivals would then choose to declare fewer people, maybe 200,000, and rob a few hundred thousand pounds but my Mister Big declares his attendance to be 500,000."

"Why on earth would he declare more people than actually attended?" Peter asked.

"Because no one would believe the numbers would have been inflated and he can declare he took two and a half million pounds. All the gate receipts are taken in cash, and he can just mix in one million of his dirty cash to the

£1,500,000 he has made legally and pay tax on all of it laundering it as clean as the driven snow! He can also inflate his costs to keep his profits down and not pay so much tax. What do you think of the idea?"

"I think the idea is fucking terrific. Using a festival to launder the money is a really devious idea and so clever. Imagine the fun it would be making this film. Maybe you could say it was Mafia money. I think a film about the Mafia could be a real money maker. That would be a different film altogether and much darker. At least no one could accuse The Great Western Festival of laundering money because they only got 40,000 punters and made a huge financial loss."

"No chance of stealing any money either with only 40,000 punters." Malcolm said gloomily. "Nevertheless, life goes on and I have a meeting with a bigwig at Guinness to finalise details of my upcoming tour. With which you refuse to help me with in any way!"

"'Tel Aviv' as they say in France. I'm sure you'll find another mug to work for you." Peter said.

"Maybe so, but where do I find someone as naïve as you?" And with that Malcolm paid the bill and they walked out into Kensington Church Street and went their separate ways both thinking of what might have been.

Epilogue

The events in this book are true. The conversations are unreliably remembered. You can verify a lot of the information about the festival and events that took place on Google. Most of the people whose full names I've given can be looked up on Google except for Steve Wilkins who deserves a whole page on Wikipedia but isn't mentioned. All the filmmaker Peter Whitehead entries are not me as I managed to completely evade publicity. Eventually the Law won!

R.I.P. Steve. You were the most extraordinary character.

Lightning Source UK Ltd.
Milton Keynes UK
UKHW011442021022
409795UK00002B/61